Marie ~

Shine & Smile
Love & Light!

She Travels Light

She Travels Light

A Novel

RAQUEL SPENCER

TUCSON, ARIZONA

Cover Image: Tammy Kalve

Book Design: Ja-lene Clark

Editors: Ja-lene Clark, Jo Ann Deck, Joanne Sprott

ISBN-13: 978-1490970806

ISBN-10: 1490970800

www.RaquelSpencer.com

www.SheTravelsLight.com

FIRST PRINTING

Printed in the USA

Gratitude

My deepest gratitude to Candi for being there from the beginning, and encouraging me at every turn. To Jane, who came into my life just as things got really interesting. To my Mom for her love and support along the way. To all the other beautiful souls in this world and beyond who have enhanced my journey.

Chapter 1

The deepest recesses congregate
The darkness cold and strong
Our soul's connection weaving a tapestry
Within the fabric of time

Deep within the illusion
The musical notes reside
Sounding Light and memories
Of our connection to the Divine

Finally, I will know what it is like to have my husband Max penetrate my body and soul. Our hearts have always been linked together. As we merge as husband and wife for the first time, our love, our Light will be forever sealed in this lifetime.

The first time I laid eyes on Max I knew. Every single cell in my body lit up when our eyes met. Those amazing, beautiful, deep penetrating, piercing electric blue eyes. Not to mention his tousled dark hair and all 5'11" of his gorgeous body. He caught me so off guard it took my breath away, literally. I thought I was going to faint. Then he smiled and I knew I was in trouble, big trouble! I could feel the blood rush to several parts of my body, the most visibly noticeable, my cheeks. I was so flushed he actually asked if I was okay. I giggled and tried to regain some sense of composure as I attempted to order a latte. As I walked past his table in the coffee shop, he asked me to join him. That was a little over eighteen months ago.

Everyone said we just naturally fit. We even looked like we belonged together. Max with his 5'11" frame, dark hair and blue eyes and me with my 5'3" frame, dark hair and vivid green eyes. It was liked we had been together forever, even from the start.

Now I lie in this bath, purifying and preparing my body for the sacred ritual of merging with him for the first time as his wife. His wife. I like the sound of that. Today is our wedding day. We both understood in the depths of our soul the sacredness of our union. The importance of going beyond the normal wedding night preparations to seal our commitment to each other with awareness, honor and respect. We had talked about it at length over the last year. There was a deep remembrance, a familiarity and a knowing we had done this before in another time and place. Performed sacred, spiritual ritual to honor our union as lovers and partners. Actually we knew it from the first time we made love. The experience was different, it was electrifying and it was powerful, really powerful!

I'm in hot water, but it feels so good! Like Max, the water soothes and nurtures me, healing me and making me feel whole. I'm so happy he found a suite with an outdoor bathtub! Private yet exposed to the elements. He made sure all four elements are represented. The golden fire dancing from candles. The air which is filled with the sweet and intoxicating smells of frangipani flowers afloat in my bath water. The sea salt from the island added to release the tension from my body. Oh, and the beautiful ambient music he chose playing in the background which soothes my soul to its core. The setting is perfect.

The truth is, I feel so completely adored by him. He has attended to every detail, selected everything just for this special night. His instincts, connection and openness let him know what I need, and how he could best create the environment and honor his wife, his lover, his goddess!

I know women dream about their wedding day, but it just never really crossed my mind. It was strange, but when I was young I couldn't really envision what my life would turn out like, much less my wedding. It wasn't until a few years ago when I had a vivid dream of getting married that I realized how different I was, never having fantasized about the dress, the ceremony or the day.

In hindsight, it is incredibly surreal how similar my dream was to how the actual day unfolded. I would have preferred fewer people, to have only my closest friends, but Max wanted his family and friends there too. Of course he did, I just hadn't envisioned his "people" yet. It seems silly now, but since I hadn't actually met him when I had the dream, I hadn't considered his friends and family in the equation.

Our ceremony was beautiful and timed impeccably to be at sunset, as the colors of the sky blended, blues and pinks merging into orange and tangerine, the water mirroring the change on its smooth yet rhythmic surface. This is Kona and here, I am at home. There is something wonderful about this island, the energy, the sisterhood with Pele, the smells and sounds. It all feeds my being on such a deep level.

There was never a question for me, our vows had to be spoken at Kona. Kona is where I go to "plug in." So much has happened to me on the big island, but it's difficult to precisely explain, as there is no language, no reference points to communicate what has transpired. It is purely experiential, which empowers me at a deep core level. I know that each time I emerge from Kona, I am different than I was previously. This time would be no exception.

Hawaii was a perfect place for our wedding. It still has all the allure of an exotic island, yet all the comforts of being in the States and close enough for our friends to gather with ease. My time traveling in foreign countries has helped me to really appreciate the simplicity of being in an English-speaking country, driving on the right side of the road and having the ability to be independent without a lot of planning involved.

I never understood why people spend extraordinary amounts of money on a wedding ceremony. Thousands of dollars to impress others with a ten-minute vow exchange and a drunken party afterwards where too many people show their true colors. Max and I simply wanted a ceremony that would celebrate the evolution of our relationship from friendship to partnership. The union of two souls. A ceremony steeped in ritual reflecting true initiation. A simple rite of passage.

Max and I wrote our own vows, which expressed what was true in our hearts. That we would honor and respect each other as individuals, while coming together as partners to share our lives. We had chosen a wise elderly Kahuna priest to perform the ceremony or rather, it was he who chose us. We found him in a moment of pure synchronicity. He overheard our conversation while we were in a flower booth at the local market. I was expressing to Max how I felt it was important to connect with the ancient tradition and energies of the island during our ceremony. He turned, looked at both of us and smiled. In that moment there was a deep recognition, a knowing that transpired, no words were needed, no conversation required. It was as if he received information directly from his ancestors that he needed to bless our sacred union. He agreed, right there on the spot to perform the ceremony for us. The booth owner just stood there with a shocked look on her face. She explained that the priest had "retired" from doing sacred ceremony decades ago.

"The ancients must know your hearts well," she said with amazement.

Max and I felt the connection to him immediately. How perfect having a true Kahuna priest perform the ritual. We wanted the ceremony to have the intimate feel of the sacredness we shared for each other, and it did.

As I lie in this hot water, I close my eyes, remembering every detail, every moment of our ceremony, our ritual, our initiation. When the ceremony started, everything around me seemed to disappear. Everything went out of focus, except for Max. It was as if nothing else existed in that space and time but us. His beautiful blue eyes looking deep into my soul made everything in my body come alive. As he kissed me for the first time to seal our contract, to solidify our commitment to each other, my heart raced with anticipation. He was mine! He was finally mine and I was his. Our souls were bound by this sacred ceremony and our hearts were forever linked.

As he drew his lips from mine, I noticed a woman standing just beyond the circle of flowers which were laid around us in the warm sand. I could tell she was a Hawaiian native. She was probably in her 40's, maybe even 50's, wearing a traditional Hawaiian dress. It was strange she was there, as our ceremony was private, but her wise, penetrating and magnetic eyes drew me to her. She waited for a few moments as the priest and Max began to move toward our guests before she approached me. She greeted me in the Hawaiian tradition, kissing me gently on each cheek. The recognition we shared for each other in that moment was ancient, haunting and it stirred latent memories inside me. She reached for my hands and as we touched, pulses of electricity raced through our fingers. I tried to pull away, but she clung tightly, holding the connection steady. She peered into my eyes with such intensity, such longing, such power, it almost frightened me. I was mesmerized, caught in a drift, barely remembering I was at my own wedding.

"We have known each other since the time before time, you and I." Her eyes were kind as she spoke softly to me. "This revelation, this truth you are now remembering. Pele wants you to remember why you are here."

Her words had caught me completely off guard. As she released my hands I noticed a glass vial lying upon her chest. It was beautiful! Its top was a gold diamond-shaped bale artfully attached to a small glass bottle. The vial was empty. She removed the necklace from her body, opened the vial and filled the glass with the sand at our feet. Then she closed the vial and gently placed it in my hand.

"Pele says you will know when to let this vial touch your heart." She kissed my hands and then my forehead, bowed gracefully and left. As I watched her walk away, I realized she left no footprints, no mark in the sand to prove she was ever there.

I stood there looking down at the vial in my hand with thoughts of Pele running through my head. The surges of energy coming up from the ground below me were undeniable. This island, this volcano was powerful and I knew it. I felt the connection every time I came here. Now I was standing, barefoot, within the circle of flowers laid specifically for my wedding, with the intensity of my connection to Pele, to the ancients of the island and the sacredness of this ritual truly overwhelming me. There was a powerful tingling in my body and it took me a minute to regain my focus.

I realized the reception was in full swing with everyone busy kissing, hugging and enjoying the celebration, completely oblivious to my interaction with Pele's messenger. I looked back to see if I could find her again, but she was gone. I wanted Max to see her and wondered if I had just imagined the whole thing, but then I looked down and the glass vial filled with sand was indeed still in my hands.

I desperately needed a moment to myself. I wasn't sure what I was feeling. The wedding had been perfect and very emotional, but the interaction with Pele's messenger had me spinning. I knew the vial she had given to me was precious and needed to be safeguarded. Comfortable that everyone was busy socializing, I quickly slipped away and went back to our suite. Who was this woman? Why did she show up at my wedding? Looking down at her gift, I carefully placed it in my jewelry bag for safe keeping. With my thoughts still racing, I freshened up and went back to join my new husband. Our family and friends were here to celebrate with us, and I wanted to enjoy every last moment.

Now, as I lie in this beautiful bath, I wonder about the vial. She said I would know when to have it touch my heart. I know now is the time, before Max and I merge in sacred union. I reach for a towel to dry myself, my thoughts still wondering who she was. She seemed so familiar, so known to me, but she was gone before I could even ask her name. She said we had known each other since the time before time. What did she mean by that? It seemed like such a simple thing, the gift she presented, but I knew it had a deep and significant meaning. A glass vial filled with Hawaiian sand that was gathered from where Max and I stood, surrounded by flower petals during our wedding ceremony. She said that Pele wanted me to remember. Pele, the Hawaiian Goddess of fire. The sheer mention of her name sent shivers up my spine. I had a strong connection to Pele, the volcano and to this island. That I knew for sure. I felt it deeply embedded within my being, and I could feel the power of Pele even now.

As I slip back in the tub with the vial in my hand, I relax into the memory of Max's touch. His lips on mine, as we sealed our vows. His eyes penetrating my soul, as we spoke our promise and desires to each other. My heart is singing as I realize once more that he is finally mine, all mine. What will it be like to finally make love with him as his wife? I hear him knocking gently at the door.

"Arayla, sweetheart, are you ready for me?"

I smile knowing full well I am, as I linger for just a moment longer. My body is prepared, my heart is open, my soul is ready and my passion is on fire. I place the precious vial necklace on my heart and lean back into the water. My delicious man, my beautiful love, is ready to merge on a whole new level. To finally merge as husband and wife. I close my eyes taking it all in and start to float...

Chapter 2

Family, friends and lovers
  Are chosen for their Light
To help us with this journey
  Throughout this space and time

We sometimes do remember
  But most of us forget
The contracts that we promised
  Before we made "our beds"

Each plays a certain role for us
  To amplify our truth
Being friend, foe or guardian
  To help us with our growth

But when it all is over
  And the curtains raised to show
We truly are all just one within
  The circle of ebb and flow

Where am I? My surroundings seem vaguely familiar, but I can't identify this place. I blink my eyes trying to see more clearly as I reached up to feel the vial on my chest. I feel like I am floating, but not in the hot water of my bathtub. With my eyes finally beginning to focus, I see a man standing or rather, floating in front of me. He's wearing a pink flowered Hawaiian t-shirt, tan shorts and sandals, all the while swinging a pair of Ray-Bans in his hand. Strange attire, I think as I know we are definitely not on a beach. For that matter, we aren't anywhere that looks familiar at all. It's dark and black, except for the two of us. This place seems so unreal, so surreal, and downright unnerving.

Then the man in the Hawaiian shirt speaks, and I instantly recognize his voice. "Look into my eyes, Arayla." I feel so confused and disoriented by my surroundings but strangely at ease. Again he says, "Look into my eyes." Then more sternly, "You know me!"

Then I see them, those beautiful amber eyes. I did recognize him, but from where I couldn't remember. His presence is so comforting, so soothing, yet so strong. He is handsome, someone I would definitely take a second look at from across the room. I wonder… Who is this guy? Why am I floating in what seems to be thin air or no air at all? Then before I can finish my thoughts he blurts out…

"I am Zaratu, but you can call me Z." He looks at me and calmly whispers, "How could you forget me?"

I laugh, surely I must be dreaming. "Where am I? Where is Max? How did I get here? This is my wedding night." I ramble off still confused and agitated trying to make some sense of it all. "How do I know you?"

"Don't worry, it's alright. The Crew has been waiting a long time for you to be ready. The vial you are holding on your heart is the portal key to bring you here to me. On some level Arayla, you know me, you know who you are and you're ready to finally begin your mission."

I laugh again, "What mission? What are you talking about? What Crew? I don't remember you! What do you mean I know who I am? Of course, I know who I am!"

Zaratu just smiles and winks at me as his body fades into nothingness. But, those eyes, those deep penetrating amber eyes, are forever etched into my mind. I hear Max in the distance calling out to me...

"Babe, I don't think I can wait for you any longer..." but I'm being pulled into the unknown, into the unfamiliar by something I remember deep within my soul.

Chapter 3

Persistent is the calling
So driven are your thoughts
So take complete full action
Within this new chaos

Your mission is important
For each of us are known
Throughout this solar system
Governed by the Light so strong

Be steady in your focus
Be true to your own heart
For so much more is needed
Before the brand new start

The pulse of Light is singing
The choice of each confirmed
To bring about the Golden Age
Of Life Eternal's song

"Ray, wake up, wake up! We're landing," Toni said.

"Wow, I just had the weirdest dream!" I mumbled as I look around trying to get my bearings. I couldn't quite put my finger on why, but I had a deep sense of loss and at the same time a deep sense of calm came over me. I tried to remember all the details, blue eyes, amber eyes, flowers, hot water and sunglasses swinging, weird I thought to myself.

"Oh yeah? Well you will have to wait to tell me about it until we get off this plane." Toni said as she reached up into the overhead bin. "I don't know how the heck you sleep on one of these things," she growled as she stretched her 5'9" body, edging her way into the aisle. She has never enjoyed flying and especially not in a commuter airplane.

The grinding from the plane's brakes and noisy conversations from all the people pulled me all the way back into reality. Airplanes are always interesting. So many people, each anxious on some level, whether they are excited about their destination or just impatient for everyone to get off the plane. I always feel like cattle being herded, everyone standing up, even though we know we are going to have to wait. I've never been good with patience, especially when there is something fun coming. Once we finally made it off the plane, Toni, her friend Stephanie and I gathered our suitcases from the carousel and headed to the rental car.

"Do you really think we can get all this luggage into this small of a trunk?" I asked Toni.

She gave me a smirk. What was I thinking? If anyone can figure out how to get six suitcases into a small Chevy Malibu trunk, it's Toni. She pulled all of our suitcases out again and reanalyzed the situation. Stephanie, who was a long-time friend of Toni's from college, just smiled. She had learned early on to just get out of the way and let Toni do it. But this was the first time I'd travelled with Toni, and although we had only known each other for about a year, I knew her personality all too well. Toni is a Virgo and a true Virgo at that. Details are her specialty and organizing is just another word for details.

Toni laughed as she picked up my suitcase. "Geez girl, what the hell do you have in here?" teasing me by pretending that her back just got pulled out of whack.

I blushed, "I don't travel light. Everything I need, I hope." Funny thing is I know Toni so well, I bet her suitcase was probably twice as heavy as mine.

It was the first summer after graduating from CSU, Sacramento and we all needed a break and some fun after graduation. Toni wanted to visit an old friend from high school who was living in Twentynine Palms. We decided it was as good a place as any to start our Southern California adventure. Sea World, the beach and the San Diego Zoo were also planned stops on our trip and besides, her friend was willing to let us all sleep there. We couldn't argue with that. Stephanie also had family living in San Diego, so we would have a place to crash for a few days, making it easier for each of us to afford the trip. We were typical college graduates, none of us making a lot of money, and our school loans were definitely still taking a toll on our finances. So anywhere we could get "cheap or free" accommodations, we were thankful for. Although I do have to admit, sleeping on the floor or even a couch has never been my idea of a good time. I would have of course preferred five star hotels all the way, but at this point, I'd never actually stayed at one yet. But a girl could surely dream!

Most people see the desert as desolate, but I see it as alive and vibrant. I suppose it isn't your typical beauty, you know, the kind that everyone recognizes instantly. It requires looking beyond the surface, going deeper into the scene to really uncover all the beauty the desert has to offer. I was in the middle of enjoying the landscape when Toni broke the silence...

"I have something to tell you," she said as she pushed on the accelerator. "I think my third eye opened!" She giggled. "While we were at the airport I started to see things that were pretty bizarre."

"That is awesome! Like what?" I asked excitedly.

"Well at first it was like waves of energy, something like you would see coming off hot pavement, but colorful. Then the energy started to shift and make shapes and move. It was really cool. It would fade in and out, so I only caught glimpses. I know you have told me what you've seen when you see energy, but I never thought I would ever really see if for myself."

She was grinning ear to ear as she shared her experience.

"It's cool, dang cool isn't it?"

"Yes, but not what I really expected I guess. And definitely not for the first time while at an airport in Palm Springs!"

Toni and I have always had one thing in common, okay, well maybe more than one thing. But what has always drawn us together has been our fascination with the metaphysical world. Although she is much more skeptical and level headed than I am, she still has an innate knowing that there is so much more than meets the eye. Now she had a first-hand personal experience of seeing "energy" for herself. I was extremely happy for her, and she seemed downright proud of herself. It was wonderful and somehow that made me feel more connected to her.

After the plane ride, that crazy dream and our drive through the desert, I was ready to relax and very happy to be arriving at our destination. At least I was until I saw our hosts, a couple standing on the porch of a small house. It looked so odd. He had a beer in his hand, and well that's not so odd, but she was holding a dagger in hers. Sheila was a long time friend of Toni's, but one she had not seen for a while. I knew immediately that this was not my kind of company.

Toni glanced over at me noticing my hesitation and said, "Sheila's okay. Maybe a little rough around the edges, but she has a really good heart."

As I got out of the car to meet Sheila, my intuition kept ringing "danger"! That was confirmed when all the hairs on my body stood straight up, and I hesitated even more, not sure if I wanted to even stand close to her. I noticed she put the dagger down the back of her pants, and I wondered why she would have a dagger to begin with. She gave Toni a big hug, smiled at Stephanie and barely acknowledged me. Not much of a warm welcome coming from someone I would have to spend the night with, I thought. If she hadn't been a good friend of Toni's, I would have gotten right back in the car and left. But I'd known Toni for a while and I knew she wouldn't be friends with someone dangerous. At least not knowingly, that is.

As far as destinations go, Twentynine Palms has very little to offer.

From what I noticed driving in, there really wasn't much to it. We decided to order pizza and beer and just kick back for the evening. Sheila wanted to take us up to Joshua Tree for a hike the next day. I have a lot of fond memories of four-wheeling on the sand dunes nearby with my childhood friend Lynn and her family. So it would be nice to revisit the area. Though, with as much damage as I had done to my knees over the years, I was not jumping up and down at the idea of hiking around on hot rocks all day.

With Toni and Sheila sitting around the kitchen table reminiscing about old times, oblivious to the rest of us, Stephanie, Sheila's boyfriend and I sat awkwardly trying to make conversation. Without the diversion of a television, the evening crawled by, and I was relieved that we were only spending one night here. Stephanie didn't seem to mind. She was kind of quiet and I had never really gotten to know her. She's Toni's best friend, but other than Toni, we didn't really have anything else in common. She was nice enough, but we just never really clicked. So I felt like I was sitting there with two strangers.

I was so uncomfortable being in that house. Something just didn't feel right, and it usually takes a lot to make me feel that way. Of course, I don't think I would ever feel comfortable around anyone with a dagger tucked down their pants. "I think I will sleep with one eye open all night," I whispered to myself as I crawled into the sleeping bag in the middle of the living room floor. It's going to be a long night.

I woke up to the smell of coffee. Hopefully it's good coffee, I thought to myself as I stretched my sore body. I'm definitely not used to sleeping on the floor!

"Good morning!" Toni handed me a cup. "Did you sleep well?"

I ran my hands across my neck and gave her a half-assed smile. "Sure."

"Do you want some breakfast? There is toast and eggs."

"Yeah, thanks," I responded halfheartedly.

"You're in a pleasant mood... What is wrong with you?" Toni asked.

"I don't know. I just feel really weird," I replied, not sure how to explain what I was feeling.

"It's obvious you don't like my friend Sheila," she said with a disapproving tone.

"I'm sorry, I'll try to be nicer, but she isn't really being friendly to me either," I said in my defense.

"Well, she did offer us a free place to stay and is taking us hiking."

"I know and I'm grateful, but I just don't feel comfortable around her."

"Is it her or her boyfriend that is bugging you?"

"Honestly, it didn't help that she had a dagger in her hand as we drove up. I would really just prefer to keep my distance." I wondered why Toni wasn't more uncomfortable around Sheila herself. Her intuition about people seemed to be pretty solid. But she always did have a soft spot for those down on their luck and in my opinion perhaps trusted too easily.

Toni wrinkled her brows, looking at me funny, then shrugged her shoulders and finished making our breakfast.

"We are out of here in about thirty minutes, can you be ready?" she asked. "I'll tell Stephanie. She must have needed the rest, she slept right through breakfast."

"Of course. Thanks for cooking and making coffee."

Thirty more minutes and we're out of here. It couldn't come quickly enough as far as I was concerned. I didn't want to spend any more time there than absolutely necessary. Sheila's boyfriend was okay, but she gave me the creeps. In true Toni style, we were out the door within 25 minutes and on our way to hike for the day.

Joshua Tree was so much more breathtaking than I remembered. I truly love the desert and Joshua Tree is such an amazing example of just how beautiful the desert can be. Large red boulders stacked high upon each other and of course, the Joshua tree. It is the most bizarre and funniest looking tree I've ever seen, yet so incredibly unique. There is a stillness, a peace and calm in the desert that you rarely find anywhere else. If Sheila and her boyfriend hadn't been with us, I think I would have actually enjoyed being there.

"Geez Ray, what is wrong with you today? Would you lighten up!"

Toni said as we got out of the car, trying to get me to shift out of the mood I was in.

"It will be fun, I promise." Coming from Toni that was a real stretch, because I know how much she absolutely hates hiking.

Why were we here? What made her think I wanted to go hiking in the desert, anyway? She knows my idea of a good time outdoors is on a beach with a cushioned lounge chair and a good-looking waiter making sure my tropical fruit drink never gets too warm. But there was something about Joshua Tree, something so beautiful and magical even, and well we were here, so I might as well try to enjoy it. What's the saying? "Carpe Diem, seize the day!"

We spent the next hour hiking around the large boulders that made the Joshua Tree national forest so unique. It was warm, but not too hot and Toni of course had brought plenty of water to drink. That girl is a girl scout to the tee. Me, I never plan things out. I'm an "in the moment" kind of girl. My impetuous nature can sometimes cause problems, but when I am with Toni, I never have to worry about anything as she always takes care of all the details. I've grown to love having a Virgo as my best friend. She handed me a bottle of water as we both laid back on the beautiful and magnificent rock we had just climbed.

Sheila and her boyfriend had taken off exploring another area of rocks. We could see Stephanie in the other direction about three large boulders over.

"Hey Blondie, can you toss me a bottle of that water?" she hollered.

Toni just laughed and cursed under her breath. She hated being called Blondie and Stephanie knew it. It was a way to stereotype her. She was in the corporate world now, in a position that was usually held by men, and she resented that others might think her good looks had landed her there rather than her brains. "You're S.O.L. Steph, sorry! I can't throw that far," she responded.

Toni really is a great friend. I don't believe I would have graduated from college without her help. I was a total mess when I met her. We were introduced through an old boyfriend of mine. He is gone, thank God! But

Toni's not. During the final semester of my senior year at Cal State, I was devastated when I caught him cheating with an old girlfriend. Men can be such assholes. He had looked me straight in the eye and just lied about everything swearing that he had been faithful and trustworthy and that I was just being paranoid and jealous! Oh, but the test from the health clinic at the university proved otherwise, unless you can actual get an STD from using a public toilet? I think not. I couldn't believe the bastard actually tried to convince me that was how I got it.

I was living with him at the time, so leaving meant I was homeless, plus I was broke and a complete emotional mess. Toni saved me. She offered me her couch to sleep on (which was actually more comfortable than some of the beds I had slept in over the years). She gave me food and even helped me write several of my final papers. I am eternally grateful to her as she got me through the last six weeks of my senior year. She has been my rock ever since. It probably took that kind of crisis to allow me to fully let her in, as trust is not my strong suit. But it was a friendship that flourished, even under the worst of circumstances. She had seen me at my worst and was still there for me. That was something I had not experienced much in my life, until Toni.

Chapter 4

Deep within the recesses
Of the human mind
Are the coded memories
Of the true divine

Single synapse firing
Pathways of Light defined
Is only but a fraction
Of required Light refined

Your heart is but the pathway
Your soul your inner guide
The truth of your evolution
Is ever redefined

I felt so relaxed lying there on that huge rock with the warmth of the sun bathing my skin, listening and watching the birds as they flew effortlessly from stone to stone. It was a nice reward for all the effort it took to actually get to the top. I took a deep breath enjoying the moment, and then suddenly out of nowhere, my body started shaking from the inside out! My heart was beating really fast as if I were running a marathon! My vision started going in and out of focus and all my perception and senses began to heighten. I started to panic but then a calmness from deep within came over me and I understood. I knew. I remembered.

"Ray, what is going on here? Something is happening. Can you feel it?" Toni's voice was fearful.

My head was racing and I couldn't seem to answer her. My body was twitching with energy that was pulsing through me. The sensation was electrifying and my heart felt like it was going to explode. It was such a beautiful and powerful feeling. I felt strong waves of love pulsing through me but this was beyond anything I had ever experienced before. As if accessing some kind of memory, I suddenly placed all of my focus on my heart. As soon as I did so, I began hearing tones in my head, beautiful elongated sounds; pitch perfect sounds which calmed me, making me feel secure. It was like a symphony orchestra playing a melody as I felt the rhythm of emotion move through me. Although my body was still shaking, I felt such love, joy and peace!

"Trust your instincts, Arayla. Allow your heart to expand," I heard a man's voice whisper.

High above me in the sky, I began to see huge multi-colored lines come into focus. It looked like something you would see in Star Trek movie but this was happening right before my eyes! I watched as the lines began to cohesively form a massive grid pattern overhead. It was a beautiful bright grid of Light that expanded above the earth. It seems like it was just outside of the atmosphere, extending into the darkness that is space, but somehow completely visible to me while I lay still on the warm rock I had just finished climbing.

"Ray, something is going on! What is happening? Something is wrong!"

Toni yelled.

Although I heard her, I wasn't able to speak. I was so engrossed in my own experience that I couldn't even make a sound, much less respond to her. My body began shaking even more. The lines of Light began to make a pillar, a funnel of Light, and it started descending down directly into my heart. When the Light connected to my heart, I gasped loudly trying to catch my breath! The intensity was so strong I could barely breathe as the energy pulsed straight through me and deep into the earth.

"Ray, help me! I don't know if I am going to make it!"

Hearing Toni's plea, I found my voice and responded. "Hold on, I think it's almost done." My God it's beautiful, I thought to myself. I wondered if she could see it, or if anyone else could for that matter. With her recent experience at the airport the day before, I hoped she could see what I was seeing.

"Ray, help me! Please help me now!"

Toni screamed for help again and everything started to shift, started to fade from my sight. Finally the intense shaking subsided and I jumped up and ran over to her. I placed my hands firmly on her shoulders and instantly her whole demeanor changed and she let out a long sigh of relief. She opened her eyes, and the look of terror and fear was unmistakable.

"Are you okay? Did you see it?" I asked her hoping she had seen the massive grids of Light I had.

But her face showed anything but excitement. "Let's get out of here!"

Toni was clearly shook up. She held onto me for dear life as we made our way back to the car. Sheila and her boyfriend ran toward us to see what had happened. I had almost forgotten about them being there at all. They could tell Toni was upset and was curious as to why. Stephanie showed up a couple of minutes later startled and wondering why we were leaving so soon.

Toni finally managed to pull herself together in pure Virgo/Girl Scout style. She made a quick apology about how she had gotten overheated and how it was getting late and she wanted to get on the road. Sheila was obviously irritated, but didn't put up an argument as clearly Toni wanted to leave and fast. Sheila gave Toni a hug and said goodbye to Stephanie, who seemed oblivious to everything that had happened. Then Sheila turned and just shot me a dirty look. I was so overwhelmed with my experience, I didn't even care that she was being a bitch.

"Why are we leaving so soon?" Stephanie asked looking perplexed. I didn't hear Toni's response to her, as I was still trying to get everything together and back into the car. We left in a hurry. My heart was still pulsing with the waves of Light I had seen, and I tried making sense of what had just happened. My whole sense of reality was shaken from the experience. I know what I saw and experienced was real. I had felt the energy pulsing through my body. I had watched the whole thing as if I were up in space, while at the same time fully aware of being in my body. How could that be?

The things I had experienced in just the last 24 hours had made little sense if any at all. The dream with the guy with those amber eyes telling me I had a mission and that a Crew or group of Light Beings had been waiting for me and the fact that the whole experience had happened while floating in no-space. Not to mention my dream about getting married. And now this amazing experience with the lights and sounds and seeing it all happen high above the earth. I was doing my best to put the pieces together to understand what was real and what wasn't. The guy with amber eyes, he seemed so familiar. What did he call himself? I wonder if it was his voice that I heard telling me to expand my heart. And did anyone else see the pillar and grids of Light? Did anyone else see me shaking on that rock? Was anyone else paying attention to what was going on? There were too many unanswered questions. I needed to get to the bottom of what was happening to me and fast.

Chapter 5

The secrets of the human mind
Require constant care
Because they hold the keys beyond
What logic shows is there

You wonder what the future holds
But time does not exist
So how does one unlock the doors
Of perception's turns and twists?

Reality is the dream state
The dream is what can be
But do you want the dream you dream
Or a different reality?

Simple mind alterations
Done with pure intent
Can modify this unruly world
To bring happiness again

With Toni at the wheel, we pulled onto highway 10 towards San Diego. She was really upset, but I wasn't sure why. I've learned that with Toni, you just don't press her for information. When she's ready to tell you, she'll tell you. Until then, I decided to just let her be.

So much had happened I needed to get it all clear in my own mind. I've seen strange things before, indeed many times. But I'd never seen anything quite like this. Those grids of light were amazing, but the light has never connected to my physical body with such intensity. Everything seemed so real but how could it be real? I wondered if I was losing touch with reality. The man in my dream felt so familiar, like I knew him. I'm sure I know him, I thought to myself as I watched the desert pass by out the window. Toni seemed like she had recovered and had pulled it together, then suddenly she burst into tears. She was freaking out, her whole body was shaking and she could barely drive.

"Pull over!" I insisted. My own self-centered thoughts shifted quickly to my friend who was clearly having a meltdown.

"Toni, what happened to you back there?" I asked with empathy. Toni pulled the car off the highway and turned off the engine. Stephanie was just keeping quiet sitting in the back seat, clearly not knowing what to think at this point. Here was her rock solid friend falling apart right in front of her and she had no idea on earth why.

"Ray, I thought I was going to die!" Toni cried.

"What are you talking about?" I asked.

"I always knew, I always knew there was true evil in the world, but I didn't really get it until now. I was just sitting there admiring the view when all of a sudden I felt this dark menacing energy surround me. It caught me so off guard. I could feel it to my bones and I started to 'see' the energy. It was black and thick and not at all like I experienced at the airport. I felt the energy coming from a distance. Then I looked and I saw Sheila on the other rock holding a dagger high above her head. I was in shock, not wanting to believe what I was seeing. I could see the black energy pouring through her dagger into her body and then moving directly towards you. I knew she was actually calling on the dark forces to give her power."

"What? Dark forces, what are you talking about?" I exclaimed.

"I was terrified. She really wasn't Sheila. I mean, she wasn't herself. Not the Sheila I know. She was some kind of sorcerer, or at least that is all I could relate it to. She was standing there arms extended high with a dagger in her hand. It was straight out of a horror movie or something. I could feel the darkness all around me. I actually saw her look straight at me and as she did I felt a sharp pain through my heart. At that moment I knew I had to protect you. I knew that bitch was after YOU!"

"Me?" I screamed.

"Yes you! I knew I had to doing everything I could to protect you. I'm not even sure what the hell I was doing, but she was out to kill you."

"Kill me, what are you talking about!"

"Yes! The dark energies working through her wanted to kill and destroy you and I knew my job was to protect you! Ray, I actually thought I was going to die! I could feel all the life force draining out of my body! I tried to get your attention, trying to get you to see, but you didn't hear me! I was using my energy, my life force to block the dark energy from hurting you. What the hell were you doing on that rock?" There was such fear and confusion in her voice.

"I knew it."

"You knew what?"

"She was standing on the porch with that dagger in her hand when we got here."

"What are you talking about, Ray?" Toni questioned in a low voice.

"Didn't you see her with the dagger when we drove up?"

"No. Are you telling me Sheila had a dagger, you saw her with a dagger?"

"Yes! It was the reason I didn't want to be around her. I said so this morning at breakfast. Don't you remember?"

"Is that what you said? I didn't know what you were talking about.

You saw the dagger?"

"Yes, I saw it the moment we arrived. Didn't you?" This wasn't making any sense..

"No, I didn't. That explains a lot of your behavior." Toni was trying to put all the pieces together. No wonder she didn't understand why I wanted to keep my distance from Sheila, I thought. But why was the dagger hidden from her? Why couldn't see she it when we drove up?

"You actually think whatever was working through her wanted to kill me?" I asked confused and a little freaked.

"I don't think it, I know it!"

It all seemed a little dramatic to me. But in all the time I've known Toni, I've never known her to be dramatic or fearful. It just isn't part of her nature. So to hear her say with full conviction that whatever she was battling on that rock was out to kill me, made me sit up and pay attention. Clearly, something really dark and evil had not wanted the grid of Light to anchor through me. Toni had been there to protect me and shield me from the danger and darkness. Thank God on some level she knew what she was doing!

Stephanie just looked at me with confusion. It was obvious she didn't know what to think.

"Toni, don't you think you're being a little over dramatic?" Stephanie said with pure doubt in her voice. She didn't seem to care that her friend was falling apart from a very bizarre and unexplainable experience. Her best friend for that matter. It seemed strange and it kind of explained another reason we had never really connected. How could her natural instincts not have kicked in? How could someone be so unaware of what was happening around her? Clearly, she just didn't care.

"Stephanie, you didn't experience what I experienced!" Toni said defensively. "You've known me a long time! Have you ever heard me so scared? Have you ever known me to exaggerate or lie? What I just experienced was real."

Stephanie just looked at both of us and shook her head.

Chapter 6

The dreamer sees the other side
The veil so thin and slight
Becoming one within the school
Of co-creative Light

Seeing it so clearly
Yet losing it so fast
To dream the dream within the dream
The Master will reside

To wake one day with eyes so bright
To understand the rules
To bring about the one true dream
Within this universe

As I got behind the wheel of the car, my mind raced. I needed to make sense of what had happened. I had such a beautiful experience at Joshua Tree. It's what I would imagine being on LSD or mushrooms would be like. It would almost make more sense if I had actually taken a hit or whatever it's called. It was so surreal, so colorful, so vibrant and alive. All my senses were heightened and my heart felt like it was going to explode from the love I was feeling. Yet, Toni's experience had been so different. She had experienced something so frightening and dark.

The grids of Light I saw coming down from the heavens, going directly through my heart and into the earth were a profound experience to say the least. But why me? Why had the grid not anchored through Toni? I wondered. My whole body had shaken from the energy, yet somehow I just knew I could handle it. I knew I was strong enough to endure the intensity of what was moving through me. But how did I know? I also knew what was happening had originated from a positive place, even though Toni had seen so much darkness. Although my logical mind could not explain what was happening, I had a deep understanding that the experience was important, but what it meant, I didn't have a clue. I just didn't have a framework or a way to describe it. I could see the grid structure completely encircle the entire planet. I actually watched it growing from my heart. How could I see that? How could I know that was happening? It seemed crazy, but I knew, beyond a shadow of a doubt that it was real.

Toni, now asleep beside me in the passenger seat, had protected me from the dark energies. How did she know what to do? Thank goodness her vision had started opening up at the airport. She had started to see the energy just the day before. Obviously the timing was perfect.

I hadn't liked Sheila from the moment I had laid eyes on her. I had felt the danger present. My heart always knows when something is wrong. It has always been my first indicator. But when I don't recognize the signal coming from my heart, I always trust that my gut will take over. I'm just beginning to realize the gut reaction is a backup system, a signal that kicks into high gear when I don't listen to what my heart is instinctively telling me. Like my mom always asked, "What does your heart tell you?" I have always known, if I want to know if something is real or true, to simply run it through my heart. My heart never lies, ever. I have to listen to it even when everything else tells me otherwise.

When I first laid eyes on Sheila my instinct told me not to trust her. Was the dagger she had real? Was it really a physical object or could it have been something my inner vision was showing me as a symbol to warn me? Instinctively, I have known that various forms of energy exist. Good energy, bad energy, neutral energy and even evil energy. However, up until this point, the only reference I had with battling evil energy was from movies and books. But somehow I don't think that compares to what Toni experienced today. Thanks to Toni, I still haven't experienced it firsthand.

Even before this moment, I saw Toni as my protector. It fits her nature—you can tell the girl is a force to be reckoned with. I was so relieved that she had calmed down and was resting. She must have really been shaken to have cried like that. It's not a usual reaction for her. For that matter, she must have been really upset to even have let me drive.

I barreled down highway 10 to San Diego with the vision of Joshua Tree, the grid growing out of my heart and the disturbing thoughts of an evil sorcerer haunting me. It was so ironic, two such different experiences, one so beautiful and one so dark and evil occurring all at the same time. I wondered what had I gotten myself into? So many questions flooded my mind. Why did I need protection, and more importantly from what? My mind flashed back to the man with the amber eyes telling me of the mission I was ready to start. Boy, I hope this isn't what he's talking about. I can deal with the beautiful waves of Light and love moving through me, but I'm not too crazy about dark sorcerers out to kill me.

All those thoughts were fresh in my mind even as we pulled into Stephanie's parents' driveway. Stephanie's mom Nora is a bubbly woman. She was so excited that her daughter was home. In typical fashion and back to her normal self, Toni pulled out all our suitcases as Nora led us through the house showing us around.

"This is your room," she said as she opened the door.

"It's beautiful!" I said. The room was full of light, with a beautiful four-poster queen sized bed.

"Here are some hangers and an extra pillow if you need them," she pointed, "and through here is the bathroom."

"Oh my, I think I'm in heaven." There was an oversized Jacuzzi bathtub with my name written all over it. "I'd like to take a bath before dinner. Do you think anyone would mind?"

"Of course not. Take all the time you need. Dinner won't be for a couple of hours. Rest and relax, we will see you later." Stephanie's mom went to check on the other girls and closed the door behind her.

I was so happy! This was exactly what I needed. Time to soak and relax and let myself forget about everything for a while. I searched for the lavender oil I had packed hoping somewhere during our vacation I could use it. I started the bath before I opened my suitcase. I pulled out my makeup case and the new jewelry bag Toni had given me before the trip. I had a bad habit of losing my jewelry, so she thought it would be a nice and practical gift. I pulled off my earrings and opened up the bag to put them in for safekeeping. I dropped my earrings in and noticed a small glass object inside. As I pulled it out, I let out a loud gasp. How could this be? I thought as my mind raced. I searched my memory trying to remember where I had seen this vial before. Was it in that dream? I instinctively lifted it up to my heart...

Chapter 7

Deep within the cellular
Is the latent DNA
Which is the sleeping genesis
To awaken from dismay

Of true disconnection
From our point of origin
Deep within the stars of Light
Beyond our consciousness

Tones and codes and energies
Work continuously to repair
All the broken pathways
Within this human shell

It is our human birthright
It is our state of truth
That has been so dysfunctional
It keep us in disgrace

For the new frontier is truly
Human Consciousness defined
As fully functioning Lighted Codes
Within the human mind

T he amber glow of his eyes came into focus. I know those eyes. I remembered them from another time, another place, but where? I tried to remember, but the disorientation of being in no-space overwhelmed me.

"Hello Arayla. Do you remember me? It's me, Z. It's okay, don't be afraid. You're safe, I'm here with you," he said trying to calm me. He took me by the hand as I began to look around.

It was like I was in a dream. Like I was floating in space. There were no walls, no structures, but here we were. It was light, but we were suspended in the dark. It seemed familiar, like I had been there before. I was surprisingly calm as I tried to focus, to recall the memory of being there before. I could see a large oblong table with several people seated around it. I couldn't make out their faces and they seemed translucent as if I could look straight through them. Everything seemed like it had form or structure, but nothing was solid. How strange, I thought.

I could tell this was a meeting of some sort. There was the unmistakable air of urgency and the atmosphere was very formal. The table they were gathered around was a slightly angled and rather long rectangular glass structure or perhaps even made of an acrylic or some other clear material. I tried to focus in. The group of translucent '"people" were studying the holographic images which seemed to float above it. As I looked closer, the hologram seemed to be a depiction of Earth's solar system. One of the "people" touched the hologram and the picture zoomed in on earth. I could see grids of brightly colored lines of light floating inside this three-dimensional hologram which was floating in space. It was fascinating to watch. It was straight out of Star Trek or Star Wars. Actually the whole experience seemed like it was taking place somewhere in outer space, in no-space. The whole place was suspended in air but I knew that it was real.

Z looked different than those seated around the table. He was rock solid, not translucent like the others. He was dressed in a business suit of all things, with an unbuttoned white collared shirt, loosened tie and hair tousled like he had run his fingers through it a thousand times already. I wanted to reach out and touch his face. I wanted to feel him and make sure he was real! Then suddenly he squeezed my hand...

"You're late!" One of the people seated around the table yelled at me. "What took you so long?"

I looked at him confused. "What do you mean I'm late? Late for what?"

"We are using the reverse energy mapping program to determine where the fray in the system is. They should not have been able to find you."

"Who should not have found me? What are you talking about?" I asked. The others seemed oblivious to me, but Z knew I was there. He squeezed my hand again trying to reassure me, as the apparent leader of this meeting ignored my questions and continued on.

"We are searching for the stream of energy that was compromised. If they find you again, we can't guarantee your safety."

"My safety?" I gulped. His words were starting to frighten me. He turned his attention to the hologram. I followed his gaze and could now see layers of information within it. The first layer or section looked like a very detailed depiction of our solar system, another was a 3D depiction of earth, then I realized, oh my God, one of the layers was of my apartment and another my work place and another Toni's house.

"What are you doing? Why are you spying on me?" I began to panic and I started searching for a way out of this place. Realizing this, Z placed his hands on my shoulders and peered into my eyes.

"Arayla, it is for your protection. We need to find out how THEY found you. You were supposed to be in hiding, invisible to our opposition. We went to great lengths to keep you hidden, to cloak your Light."

What is he talking about? Cloaked, what do you mean cloaked? I shook my head trying to clear my thoughts.

"Invisible to our opposition! What opposition? What are you talking about? My safety?" I started to panic even more. Oh God, I'm in danger?

This can't be real. I must be dreaming. Dreaming that I'm inside a Star Wars movie, that is the only explanation. Yet, this Z person keeps showing up and I know I know him. I can feel it deep within my soul. I know we're having this conversation. I know that he is talking directly to me! If I were really dreaming, would I be questioning my dream? Maybe

I was having a lucid dream. Wait, what is lucid dreaming? My thoughts were going in a million different directions as I tried to make sense of what was happening to me.

"We've isolated the problem! We have to send her back into the past to repair the source of the fray!" Someone yelled with excitement. "The location has been determined. San Francisco, the Mind, Body, Spirit Expo."

"Arayla, you must remember! Make the connection," Z said as his face faded into darkness, but not his eyes. I can still see those amber eyes...

Chapter 8

Sitting on the sidelines
A soul can rot away
Not putting in the effort
To make the proper change

For life is truly precious
Something we must remember now
As global evolution
Is unfolding without a doubt

The matrix of our planet
Is changing as we speak
Into a higher frequency
Of Light and love and peace

We either ride the wavelength
That brings us to that state
Or we simply wash away again
Back into mindless sleep

I t was Saturday morning and I was meeting Toni at my favorite coffee house before we headed off to San Francisco for the Mind, Body and Spirit Expo for the weekend. It was our first time going to such a large metaphysical conference, and we both wanted to get an early start. However, Toni knows that good coffee is a must if she wants me to be anywhere before eight o'clock. My favorite spot is a little funky cafe down by the Sacramento River. The atmosphere is always inviting with its friendly staff. There are beautiful photographs of the river mounted on brightly painted walls, lives plants all around, good music is always playing and they make one of the best mocha lattes I've ever had. I admit, having a good mocha latte to me IS an experience. Coffee is one of my passions but really good coffee is truly an obsession. Oh, and not to mention when you combine two of my favorite things, coffee and chocolate, that is a personal pleasure I can't do without!

She'd already ordered my mocha, when I strolled in ten minutes late.

"You're late!" she exclaimed as she sat with the Expo program all laid out in front of her.

"Sorry!"

As always she'd already planned out the details, including staying overnight to be able to enjoy the whole conference. It's a couple hours' drive to San Francisco and neither of us wanted to drive back and forth.

"Thanks for ordering my mocha."

"You better get a to-go cup. We need to get on the road or we might miss some of the speakers I want to hear." I nodded in agreement, trusting that Toni would chose speakers I would want to hear, too.

Eyeing my tall cup of goodness I told her, "As long as I can take it with me, I'm happy."

You could feel all the energy and excitement as we entered the conference center. The main hall was crowded with thousands of people, hundreds of booths and just as many speakers to hear. With floor maps in hand and the speakers we wanted to hear marked off and identified, Toni and I smiled at each other, took a deep breath and made our way through the bustling center. But even as we walked in, I realized something was nagging me. I knew there was something I should have been doing but I just couldn't put my finger on it.

Then I realized my guard was up, I mean WAY up. It was a natural instinct, but for some reason it just didn't feel like enough walking around this expo. I could almost hear Jean-Luc Picard's voice saying "shields up" as I began to put a force field around me. What can I say? To me it seems perfectly logical, if it can work for the Starship Enterprise, it can work for me, especially in all this chaos. You always need to have your radar up in a crowd as large as this, where there are all types of people, even when it's a metaphysical or spiritual new age crowd.

Most of the time I get a pretty accurate hit of what people are about, but I have learned that it's tricky when it comes to "spiritual" types. I always want to believe that everyone on a spiritual quest is coming from the heart, but unfortunately there are charlatans in every arena and this expo was no exception. There are those who are really on the cutting edge, the true wisdom keepers who are working from the heart and doing their best to be pure and clear in their work, but you also have a lot of crooks and thieves just looking to make a quick buck. All you have to do is look around, the signs are everywhere. "Get your palm read" for $50. "Let me predict your future!" for $75. "The most powerful protection technology in the world—tachyon energy will protect your fields." Here, "feel the energy" for $350. Geez, if you had enough money, you could even learn where your soul came from in the Solar System and it's a bargain at just 1,000 bucks-! As I walked around, I wondered what any of that had to do with spirituality.

I tried to "feel" the energy of the tachyon frequency, but it didn't feel like anything to me. At the booth there was quite a show from people acting as if they were super sensitive and highly important spiritually evolved beings who could really feel the difference by wearing this new technology. Part of me hoped I would feel the difference, but after spending a few minutes sitting there waiting, I gave up. I could see where someone could be easily swayed by the testimonials given from other people. We are all looking for help any way we can get it. It seemed that everywhere you turned someone was offering a new healing modality, or an old modality newly re-discovered or ways to fix your aura by wearing crystals or gem stones. Blah, blah, blah. None of it was of interest to me, even though the packages and presentations looked pretty. My real reason for coming was to see and hear a few authors. There were several best-selling authors that I wanted to check out. Not that I had actually read any of their books, because reading isn't really my thing. I would rather see and hear them than read their books. Besides, you can tell a lot about a person just by being around them.

"There is lots of great stuff here. Have you seen all the artwork?" Toni asked.

"Well, not all of it yet, but what I have seen has been cool."

"It's time for the first speaker we want to hear. Come on Ray, I want to get a seat up close."

The first speaker on our list was a bestselling author that had written several books. I felt that he had a connection or insight that I might find intriguing. Toni and I had been to small psychic fairs, but never one with this many well-known authors. We managed to get into the fourth row. I could see Toni making a mental note to be earlier next time.

John Blueman entered the room and everyone fell silent. His energy was gentle, he seemed like a kind man and I liked him immediately. He was definitely popular as 200 people were packed into the small room to hear him speak. I attempted to listen, but I couldn't really hear anything he was saying. My mind was somewhere else, but I couldn't tell you where, or what I was focusing on. I felt like I was floating in no-time, just being present. It was strange, I really did want to listen, focus on his words, but everything just seemed so surreal. It was like I'd been placed into a bubble, an iridescent one at that. I just seemed to float in the room, without actually floating. Toni, seated beside me, and being the analytic she is, was listening intently to every word he said.

"That was a great speech," Toni said as we left the room.

"Yeah, I guess," I replied.

Toni looked at me strangely. "What is wrong with you, girl? You look like you're in a haze."

"Yeah, I'm a little tired. I hate getting up early." I chalked up my fatigue to waking up early. It was a while before the next speaker, so we decided to walk around and do some more shopping. There were a ton of metaphysical artists selling their creations— paintings, graphic art, jewelry, candles and everything else in between. Toni fell in love with one of the mandala paintings and was negotiating with the artist when I walked up to join her.

"Isn't this amazing!" she declared.

"Yes, it's gorgeous. Where are you going to hang it?" I asked.

"Right over my bed. I think it will help me remember my dreams more clearly."

The artist was signing the back of the painting as I wandered off to the next vendor. Essential oils, now that is something that actually helps me. Olfactory is such a powerful tool. I started remembering one of my first lovers and the musk scent he wore. Whoa, that smell could always trigger a powerful sexual reaction in me. Okay, back to reality I thought as a smile came across my face. I took a sniff of the Patchouli oil on the display table. Scent really can bring back memories, both positive and not so positive.

Toni walked up to me just as I looked up and saw John Blueman walking straight towards us. I smiled at him and started to go to the next vendor. I was startled when he walked right up to me and put his hands on my arms. Toni stood by quietly watching.

"I want to thank you!" Mr. Blueman said. Obviously, he could see the confused look on my face.

"Thank me? Thank me for what?"

A warm, gentle smile came across his face. I looked over to Toni wondering if she was seeing this as well.

"In all the time I've been giving presentations around the world, never have I seen anyone like you. Your energy is amazing!"

"What?" I said as it was all I could manage standing there dumbfounded, not comprehending what he was saying.

"The way you held the energy during my speech. The love that was pouring out of your heart. It was truly spectacular! Thank you for holding such amazing space for me!"

His words were so genuine and his tone so comforting, but all I could muster was a simple "You're welcome."

He looked at me with a raised eyebrow and laughed. "You have no idea who you are and what you do, do you?"

I shook my head no. He closed his eyes and was silent for about a minute, as if he were searching for the words. Then he took a deep breath and said, with his eyes still closed, "You are an amazing Light. You are a true master. A master teacher. You are here to assist humanity to remember who they are."

He opened his eyes and looked straight at me with such warmth and appreciation.

"Thank you for being here!" He gave me a long enduring embrace then smiled at both Toni and me and left.

We both stood there in complete shock. Did a world renowned spiritual author and teacher just tell me that I was a master? And in the middle of the expo no less? I was so confused and at the same time overwhelmed by his statements. What did he mean? Why did he say those things to me? Did he seek me out? Toni was just standing there with a puzzled look on her face. When our eyes met, we both started to giggle.

"Whew, that was intense," she said. I agreed. We couldn't just stand there, although at that moment I didn't really know what to do. I took a deep breath and headed towards the next vendor. I was grateful that Toni didn't make a big fuss over it, as I needed time to process what had just happened.

Toni has always known there was something different about me, says she felt it in her gut from the first time we met. But this was the first outside confirmation from a respected source either of us had received, and it validated a lot for both of us. We were both anxious to talk about it, but I knew she was analyzing it and I still needed time to let it all sink in. How did he know what he said about me? Why did he seek me out? Me, a master, what did he mean? How could he know who I am, when I didn't know who I am besides the obvious?

He was a well-known spiritual teacher and intuitive. That could explain why he "knew" what he shared with me. I have always known that I was destined for something different, something that would have an impact on well, more than just my small circle of friends and family. Something outside of the "'normal" life. But what did I really know about any of it? I did know the real-world stuff. I'm Arayla Malana Weaver, a single educated female, living in Northern California and a woman longing to find her partner to share this crazy thing called life.

Chapter 9

Friendship is a gift, my friend
That ultimately denies
All reason and acceptance
Within the human mind

For when a friend is truly
Connected to your soul
You give without a second thought
Loving freely through and through

They say you can't pick your family
Or choose whom you will love
But ultimately, your friendships
Are stronger than them all

So cherish every moment
Within your life you find
To celebrate the gift of friends
Who stand the test of time

Toni and I continued to move through the expo, stopping at a couple of more vendors and listening to one or two more speakers. But being in that much chaos and around so many people wears me out, so we headed back to the hotel early. Besides, I was having a hard time focusing, as the interaction with Mr. Blueman was all I could think about.

As soon as we got into the hotel room, I dashed into the bathroom, and before I could even get out Toni started with her questions.

"So?" Toni asked. I could hear her talking to me through the bathroom door.

"What, I'm kind of busy in here?" I responded, knowing full well what she was referring to.

"What do you mean what? What do you think about Mr. Blueman saying all that stuff to you?"

"Just a minute, let me get out of here will you?" I said, still running the events through my own head. Toni impatiently waited for me to emerge from the restroom and plop down on the bed next to her.

"It was pretty overwhelming to say the least. Me a master teacher? That was pretty wild to hear."

"Well it's obvious he recognized you on some level, Ray!" Toni continued adamantly. "You have always told me you felt that you had something important to do in this life."

"I know," I sighed. "But it's a little unnerving to have someone with his credentials come up in a place like that and say those things."

"Well I think it's perfect you ran into him at the expo. Where else would you have met him? Haven't you been asking for confirmation, for information?"

Toni had a good point. It was clearly a prime opportunity. Well-known spiritual teachers and I typically don't run in the same circles, and I don't attend lectures or workshops on a regular basis.

"Well, I think it was awesome! What a brilliant confirmation Ray, I mean you are really fortunate!" Toni reached for her pajamas, changed and crawled into bed for the night.

"Yeah, it's pretty awesome, but still, I'm not sure what to do with it. I wonder what he meant by, 'You have no idea who you are?'"

I pulled out the Seattle Seahawks tee-shirt I had stolen from an ex-lover. It is my favorite and always makes me think about him. He was a delicious short-term diversion I had played with between high school and college. I started to remember the events of an extremely passionate weekend that included a hot tub and lots of physical activity. He was a great lover. No, an exceptional lover would be more accurate. The sex had been so intense, I couldn't sit for a week. He had an athletic body, firm, muscular, but what really got me were his intense green eyes. One look and I just about melted. We were both young with neither of us wanting any real commitment. Just thinking about him again got me worked up and this was really the wrong place and time to be all hot and bothered. Geez, get your head out of the gutter Ray, I thought. Today you were told you are a master. Hmm, a master Goddess who knows a good lover! I could feel my face turning red.

"You always get a big grin on your face when you put that tee-shirt on!" Toni said with a chuckle.

I'd told her all the juicy details before. "Yeah, he was yummy!"

Toni laughed as she turned out the light on her side of the hotel room.

As I crawled into bed, my mind continued to replay the encounter over and over. It was really odd but fortunate that John Blueman came up to me like that. It felt like it was an answer to my prayers. I had been asking for guidance and clarity about who I am and why I have this deep knowing or feeling that there is something really important I am supposed to do. He had seemed so sincere with his words. Did he have any ulterior motives behind telling me what he did? He didn't try and get me to buy anything from him or attend another of his workshop. What was his motive? Was there any? Or was this just the confirmation I had been asking for to help me believe what I had not yet dared to think might be real? With these questions still fresh in my mind, I slipped into a deep, dreamless sleep.

The next morning Toni and I returned to the expo juiced up with extra strong java in our systems and ready to shop. The day before, I had spotted a couple of rose quartz crystals that called to me like old friends wanting me to take them home. Toni wanted to purchase another painting. She was focused on decorating her first home and wanted to use some of the new age principles to "refine her personal space." The show had so many interesting art pieces, and it had taken her all night to decide which ones she wanted. We sat in on a couple more presentations, but no one who really captured my interest.

We were walking through the expo and I stopped dead in my tracks when I noticed the booth for Power Place Tours.

"I have to go there!" I stated as I pointed at the picture on the table. I knew that place! Where is it? I thought as my body started to tingle a bit. Toni went straight to the flyer with the same picture on it.

"It's called Machu Picchu. It's in South America. Peru, to be exact."

"South America!" I exclaimed. My mind was racing and an overwhelming feeling rushed through me. I immediately knew I was going on that tour. It was so absolute and matter of fact. I'd never been out of the country and didn't know how I could go to South America for heaven's sake, but I knew in the deepest part of my soul I was going! I was so glad Toni was with me. In her organized Virgo style, she immediately started to give me a synopsis of the trip.

"This company offers spiritually based tours to sacred locations around the world. This is a two-week tour of South America including this ancient site of the Inca culture," she read.

My head started spinning as my mind went back and forth between the practical logistics and cost of what it would take to go to South America and the intuitive knowing that I really had no choice.

"It leaves in six weeks. You'll need a passport." Toni was already sizing up all the details of what would be needed for me to go.

"I don't have a passport. How do I get one of those?"

"It takes a lot to get a passport. You will have to file the reports, go through a background check and it usually takes 8–10 weeks to get it back," the sales person said.

My mind was doing somersaults. I had to go. I had to go on this trip. There was no getting out of it. My gut was telling me without hesitation that I must go to this strange-looking mountain in the middle of South America where the ancient Inca lived. This is crazy, I thought to myself.

"Ray, it's almost $3,000 dollars, you can't do that!" Toni reminded me. "Where are you going to get that kind of money?"

The sales person spoke up. "We take all major credit cards."

Toni frowned as the sales person was not helping to dissuade me from going. She retreated back to the other end of the table in response to Toni's disapproving look.

"Toni, I have to do this!" I picked up all the paperwork and asked when final payment was due. The sales woman said within three days and that I need to have all my vaccines and travel insurance to go as well. I was overwhelmed. What the hell was I thinking? But I knew I was going. I just didn't know how. All the pieces would come together somehow, I was sure of it. I made my decision right there on the spot, handed the sales woman my credit card and hoped I could figure out how to pay for the trip later on.

Toni grabbed my arm. "Can you get a refund if you can't get a passport in time?"

I just smiled at her. "It will all work out. I know I have to BE THERE!"

I was going to Peru come hell or high water and in less than six weeks. Toni could see the resolve in my eyes and knew I was responding to something deep inside me. Something she knew I could not explain yet, but something that was becoming a part of my daily reality. And she was witnessing it unfold right in front of her eyes.

The ride back to Sacramento was very quiet. There was so much to think about and so much to process. My intuition and guidance were getting stronger and I knew it was leading somewhere important. Somewhere unexpected, but still somewhere I was destined to go. I had plenty of vacation time available, so the short notice wasn't a problem, but the logistical details were daunting. I had never traveled out of the country, let alone by myself. I felt some comfort knowing it was a fully escorted tour, so I really wasn't traveling alone. But I wasn't traveling with anyone I knew, either. I broke the silence when I started to read the itinerary out loud to Toni as she drove us back home and as I did, my excitement just got stronger.

Roger Campsuit, author of the newly released metaphysical bestseller, would be a guest speaker on the tour. Cassandra Lee, another well known channel and author, would also be there. Cusco, Ollantaytambo in the Sacred Valley of the Incas, and Lima were planned destinations. I was so excited! Even though the places were unknown to me, they still had an undeniable familiarity about them. I knew it was going to be a magical experience for me on so many levels.

Toni's protective nature kicked in again. "Do you think it's safe for a woman to travel to a third world country by herself, Ray?"

"Is Peru a third world country?"

I'm not sure, but it is definitely not Europe." She asked, "Ray, how did you know?"

"Know what?" I responded, knowing full well.

"How did you know that you need to go on this trip?"

"Just my intuition, my gut?"

"Yes, but how do you know, how are you so sure?"

"I've just always had strong intuition. I'll never forget the time that my whole family was supposed to go to Disneyland. My dad's company rented out the entire park just for their employees and every year we got to go. But this year, my dad had lost the tickets. He swore he had placed them inside one of the books in the living room for safe keeping, but when he went to get them right before we were ready to leave, they weren't there. He was in a panic and my mom, brother and sister were all really upset."

"Geez, his company rented out the entire park. Wow..." Toni sounded wistful.

"Yeah, it was great! We pretty much had the park to ourselves. No lines, no crowds, it was awesome!" I continued. "But I remember being really upset too and I wanted to go really bad. I must have been around five years old. So I told my dad I was going to go ask my friends if they knew where the tickets were. He just barked at me like I was stupid and continued franticly looking. I went into my bedroom and asked 'my friends' where the tickets were. I came back out a couple of minutes later and said the tickets were in the book with the green cover on page 160. I remember it so clearly, even now. My dad just looked at me like I was crazy. He said he had looked through that book a hundred times, they weren't there. I guess my mom was more willing and walked over to the book, picked it up and turned to page 160. They were there, right where I said they would be. My dad didn't say anything to me, we just grabbed the tickets and left."

"Wow! That is pretty specific information to get."

"Yeah, it doesn't come that clearly all the time, but I've always gotten guidance when I need it. I guess that is how I know I'm supposed to go to Peru. The guidance just comes to me, and over the years I've learned to trust it. It's never steered me wrong."

"Well, it sure turned out to be an exciting expo! You received some pretty interesting information from John Blueman and now you're going to Peru." Toni was amazed...

"Yes it did! Thanks for going with me. I'm so glad you were there."

I had shared with Toni every "no-space" experience I could remember. Telling her about Z, who seemed to keep showing up. About his amber eyes, how the first time he showed up in Hawaiian attire, telling me I had a mission, something about a Crew and the feeling like I had known him forever. She had been so supportive through all of it.

Reminiscing about my encounters with Z, Peru and wondering what it meant to be a master, an image of a jaguar flashed vividly in my mind. I about jumped out of my skin as the sensation of electricity ran through my body. Wow, that caught me so off guard. Hmm, I think there are jaguars in South America.

"Are you okay?" Toni asked in response to my jerking.

"Yep, it's going to be an interesting adventure indeed."

It was a little weird to go somewhere so foreign, so far away on such short notice. If you had asked me a few hours earlier, I would not have been able to tell you where Machu Picchu was. Yet I made a split second decision that I would go, purely on a gut instinct. And I gave them my credit card. Who makes a decision like that in less than five minutes? I closed my eyes and took another deep breath. Even against all logic, I just knew I was doing the right thing. My intuition, my heart said yes! I closed my eyes with the vision of the jaguar in my mind and started to drift...

Chapter 10

Fabric Light constructions
Reality defined
Conscious choice reflected
In the outer mind

Seemingly unnoticed
Reverently denied
Projections of an inner hope
Sloppily applied

Remembering the sequence
Weaving threads through time
Masters of illusion
Masters of the mind

Knowledge does await you
Golden Light refined
Open up to higher realms
And Create Your World Divine

" The connection has been repaired. The energy fray interruption in the grid has been corrected. Arayla has successfully shifted to the new timeline," the technician said in response to Z's question.

I looked around knowing I had been here before. Then I looked down and realized I wasn't standing on anything. I was just floating in no-space, suspended in air, yet I was fully present and focused on the things around me.

The table in front of me seemed familiar, as the holographic depiction of the earth, the solar system, my apartment and my work place all came back into focus. I could even see a reflection of myself at the Mind Body Spirit Expo Toni and I were just at. It was like watching it all on instant replay or something. There were several "people" moving about the space, but none of them were solid. Only the man standing in front of me, the man I remembered now as "Z" was solid, wearing a vaguely familiar suit. I remembered him looking handsome in that suit. Why was I thinking about a man at a time like this? But my heart jumped every time I saw him, and this was no exception. His eyes always caught my attention. Those piercing amber eyes.

"Arayla, you have succeeded in correcting the energy fray in the system. Your safety is much more secure. You must return to Pyramid Lake to further anchor the new timeline. It's critical. Keep your protection strong. Watch your back and listen to your instincts. Your instincts are always right. Listen and follow them always," Z said as everything began to fade out of sight.

Chapter 11

Light illuminates consciousness
While intention sets the stage
For understanding everything
Within this Matrix maze

Your soul controls the inflow
Your grids provide the path
With ever-changing knowledge
For enlightenment at last!

I stood at the edge of Pyramid Lake, just north of Reno, Nevada. "Can you see it?" I shouted as if I were a million miles away.

"Yes, shut up and keep toning!" Lisa yelled back.

The sounds were coming from deep in my heart, and as I released them with my breath, became beautiful tones. Powerful, long, precise, perfectly pitched tones, as if I had been singing all my life. This was something I had not done before, but the urge to "sing" out loud was so natural. The tones just kept flowing out of me, and as they did, I began to see lights coming from inside the lake. Shimmering golden beams of light began to appear. I could see them under the water itself, clear as day.

The lights were emanating from the center of the lake right in front of me. I took another deep breath and continued to make the sounds, feeling the energy moving through my body as I did. When I stopped to take a breath, the lights stopped moving. When I started toning again, I realized the tones were actually connected or affecting the light. And like a conductor waving a wand to direct an orchestra, the light shifted and moved in complete unison with my toning. Each time I stopped to fill my lungs, the light held itself suspended, waiting for the next instruction or sound. It was magical. I watched it begin to take form, a form that was visually recognizable. It was a golden pyramid that floated up from inside the lake. My mind was saying, of course there is a golden pyramid inside of Pyramid Lake. You're losing it, Ray. You might really be crazy.

I continued to sound the tones, until the entire pyramid was sitting plain as day on top of the lake. It looked just like the pictures of the pyramids in Egypt only it was just a grid outline of the shape. It was not solid, but there was no question as to what it was.

"Can you see it?" I asked. "Can you really see it?"

"Yes!" Lisa replied.

"Are you sure? What do you see?"

Lisa said, "I see a golden pyramid of Light, Ray!"

Lisa was the perfect person to be there with. She has strong psychic abilities and multi-dimensional sight, which allowed her to validate what I was seeing. She was a single mother of a challenging teenage son, with a gentle but powerful demeanor and a lot of wisdom for her age. I liked her from the first time we met.

In that moment, standing on the edge of the lake, everything seemed so surreal. How did I get here? Was I really seeing a golden pyramid floating on the water? Where had those sounds come from? Was any of this real?

Lisa touched my shoulder and when she did I started to realize I wasn't dreaming, although what was happening seemed so out of the ordinary.

"Ray, that was amazing! I knew I had to come here with you. I knew I had to bring you to Pyramid Lake. My guidance had been so clear. Now, look!" She waved her arms towards the now illuminated pyramid.

"I'm not sure what just happened. Can you really see it? That was so intense, making those sounds and watching it all."

"Yes, Arayla, it is real. It's in another dimension of reality, but just as real as this one."

"Is this what you call seeing multi-dimensionally?" I questioned.

"Yes, girl! And it was you who activated this. My guides told me to be at Pyramid Lake during the 11:11 Star Gate opening and they told me to bring you with me. They were very specific." Lisa sounded proud of herself.

"Whew, I feel kind of weak and shaky." I realized this was taking a toll on my body. My mind raced back to the experience at Joshua Tree. I had seen the lights and felt the energy then, but this was different. This time the light had formed a pyramid rather than a grid and had responded to sounds I made. I wondered if Toni had seen the pyramid. She had been standing there watching the whole thing, and then I realized she was probably watching for more than the light. I wondered if I needed protection this time like I had before.

"We should get going, so we can get to the cabin before it gets dark," Lisa said.

As I reached for the car door, someone caught my eye in the distance. I stopped and watched as she lifted her hand and gave me the universal signal of "thumbs up." I knew that woman standing there in a Hawaiian dress with long dark hair down to her waist. But I couldn't remember from where. It seemed strange to see her there and even stranger that she was giving me a thumbs up. I nodded back at her with a smile.

I climbed into the car trying to make sense of what was happening. Everything around me seemed so foreign, so artificial. I ran my hands over the inside of the car door just to convince my mind it was real. I was glad Toni was there. She had been keeping an eye on me the whole time. I just knew it. She had only met Lisa once, but agreed to come for this weekend getaway. Besides, she wanted to keep a close eye on me during the 11:11 Star Gate weekend. There was bound to be some powerful energy flowing and she wanted to be a part of it too.

"Are you back with us now, Ray?" Toni asked.

"I think so, but that was wild." I responded as Toni, Lisa and I settled into the car.

"You need some food, you look white as a ghost," Toni observed.

I felt really weak and lightheaded from all the energy that had poured through my body.

"Are you okay, Arayla?" Karen asked.

I nodded yes. I had forgotten all about her. Karen was Lisa's friend who had flown from New York to spend this auspicious weekend and much anticipated 11:11 Star Gate opening with her psychic friend. I wanted to share my experience while it was fresh in my mind, but I really didn't feel comfortable sharing with a stranger. It was really frustrating to say the least.

The 11:11 Star Gate opening was all the buzz in the metaphysical communities.

I understood that the 11:11 Star Gate was a cosmic portal. It was an alignment and an opening that many in the metaphysical world were describing as a doorway. It was why we had chosen to come to the lake that week. There had been so much talk about the importance of the "date," and Lisa had gotten a clear message and then an invitation to stay on sacred Indian land here at Pyramid Lake. I had never heard of the lake, but jumped at the chance to spend the weekend with her and Toni.

I had actually planned to be somewhere else for the much anticipated event. A spiritual group I knew of had planned a big celebration and ceremony around the 11:11 Star Gate opening. People were traveling from all over the country to be in Sacramento with the spiritual teacher leading that group. At least that is the hype I heard from several people who were planning on attending the event.

I had met this "spiritual teacher," and the people in her group held her in high esteem. But I didn't get a good feeling from her. As a matter of fact, we had a few encounters that had been anything but pleasant or enlightening. She did not like me and the feeling was mutual. After a very unpleasant encounter at the state capitol earlier in the year, she had actually banned me from attending her event during the 11:11 celebration.

For me, it was like I had been banned from going to church or school or something. She didn't even give an explanation as to why I had become an outcast. The whole thing had been upsetting, but in reality I was much happier to be with my friends here, having this extraordinary experience instead of back in Sacramento listening to her lecture on about all her gifts and talents.

When Lisa got the invitation to stay at the Native American reservation at Pyramid Lake over the exact weekend of the 11:11 Star Gate opening, we knew this couldn't be a coincidence and it felt more like providence. Luckily Pyramid Lake was only a three-hour drive from Sacramento and made the trip easy for all of us. Well, except for her friend Karen, who had flown in from New York, but still it was an easy weekend getaway.

"What were you doing out there Arayla?" Karen asked.

I really didn't want to answer her, but before I could think, I blurted out, "Oh, I was just singing to the lake." Toni started to laugh. I quickly regretted saying anything. I didn't feel safe revealing anything that I had experienced, especially to someone I had just met a few hours before, even if it was a friend of Lisa's.

"Singing? Why were you singing to the lake? That's weird!" Karen said.

I ignored her and shifted my eyes to Toni. She was smiling and trying to contain her laughter even more, but she knew me so well, she knew I wasn't ready to share my experience, let alone with a relative stranger.

"Why don't we give her a few minutes and let her be," Toni tried to steer the conversation in a different direction. I was so glad she was there.

But I had to ask, I needed more information. I guess I really didn't care that there was a relative stranger in the car at this point. This was too much to contain and I was sure Lisa knew more than she had shared.

"Lisa, do you know what happened? You said your guides told you to bring me here. Do you know why? Why me?" I questioned, wanting to understand more.

"My guides told me to bring you here to unlock the hidden wisdom. That you were a key," she said. "It is the 11:11 Star "Gate" after all. They said the ancients were expecting you, that you would be given access and that YOU would know what to do. And I guess you did!" Lisa bubbled with excitement.

I sat there silently trying to absorb everything she was saying. I could almost see Toni's mind going a mile a minute.

"Toni, did you see the pyramid?" I asked hoping she had.

"Nope. But I was keeping an eye on you the whole time." Toni put her hand on my shoulder.

As we drove to the cabin I retraced the experience. I was so thankful Lisa had seen the same thing I had. It was great confirmation and kept me from thinking I was totally crazy. I knew the golden pyramid was still sitting on top of the lake, shimmering and glowing. I didn't have to be there to see it with my inner vision. It was clear as day and it was a massive structure of Light! I was surprised that everyone couldn't see it!

Chapter 12

Time is but illusion
Time is but a dream
Time makes life possible
To experience the extremes

Singing sounds of happiness
Singing sounds of pain
Singing sounds of inner truth
To ascend to higher planes

L isa drove us straight to the cabin and we arrived before the sun set. We unloaded the car, got settled in and started to make dinner. Toni is always so prepared. She knew there wouldn't be a grocery store for miles when she found out where we were staying. She had already prepared food for the entire weekend. It was a treat, she's such a great cook. She doesn't do "normal" food, she does gourmet with flare. She began to organize everything she had prepared for the "'girls' weekend," as she called it. Lobster salad with grapes and pecans, watercress salad with fresh pears and a lemon vinaigrette dressing, sliced medallions of beef with a gorgonzola sauce, a beautiful ham and cheese frittata, fruit, cheeses, a Chinese pasta salad I love and a batch of brownies. All of which smelled heavenly at that moment. I was hungry and ready for dinner.

"Don't worry. I brought all the stuff for good coffee! Heaven help us, I wouldn't go anywhere with you without good coffee!" She laughed.

"Ah, how nice it is to have a friend who cares." I giggled.

"Cares, you're scary in the morning without your coffee." She giggled back.

"So who wants wine?" Toni asked.

"That would be great!" Karen said.

"No thanks, I'll pass." Lisa piped in.

"Ray, you want some?" Toni asked.

"No, I think I'll pass tonight. I feel lightheaded as it is. It must be the altitude." I knew this feeling. I recognized it and, well, I knew something was about to happen, but I didn't know what. Food, food would help ground me. I headed for the kitchen and just as I rounded the corner, I saw Toni with a beautiful plate of cheese, fruit and crackers for us all to enjoy.

"And I have chocolate for later!" Toni smiled. Ah, she knows what I need so well.

"Everything is just better with chocolate!" I exclaimed. "Thank you Toni, it looks heavenly."

It was beautiful there and even though it was cold we decided to sit outside for awhile to enjoy the scenery. There was something mystical about physically being in that place, on Native American land, and I realized that I was really starting to "tap into" the energies. As I relaxed and breathed into it, what I was feeling became almost tangible. I sensed tears and lots of them, I heard drumming and visions of people dancing in ceremony, I could feel and see it, as if it was still happening in that very moment.

"Can you feel the energy here?" I asked Karen.

"What do you mean? Geez, this wine is really good."

"Oh yeah, perks of living so close to Napa Valley. We always have access to great wines," I responded, glad that I had skipped the wine since I'm a lightweight when it comes to alcohol, and I didn't want anything else causing me to feel any more strangely than I already did.

"Wow, I really can sense the dancing and drumming that has gone on here. I've never stayed on Native American land before. It's really quiet powerful, the energies, the images I'm seeing," I said as visions of what I can only imagine actually happened in the past flooded my mind.

Karen gave me a strange and inquisitive look. I forget that people don't often perceive the way I do, but this experience was downright tangible. I felt like I should take my shoes off, put my feet on the ground and start dancing in a circle. It was eerie. I could see a group of Indians in full ceremony dress in front of me, just as plain as day. Whew, I'm not drinking the wine tonight, I thought as I shook my head trying to regain my composure.

"Yes, it's really powerful being on this land, isn't it?" Lisa said. She was actually part Native American. It was the reason we were allowed to stay on the reservation.

"Man, I wish I could feel things like you two." Karen sounded disappointed.

I realized I needed more food as my body was starting to feel funny again. Toni and Karen were both watching me. I could tell Toni's intuition was starting to kick in, because she quietly asked me if I was okay. I nodded my head yes and took a deep breath.

"Food, I just need a little more food and some water. I'll be fine." But the tingling in my body told me differently. I had felt energy moving through me earlier at the lake, but this was different. Damn, I was glad Toni was with me.

With our tummies full, Lisa suggested we all do a tarot card pull as she's starting to pick up on all the energy coming. She is a very gifted psychic. That is how I met her to begin with. She had been at one of the spiritual gatherings I attended. After a group meditation she approached me and commented that out of all of the people there, including the spiritual leader, I was the only one she saw Light pouring into. She had said it was blinding and knew that she wanted to get to know me. We had been friends ever since.

Lisa had brought several different tarot decks with her and laid them all out on the kitchen table.

"Pick a deck." She looked straight at me. So I scanned the decks and picked the one with a Native American feel and handed it to her.

"Yeah, that's a great set!" Lisa responded. "Go ahead, shuffle them and draw out nine cards. I'll do a reading for you."

It seemed like a good idea, doing something semi-normal and grounding to bring us all together for the evening. Besides, it would be interesting to see what kind of reading Lisa would do tonight. It was the 11:11 for goodness' sake. The energy should be pretty powerful. I smiled at Toni, knowing she is talented at reading tarot herself. Me, I never got the feel of the cards and didn't seem to connect with them much. But I was always game for more information.

I picked out nine cards as Lisa has requested and handed them to her. She spread them out on the table in a specific format. I tried to focus on the cards and what she was saying, but something was starting to happen. I could hear her talking, but I couldn't respond or focus on her words. I could see Toni sitting next to me through my peripheral vision, but I couldn't manage to focus on her either. I took a really deep breath and tried to stay calm. My body started to tingle from the inside out and then began to shake, but for some reason I wasn't afraid. A sense of understanding and calmness overcame me as my senses started to awaken and my inner vision came back into focus.

Chapter 13

Beyond the heightened memory
Is the vibrating sound
Oscillating coded Light
Mathematical divine

Interwoven particles
Flashing specks of truth
Colliding within this universe
Of diluted truth

My eyes began to blur and the physical world around me seemed to become unimportant as my focus shifted to my inner vision. The pyramid that I sang to the surface of the lake earlier that day was brought fully back into my awareness. It looked different now, like a laser light show had started inside the structure. The contrast between the night sky and the golden light of the pyramid accentuated everything, making the form of the pyramid seem even more vivid. I could hear the girls talking about me and how my body was shaking. I could hear the concern and the worry in their voices, but I couldn't speak to reassure them I was alright. My focus in that moment was steady, strong and unwavering as all of my sense went into high gear. I was completely focused upon the massive pyramid of Light, which logically I knew was at least several miles away from where I was sitting.

With my focus unwavering, I saw something rising out of the top of the pyramid. At first it seemed small and circular, like a ball, but it was too far away for me to tell. Then it started moving directly towards me, effortlessly floating through space. My body violently shook as the energy poured through me. It was such a strange sensation. I could feel my body shaking, yet I was still so calm "watching" the whole experience unfold.

I watched in amazement as the circular object glided towards me until it was directly in front of me, approximately arm's length right in front of my face. I felt myself gasp as I realized it was a skull. Not a human skull of bone, but a skull made of what appeared to be clear crystal.

"Oh My God, it's a skull!" I shouted in complete terror. I was not really sure if I was shouting out loud or not, as my body didn't seem to be responding.

In shock, I watched as the crystal skull changed colors, from crystal clear to a glowing neon green. Although I'm not really sure, I think I gasped out loud.

"Oh shit! It just started glowing green! Lisa can you see it?" I exclaimed.

"Ray, are you okay?" Toni yelled.

I could tell by the sound of her voice that she was panicked.

"Oh My God, it's coming..." my words trailed off. But I was not really sure anyone was hearing me, or for that matter if I was actually speaking out loud at all.

The green glowing skull superimposed itself onto my physical head. Why is this happening? How is this possible? I realized I was inside the experience, but I also had the ability to watch all that was occurring, as if it were televised on a screen. I was in it and watching it all at the same time. This experience was so surreal. I had the strangest sensation of chaos and calmness, and both were occurring in the same exact moment and at the exact same level of intensity. The skull seemed to be alive, and I know it was giving me something because I could "see" the sparks of electricity inside my head. But what, what is happening? The skull completed a 360-degree rotation inside my physical head, then moved back out in front of me again. In a flash, the color of the skull changed from green back to clear. Then it began to float back through space towards the top of the pyramid. I watched as the skull went down back into the top of the pyramid, and then the entire pyramid sank back into the lake, disappearing from my sight. At that moment, everything went black...

Chapter 14

Patterns, templates, geometries
Restructuring our truth
To bring about a human change
Within our universe

The grand design is hidden
Within the DNA
To bring about enlightenment
Within the human race

The cosmic trigger activates
The Light codes to infuse
Our higher mind with memories
To bring about our truth

That we are not just merely human
But galactic Beings of Light
Journeying through the galaxy
On the Quest for Light!

I awoke with Toni standing over me. The last thing I remembered was the pyramid sinking back into the lake.

"Ray, are you okay?" she asked.

I tried to sit up and decided that might not be such a good idea as I was really weak and dizzy. Where am I? Why am I on the floor? What's going on? My mind started to race, trying to put the pieces together. My head felt like I had consumed a whole bottle of tequila by myself.

"Geez Ray, what the hell happened? I almost called an ambulance last night! I thought you were having a seizure." Toni was worried.

"Last night?" I said. How long have I been out? Where are we? Then I remembered the green skull.

"You shook for almost four hours, and you were making all kinds of sounds. You were moaning, screaming cries of agonizing pain, you were even speaking in a weird language. It was like you were speaking in tongues." Concern flooded Toni's face.

"I was? I don't remember. Why didn't you call an ambulance?"

"Something kept telling me you would be alright. That everything was alright," Toni said. "Karen was so freaked out. I didn't want her here, so I told Lisa to take her into town. I told them to come back later today."

"God, Toni, you must have really trusted what you were hearing!"

"I've never heard anything so loud and clear as I did last night. I just kept hearing 'she is fine, she is fine.' This is supposed to happen. All is in Divine order. It was one of the hardest things I've ever done. It went against all my logic and you know how logical I am!"

I began to tell her what I remembered. The pyramid illuminating so brightly, the object coming out of the top that turned out to be a skull and then super imposing itself on my head. The feeling of being so calm and centered and at the same time knowing my body was shaking and that I was freaking everyone out.

For a moment Toni was speechless. Then she wondered, "What do you think happened?"

"I feel like the skull gave me something, like it transferred information somehow. Important information." I tried to wrap my head around how strange it all sounded.

"You think?" Toni laughed.

"Did you see any of it happening?" I asked, hoping she had.

"No. It's funny, I kept thinking about Joshua Tree and how I was there to protect you. But this time, everything seemed okay. I kept checking and asking, but I didn't see anything you did this time Ray, and I didn't feel any darkness at all," she answered. I could tell she was disappointed that she hadn't seen the pyramid and the skull, but I heard the relief that there hadn't been anything menacing or evil this time. She had trusted her guidance, even with my strange behavior.

"I can tell you the first thing I'm going to do when we get home is some research and see what I can find about crystal skulls," she said, now back to her logical self.

We just sat there, staring at each other until we both started giggling at the absurdity of it all. Toni put on a pot of coffee. The aroma of coffee always makes me feel better.

"You have no idea how weird last night was. The sounds and language coming out of you would scare anyone. It was wild! You were rolling all over the floor. Sitting up and screaming in a language I couldn't understand, rolling your eyes back in your head. I didn't know what was happening. If you were having a seizure, possessed or what, I just didn't know." Toni found us two cups.

I wondered what did happen last night. Why was it a skull? Skulls are scary, really scary and not anything I would associate with a spiritual experience. But I knew this was a spiritual experience. A profound spiritual experience. I just didn't know the how or why yet.

"I know you aren't possessed Ray, but last night was weird. I mean really weird. If it wasn't for my own inner guidance telling me you were okay and that this was supposed to happen, I might have gone running too."

She's not the only one who would like to understand what had happened the night before! I retraced the memories of the event in my head trying to remember everything I could. What was going on with me? My life was REALLY getting bizarre. Crystal skulls superimposing on my head, my body shaking uncontrollably, people with daggers energetically attacking me, toning, grids of Light moving through my heart. It was all getting very strange. As I closed my eyes, I went back, back to the golden pyramid of Light. Just thinking of it, my body began to tingle again. There had been so much Light and energy moving through me. I didn't really know what to think of it all. But it felt right, it felt perfect and even though I didn't understand it yet, I trusted it was Divine.

"I need more rest. I'm going to go lay down until the girls get back," I said and drifted into a deep sleep.

In the dream world, my awareness started to come into focus again. The familiar sensation of being in no-time, no-space returned. It was disorienting, but this time I realized that I was not dreaming, but instead that I'd returned to the group or "Crew" and I remembered Zaratu.

"There is so much for you to do. So much for you to restore. The skull was the first of many initiations you will experience, Arayla." Z explained. He stood in front of me studying my fields and inspecting me from head to toe.

"Initiations? What initiations?" I asked. What is going on? Where am I? Why does this keep happening? Then another man appeared, and he took my hand. I knew it wasn't Z, but it was someone I also knew really, really well. His touch sent electricity throughout my whole body. I tried to see his face, so I could memorize it. But all I could see were his intense and beautiful blue eyes. Wow, I knew him! I remembered him, his energy. I loved this man, but how could that be? I didn't even know who he was, but his touch, his energy were so familiar. I knew him in my core.

"Arayla!" Z snapped. "These initiations are vital. You have to be prepared. You have to be ready. You need access to the information in a precise sequence. You have to know what to do with it. Arayla, this has to be your focus right now. Separation is the illusion. Your true love is always with you. I know he is coming into your awareness, but you must keep your focus! Trust he will be with you in physical form when the time is appropriate. But, that time is Not Now." Both Z and this oh, so familiar man with the loving blue eyes faded away into the darkness.

I tried to remember his face. Who is he? Where is he? I know him in my core. Was he real? Is any of this real?

"Ray, Ray, wake up, it's time to go." Toni said as she gently rocked me. My head felt fuzzy and my body felt like it had been hit by a truck. I hurt everywhere.

"The girls are back and everything is packed. Are you ready to go home?" Toni rocked me trying to get me to move.

Karen was waiting in the back seat and gave me a look like she thought I was crazy, so I crawled into the front seat next to Lisa instead. She turned on some soft music, and the peace and serenity were so welcome.

"Are you okay, Ray?" Lisa asked.

"Yeah. Did you see anything that happened last night?"

"I saw the pyramid again. I saw flashes of light and I saw your head glow green," Lisa said. "Unfortunately it was a little too much for Karen. You started to shake so violently and talk in ancient languages. It really freaked her out. Sorry I couldn't stay for you."

I smiled knowing she really wished she had been there all night. We all rode back in silence as the events of the weekend danced through our heads. I closed my eyes and started drifting off, but I was fully alert as I began to hear him speak...

"I'm right here with you! Arayla, you are safe with me. I won't let anything harm you. I will always protect you! I have loved you forever."

I knew this voice. I recognized him, but from where, from when? I remembered him holding me while I was lying on the floor at the cabin. It's not Z. Who is he? Maybe I'm going crazy. Toni would surely tell me if I was. I had clarity, yet I was so confused. How can it feel so real? What is real? That pyramid of Light was real. Real as day is day and night is night. I have no doubt about what I saw... twice! At least I have witnesses who saw it too. Thank God Lisa was there. Thank you Lisa for taking me to Pyramid Lake, or at least I think I will want to thank you in the long run.

I could hear the rain coming down as we cruised down highway 50 towards home. I drifted back into a deep state of relaxation. There are those amber eyes again! I felt disoriented. I saw those beautiful amber eyes staring at me, but I didn't know where I was. It was different than being with the Crew in no-space, which I had almost started to be comfortable in. This place was dark and my heart started to beat faster and faster. I felt on high alert. Like I was ready to pounce at any minute. Those eyes were so intoxicating and so primal. I was spinning more and more, losing my bearings, then suddenly I felt something change. He was becoming clearer. It was definitely the energy I'd come to know as Z, but he was not like I'd ever seen him before. He was in the form of a spotted jaguar, pacing in a circle around me. I could feel the heat of his breath on my skin. His tail flicking away as it outlined the space around me. Where am I? My head was swimming, but I heard him in my mind whisper...

"You're at the Temple of the Sun."

I know this place. I'd been here before. I was at the Temple of the Sun at Machu Picchu, high atop the ancient city. I could feel the energy of the jaguar, so strong, so primal, so powerful. He continued to pace around me with incredible intensity.

"Do not be afraid, Arayla. You know me, you know my energy. Surrender to me." I heard him whisper in my ear. Like a spider, from his tail, he was spinning a web of Light that encircled me fully. The web of Light, building up around me, was cocooning me completely. I could see the night sky and all the stars shining brightly above my head. I could smell the night air high up in the Andes, and I could hear him speaking to me as though he were whispering directly into my ear and my heart.

"Arayla, you are Light. You are sacred. You are safe. Surrender to the Light. Surrender to the Light. Surrender. You are Light. You are Light."

Like a mantra repeated over and over again, he continued.

"You are Light. Surrender!"

I felt myself release my fear and surrender to him completely. It was like I was a firework exploding from the inside out. Light was flashing from everywhere all at once. My heart felt like it was going to explode from the love and I knew that I was completely safe, completely secure and completely loved. I could still feel his breath on me as the jaguar continued to weave this web of Light around me.

"Arayla, stay in this cocoon of Light until you are physically here in Machu Picchu."

Chapter 15

My soul is called to service
Walking deeply between the worlds
To bring through ancient wisdom
And the long awaited cosmic force

The bridge to all this wisdom
Is held within my codes
Which is forming waves and patterns
To release for all to know

It is within the ancient
Ritualistic primal force
That the codes of information
Will come forth for me to know

And with this my soul remembers
The truth of who I am
The one who pulsed my Light with Breath
Creating life, where there was none

" It's going to be a blast!" I exclaimed as I continued packing my suitcase. Toni just rolled her eyes as she sat there with her checklist of things I needed. As excited as I was, I do have to admit I was a little scared. I was traveling to a foreign country where men with machine guns patrol the streets. The split-second decision to go on this "spiritual" tour to a foreign country was extremely impulsive and probably the most expensive impulsive thing I'd ever done. But there was no backing out now. Much to everyone's surprise, I had even received my passport on time.

"Did you purchase travel insurance?" Toni asked as she repacked everything I'd put in my suitcase so far.

"Yes."

"Did you bring your small first aid kit?"

"Why did I even bother to pack?" I proclaimed. "Sometimes I feel like you mother me too much!"

"Sorry Ray. You know me. You might as well just let me do it, I do it better anyway." I laughed knowing she was right and it would just be a lot easier to have her pack my suitcase.

"I'll get some wine." I made my way back to the kitchen. "So what is going on with you and Mark?" I asked. She sighed.

"Well, if you must know, he is at my house waiting for me." She laughed. Toni loves being in control, especially in her relationships with men.

"What? You're just letting him wait for you at your house?"

"Yep! It's good for him. Keeps him wanting me." She laughed again.

"Don't you think he will get bored and leave?"

"Nope. At least I hope not. I left my laundry on the bed. I just washed all my sexy undies. That should get him all hot and bothered." She giggled. "Besides, I have ESPN and beers in the fridge. What else does he need?"

It was true. Mark was smitten with Toni and she knew it. She was very controlling and men seemed to love it. Or at least she seemed to find men that did.

"Besides, he knows I'm worth waiting for." She giggled again. I rolled my eyes as I handed her a glass of chilled V Sattui Gamay Rouge.

"Umm. I love this rosé!" She said as she took yet another piece of clothing back out of my suitcase for rearranging.

I had tried to convince her to come with me, but she had refused. Jumping on a plane to go to a foreign country on a whim was not her cup of tea. I should know that by now, but I still wanted her to come with me. I was going on a trip with strangers. How did that happen? Why did I feel so confident about doing something that sounded so illogical?

"There, all finished! I think you have everything you will need," Toni said.

"Well, except you!" I replied. She smiled and hugged me.

"You will be fine. You love adventure," she reassured me.

"I know, but this feels different somehow."

"I have a copy of your itinerary, so I will know where you will be at all times," she reminded me like that would somehow make it easier to go by myself.

"Besides, you know it's killing your family. That makes the trip worth going on just to piss off your siblings. You know they are jealous because they don't have the freedom to go whenever and wherever they want like you do," she said.

"It's not really true," I countered. "My brother Bob and my sister Helen just have a hard time understanding me. They're both married with jobs and families; you know the American dream. I'm definitely the odd ball or black sheep of the family."

"Yes, it's going to be a grand adventure!" I smiled. "You better get home to Mark, before he gets too involved in whatever game is on ESPN tonight."

"Okay, I'll be back at 4:30 a.m. to take you to the airport!" She moaned, grabbed her purse and started to leave.

"Thanks Toni. I really appreciate you taking me so early!"

I guess I'm really going, I thought. The wine is making me sleepy, but

I know I won't sleep a wink tonight. I'm too excited to sleep. In my soul I know that this adventure will be life changing. I just don't know how, yet. Maybe I'll meet him, the man in my dream. Maybe I'll fall in love with a local and want to stay in Peru. Maybe I'll go too close to the edge of the cliff and fall to my death… Why the hell did I just think that last bit? I crawled into bed hoping to quiet my mind.

Upgrading to business class is so worth it! There is so much more room. They even bring you warm towels to wipe your hands, fresh juice and champagne before you leave the landing strip. The flight over to Miami was coach, so this upgrade was very welcomed. It was an international flight from Miami to Lima, and business class is actually pretty cheap. The ticket agent had encouraged me to upgrade. I thought she just wanted to make the sale, but now I think she was sincere. This is great! As I settled into the comfortable seat and reclined back, the gentleman next to me smiled. We sat there in silence until the meal service began. He was handsome, had a great smile, but was way too old for me.

"Is this your first time to Lima?" he asked.

"Yes" I responded. "I'm going on a tour to Machu Picchu. We will even be there for a sunrise ceremony on the Summer Solstice with a real shaman," I said with excitement.

"Ah, Machu Picchu. It's a magical place."

We spent the next hour in small talk. I couldn't believe my luck. The man next to me was head of security at the Lima airport.

"It would be a pleasure to assist you with customs. I will make sure you get through quickly," he promised.

"Oh wow, that would be great. I've never really traveled alone. But I'm a little more comfortable since I'm part of a big tour group."

"Well customs can be tricky, but you won't have any problems here." He smiled. "Perhaps when you come back after your tour, we can get together and I can show you my beautiful city."

"That would be lovely," I lied. There is no way I am going to go around a foreign country with a man I'd only known a few hours. What does he think, I am crazy? There are many levels of stupidity. Yes, traveling to a foreign country without knowing anyone on the tour sounds kind of stupid, but hooking up for dinner with a strange man while there, is just plain dumb.

"Here is my card. Just call me when you get back and I'll arrange everything."

Yeah, right buddy, I think. "Of course," I smiled back. I am used to getting flirted with, but not by a man in his league. So much was running through my head. Every hair on my body started to stand on end. He was wanting much more than a tour of his city and dinner and he and I both knew it. I just flashed my smile and pretended to be interested. To avoid any more conversation, I put my headphones on to listen to music for the last hour of the flight. As promised, he helped me get through customs quickly and without the hassle of all the panhandlers at the airport wanting you to buy everything under the sun. He even helped me with my luggage.

"What the heck do you have in here?" He laughed as he attempted to pick up my large suitcase.

"Everything a girl would need on a trip to a foreign country." I laughed. He would die if he knew that twenty pounds of the weight of my suitcase was actually bottled water. Toni had insisted I take water to drink. She told me most people who travel to Peru get sick from the water.

He even escorted me to where the representative from the tour company was waiting for everyone.

"Until we meet again, Ms. Weaver. It's been a real pleasure. Enjoy your tour."

I blushed and smiled, turning to the tour operator who was responsible for all 88 people arriving on the flight from Miami. She just snickered when he turned and left.

"Making friends are we?" she teased. "What is your name?"

"Weaver, Arayla Weaver."

"Ms. Weaver. Well, at least you made a powerful friend. You do know that he is head of security for the entire country?"

I'm sure my face looked shocked. "I thought he was just head of security here at the airport?" Wow, that threw me for a loop. Maybe I will keep his card after all. Never hurts to know people in high places. I waited very impatiently for the rest of the group to show up. They didn't have the head of security escorting them, so they took longer, a lot longer. About two hours later I was finally in my hotel room.

Chapter 16

Stepping out of comfort
Rings the bells of life
To change what is not working
To make the new path right

But courage is required
A requisite, it's true
But staying in discomfort
Will never satisfy you

We all desire happiness
It is the true pursuit
That forges all our destinies
To choose to walk our truth

H otels in foreign countries are different somehow. They have the usual things, beds, a restroom, etc., but it felt foreign to me. Actually everything seemed foreign. I guess that is why it's referred to it as a "foreign" country. I couldn't manage to sleep and was tiptoeing around the room trying to be polite and not wake up my roommate. Our hotel room was modest to say the least, but the towels and sheets seemed clean and so I guess in the scheme of things, it didn't really matter that the frames of the pictures were cracked and the carpets were really, really dirty. I felt safe, or at least I kept telling myself that. It's interesting how naturally your instincts and guard go up when you are in unfamiliar territory.

I must have drifted off at some point because I jumped a mile when the phone rang for our wake up call. Disoriented, I almost forgot I was in South America, but my surroundings quickly reminded me. I packed my things, collected my bags and headed down for breakfast. I still had not met anyone else on the tour except my roommate, and we didn't exactly click, so I picked a table and sat down by myself hoping someone from the tour would join me. Everyone was wearing the name tags we had gotten yesterday from the tour operator, so knew I was in the right place. The waiter came quickly and offered me coffee. I responded with a nod and watched as he poured a syrupy dark liquid into my cup and followed it with what appeared to be hot milk. I looked for some sugar, as this brew looked strong. Slowly I took my first sip not knowing what to expect. A smile quickly spread across my face. This coffee was fantastic. If I could get coffee like this each morning, this was going to be a great trip indeed!

My body started to get that now familiar tingling sensation as I sat there savoring my delicious hot brew. Consciously I knew there were people gathering and eating breakfast around me, but my focus was on the big amber eyes that were staring right at me. This time I could hear the voices that were coming from "wherever" he was. I couldn't make out what they were saying, but I could feel Z pulling me in to the space we always went to, the place of no-space, no-time. I could actually feel his hand touch me and I jumped. I was intent on following him out into that distant, yet now familiar realm, but I knew I had to remain present. I didn't want to "check out" and wake up hours later. God knows what could happen to me traveling alone in a foreign country, even if I was part of a spiritual tour group. I felt somewhat safe when Toni had been there to watch over me when this type of thing happened. But she was not here to protect and watch over me now. Somehow I willed myself to stay present.

"Arayla, do you remember the cocoon?" I heard him ask. "You are safe. You must be prepared. You must be aware. You must complete the sequence." Z sounded comforting and commanding all at the same time. Just then someone touched my back and asked if they could join me for breakfast. I jolted back to reality and smiled... "Of course!"

This woman was obviously hungry. She inhaled her breakfast and managed to get only one sentence out before her plate was completely empty. She was in her early thirties I would guess, with strawberry blonde hair, beautiful blue eyes and an obviously bubbly personality. You could tell that right away. I liked her instantly and was glad she asked to join me.

"Have you ever been to Machu Picchu before?" she asked.

"No, this is my first time. What about you?"

"No, but I've traveled a lot. I just love going to sacred sites! It feeds my soul, you know? Where are you from?"

"California. How about you, where are you from?"

"Oklahoma." She tried to get the waiter's attention for another cup of coffee.

She looked at my name tag. "How do you say your name?"

"Ah-ray-la" I replied. "But my friends call me Ray. Yours is much easier. It's nice to meet you, Vicki."

"What do you do in Oklahoma?" I asked trying to keep the conversation going.

"I'm a massage therapist. How about you?" Vicki asked.

"I'm in administration at a computer company." I frowned. "I don't like it much, can you tell?"

She laughed. "Well there aren't many computers here, and there is nothing to administer, so this ought to be a great trip for you. Do you know anyone else on the tour?"

"Nope. You?" I asked.

"Me neither. Well, now I know at least one person!"

The realization I didn't know anyone on this tour made me start to panic. I was in a foreign country and I was starting to shift into no-space again and while sitting eating breakfast. What was I thinking coming here by myself? Where was Toni? Who was going to have my back? And as if on cue, I heard the familiar voice inside my head.

"I will. I have your back. Arayla, you are not alone, you are never alone. I'm with you always," Z reassured me.

There was a brief moment of relief, but it was fleeting. Then as reality hit, I realized that I might really be in way over my head. I vowed to shake it off, since there wasn't a lot I could do about it now. At least I was on a "'spiritual" tour. Maybe someone else would have had experience with these types of episodes and would know what to do if I needed help. Of course, I didn't really believe that. Who could I trust in a crowd of strangers to help me? I ordered another cup of coffee to try and shake off the panic. The group would fly from Lima to Cusco on a much smaller plane than the one we flew yesterday. I found myself sticking close to Vicki for comfort, even if I did just meet her thirty minutes ago.

I really don't mind flying, but small planes? Well that is a different story. I felt claustrophobic, uneasy and crammed in that small plane, but I wasn't actually afraid that we would crash. It was just uncomfortable. Vicki sat next to me and we both took a deep breath when the plane took off. It was a short flight compared to my travel from California to Peru, but it still felt like it took forever. I found myself praying, which I thought was odd, but for some reason I felt the need. Something inside me was on high alert and I couldn't put my finger on it. I shrugged it off to all the new experiences and tried to let it go. I closed my eyes and drifted off...

"You have to be aware. You have to be prepared," I heard Z say. I woke up feeling disoriented. Vicki was already up grabbing her carry-on luggage.

"We're here!" she exclaimed. Wow, I had not even noticed we had landed. I thought of Z's warning and the uneasiness overcame me again.

Damn, I wished that Toni was here, and I started to regret coming on this impetuous trip. This was so not like me, but then again, how would I know what it was like in a foreign country, by myself with eighty-plus strangers going on a spiritual tour to a sacred site? Another wave of panic swept through me. I felt trapped and uneasy and wished I could just go home.

The locals camped out at the airport, trying to sell you their goods, really caught me off guard. I had experienced panhandlers before in Mexico, but today it felt so much more like a physical assault. I could barely walk as they were shoving their goods in my face and begging for money. There were all ages; young, old, children, mothers with babies on their backs. I knew they were desperate for money and I felt cheap and selfish that I was not buying their stuff. It was all too much to handle and I just wanted to cry. I'm not sure why I was feeling so emotional. I felt like an idiot and I didn't want anyone to see how afraid I was, so I took another deep breath and put on a smile. I was tougher than this, I thought to myself. I was as good as anyone else on this tour. However, I didn't see anyone else falling apart, but then again I wasn't looking either.

I followed the group into a rundown bus that would take us to our hotel. I wasn't used to being on a bus, especially in a foreign country. It was just like the old yellow school buses you see in the States, except the paint was chipped and the frame bent in a lot of places.

I stayed close to Vicki. She said, "It's hard to see them beg like that, isn't it?"

"Yes, I haven't really traveled much outside the US, so it was a really strange to experience. I didn't know, I guess I should have had some change to buy things with." I shrugged my shoulders and tried not to feel guilty.

"I always bring things for the children whenever I travel. I brought socks and sneakers this time."

"Geez, I didn't even think about that."

"Well I just always feel so blessed about what we have when I come to a third world or underprivileged country and I like to give something to the children."

"I guess I was a little unprepared," I said, trying to shrug off the feeling of being smothered and hounded. It was so strange to see children begging on the street. The whole experience was very foreign to me. My childhood had been very different from what I was witnessing in Cusco. I couldn't imagine not having what I needed. I wasn't spoiled, but I always had what I needed to be comfortable and fit in. I guess you could say I grew up in typical middle-class America. My dad was a professional engineer and my mom worked too, usually in clerical positions or as an Am-way or Avon representative.

I always had my own room and bed to sleep in, clean clothes and good shoes to run around in. My parents made sure we all did our fair share of chores around the house. Everyone had a job. Laundry was the chore I hated the most. I still hate doing laundry even to this day. I was in charge of cooking dinner every night during the week, doing the dishes and laundry for most of my childhood and teenage years. I thought I had it rough, but now I can see that I really had it made. I can't imagine a lifestyle of begging on the streets hoping that strangers from a strange land will give you money. My biggest complaint was Saturday morning chores, which were beyond our normal duties and included a thorough cleaning of the house from top to bottom, all of which had to be completed before we could go out and do anything fun. I wondered, what do these kids do to have fun? I always received an allowance back then, money to use however I wanted. I can't remember what I did with it, except spend it to go to the movies with my girlfriends on the weekends. I bet these kids don't even have a word that means the same thing as allowance does in the USA. My own childhood seemed like an easy life compared to what I was seeing in Peru. Life in this country was harsh, but I also sensed a simplicity and grace about it that was beautiful.

We moved around a lot when I was growing up. Dad always kept getting job promotions that required us to move, usually to another state entirely. Being in the aerospace business, you went where the contracts were. It made it so I got used to being uprooted. One thing is for sure, you learn how to blend in or fade into the scenery, so to speak. Every few years I had to adapt and make new friends, blend into the group and find a way to fit in. After a while, I just stopped trying to blend in and became more of a loner. As I got older, the groups became more cliquish and it seemed less and less important to try and fit in. Eventually, I really didn't seem to fit in at all. I became really good at reading people. Not to stereotype people, but there seemed to be a pattern everywhere we moved and if I watched long enough, the same types of scenarios between people played out. You had the popular crowd, the athletic crowd, the geeks and the nerds. Then there were the misfits, which I seemed to relate to the most. I really hated being a part of that crowd.

Eventually I just learned to be by myself and become part of the group only when truly necessary. As I got older, that need occurred less and less often. I never remember having a group of kids I really felt like I could just hang out with. Watching these children here now, made me wonder if they felt the same way. Did they find it hard to fit in, or was it such a different experience living in this type of environment, that fitting in was the least of their worries?

I wondered what growing up at the base of the Andes would have been like. I wondered if the spiritual energy from the past would permeate everyday life. Would growing up in such a rural and natural environment alter a person? Of course it would, how could it not, but in what way? Would one have more compassion? Would one appreciate the simple things in life more? Would you think the more industrialized world was strange and unnecessary? These children seemed like they were in need, but were they really? There was an underlying quality to them that I couldn't really put a label on. Their lives seemed hard and brutal compared to my childhood, but who was I to judge or know if that was real or just my tainted perception?

"I read that Cusco was a popular tourist town and locals would be trying to sell goods everywhere. So I was prepared." Vicki continued. "It's beautiful here, isn't it?"

I nodded in agreement. I realized I wasn't enjoying the scenery much, still feeling uneasy and uncomfortable about being there. I needed to relax and be in the moment and Vicki was doing a great job of helping me do just that.

"Look at all the colors and old buildings. Isn't it cool?" Vicki kept staring at everything.

Traveling through the streets of Cusco was a visual delight. The old churches, the cobblestone streets, the people, the colors. It really was a beautiful city. The old church in the center of town was right out of the history books. The bell was ringing as we drove by. As the bus started to pull out of town, it was a couple-hour drive to our destination and the rocking of the bus made me sleepy. I closed my eyes and started to drift into a dream state again.

Chapter 17

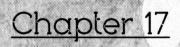

To walk within the portals
To see a whole new realm
Of magic, music and mystery
Just waiting to unveil

I can feel his warm hand touching mine and he feels familiar, protective and wise. His face is just inches away from mine and his piercing blue eyes are intoxicating. But why do I feel so cold? Everything seems white and sterile and really unfamiliar, except him. Those eyes and his touch I would know anywhere. I wish he would just kiss me already. Why does he look so concerned? He knows I love him.

"Mom, what are you doing here? Can't you leave me alone for one second? I'm trying to sleep. I'm just so tired. I just need more sleep," I say as I hear her voice trail off in the distance.

Max, why won't you just kiss me and take my in your arms? Hold me, babe. Just hold me... I just want to rest in your arms forever...

Chapter 18

Dancing to the rhythms
Of the universal cry
To search for understanding
Within your frozen life

The movement sparks the knowing
Of deep enchanting truth
Within the dark subconscious
Stored in your native roots

The erotic feelings surface
To unleash the primal force
Of penetrating oneness
To unmask your one true source

I felt like I was being watched, but I couldn't see by what or by whom. I felt as if I was prey being hunted. I could feel the wind hitting my face as it swirled around me, and the smell was sweet and sweaty all at the same time. My urge to run was strong. Why was I here? What was happening? Why was everything dark? The smell of ripe bananas seemed to be all I could relate to. Yet I felt in danger of something. Something I could not see or name. Why was it so dark? Where was the light, where was everyone? I felt like I was going to vomit, and I started to sweat. Behind me I could hear a voice. It was soft and low, but sinister to my ears.

"You'll see who has the real power," the voice said. I froze in place.

The bus hit a hole in the road and shook me wide awake. I let go of the creepy feeling from the dream as I looked out the bus window. I could see the old mission-style church complex that had been converted into a hotel. This would be "home" for the next couple of nights. It was beautiful!

A reception was being held in the courtyard to officially begin the tour. Tropical punch with papaya flowed from glass pitchers. All kinds of local fruits were laid out on a beautifully colored backdrop. The courtyard was a paradise of sorts. Large trees with brightly colored flowers hanging from the branches. The mix of the floral and fruity smell was intoxicating, and this combination with the scenery made the atmosphere seem magical. After a brief introduction from our tour guides about the featured guest speakers and the layout of the hotel, everyone was given several hours to find their rooms, settle in and mingle with the others on the tour.

Much to my dismay, I realized I had the same roommate as the first night in Lima. She was still less than friendly, so I decided to mingle with everyone else out in the courtyard. It was going to be a long trip without a roommate to converse with! I figured I had better find someone else to hang with during the next two weeks. I felt awkward and self-conscious as I started to socialize with the other members of the tour. That was a surprise, as usually I feel comfortable striking up a conversation with just about anyone. I was attracted to a couple of guys who looked friendly enough, so I strolled over and introduced myself. I learned that Gary and Tim were from Connecticut, in their forties and were both married businessmen, although they were traveling together without their wives this time around.

"They are just not into this type of thing," Gary nodded to his friend.

"Not into what, traveling with a group, foreign countries or the spiritual stuff?" I asked.

"All of the above. Well, I should say they like to travel as long as it is 5-star accommodations with someone to wait on them hand and foot, not what you would get on this type of tour," he said. I laughed to myself thinking 5-star accommodations sounded nice right about now and was comforted by the small talk. I hoped that mingling would make me feel like I belonged. However, I realized it wasn't working very well. My excitement about the whole adventure began to wane.

Dinner was still a few hours off, so I decided to lie down on one of the loungers in the courtyard to rest. I was still feeling tired from traveling and the altitude change and wanted to take advantage of the free time, as the rest of tour schedule was non-stop.

The meal hall was bustling when I entered for dinner. Long tables set with colorful tablecloths and pitchers of water. I found a table with a group that looked inviting and sat down ready for what I was sure would be a culinary adventure. The meal started out with quinoa soup. It was a strange texture and not very flavorful but it was warm. The next course was a potato casserole I think, made with purple potatoes and some kind of creamy sauce. The last thing I needed was spicy food, so I was relieved by the menu. I just needed something warm and bland to fill me up. There was lots of small talk happening around me, but nothing that caught my interest. I just sat there and listened, taking it all in. My senses were heightened and my body tired, and it was all I could do just to sit there. The meal came with entertainment, a local dance program with beautiful children dressed in vivid costumes singing and dancing to the traditional music of Peru. It was good, but my heart just wasn't into it. I chalked it up to my exhaustion and returned to my room before the end of the show.

I stopped as I caught myself reaching for the faucet in the bathroom to brush my teeth. I could just hear Toni warning me, "Use the bottled water to brush your teeth. I promise you will thank me." I pulled out one of the bottles from my suitcase and used it. Better to be safe than sorry. Toni was such a great friend. I crawled into bed with my excitement returning as I imagined the adventure that was about to unfold. There were so many people on the tour, I wondered how or if I would get a chance to meet them all. People like me who were searching for answers, looking for adventure and longing to find others who shared the same beliefs. It was hot in the room and the bed was small, but I took a deep breath and remembered that I DO love an adventure, as I closed my eyes and drifted off to sleep.

I woke up drenched in sweat. I sat straight up in my bed and was completely disoriented for a minute until I remembered where I was. I felt like I had been running a marathon and was really tired, although I knew I had slept through the night. It was light outside and about ten minutes before my alarm was set to go off. I just lay there for a minute trying to remember what I had dreamt. Nothing was coming back except for the notion that I had been running. I was being chased, but by whom or what I couldn't remember. It left me feeling really uneasy.

The meal hall was bustling again with everyone ready for breakfast. I took a seat at a table with Gary, Tim and Vicki. The coffee smelled great and the papaya looked superb. It was fresh off the trees with lime juice squeezed all over it. It was delectable and I ate twice as much as I should have. I did manage to get some scrambled eggs down and tried a bite of the quinoa cereal. Still not sure I liked that grain, but to get the full experience, I believe you should always try the local fare.

"Arayla, did you sleep well?" Tim asked as he took another bit of papaya.

"Yes. How about you?" I asked in return. He nodded yes and smiled. "Have you met very many people on the tour yet?" I tried to make small talk.

"A few people. They all seem really nice. Of course, there are those who are part of the 'in crowd' who signed up for the extra sessions with Cassandra Lee and those of us who didn't."

"How about you Arayla, are you part of the 'in' crowd or just a regular like us?" Tim asked.

"Me, nope. I don't even know who Cassandra Lee is," I replied. Tim winked at me and took another sip of coffee.

"I'll tell you one thing. I could live off of the coffee and papaya alone. This coffee is awesome. I've never tasted papaya like this before, either. The squeeze of lime is awesome on it, don't you think?" I asked.

"Well we are in South America. The coffee should be good!" Tim said.

"What do you think of the quinoa cereal?" Gary asked. I crinkled my nose and shook my head.

"Not acquired the taste yet, I guess?"

"Yeah, me neither. I'll stick with the fruit!" He laughed.

"So what do you know about our first stop today?" Tim asked.

"Me, nothing." I responded.

"Nothing, what do you mean?" Tim questioned.

"Well, I didn't really do any research about this trip."

"You're kidding me. You came all this way without knowing about the places we are visiting?" he asked in shock. "What made you come then?"

"I was just walking by a booth at the Mind Body Spirit Expo in San Francisco, saw a flyer for this trip and knew I had to come. I didn't even have a passport and that was just five weeks ago," I said.

"Well, now that is an adventurist!" Gary was enthusiastic. "I like that in a person. I like that a lot. Stick with us kiddo, we'll keep you abreast of what we know about the places we're going to. The first stop today is called Ollantaytambo and is one of the starting points for the Inca trail." Gary talked with a level of confidence. "You do at least know about Machu Picchu, don't you?" he asked.

"Well, actually I don't have a clue except that it is an ancient Incan city," I responded. I felt stupid that I didn't know more about where I was and why we were traveling to these places.

"Girl, you are too funny! How can you come on a trip like this without knowing where you are going? That is crazy," Tim said.

"Or someone who really follows their faith," Vicki chimed in. "I think it is awesome that you would take a leap of faith like that and all by yourself."

"You're traveling all by yourself," I teased.

"Yes, but I've done a fair amount of traveling and I know about the places we are going to." She smiled proudly.

"Well all I know is I had to come and I paid the money before I could even talk myself out of it. Believe me, I have questioned myself a hundred times since then." I tried to sound strong and confident. "I'm sure it will be an adventure to remember. Look, I'm already meeting exciting people. That is one of the reasons I came. I know that for sure!" I stated and took another sip of the coffee. I sounded an audible "Mmmm" and Gary laughed.

"You do like the coffee!" he said.

I giggled, "Coffee is one of the best things on this planet, next to sex and chocolate!"

"Here, here! I'll drink to that," Vicki said.

"Interesting order to that line-up," Tim said.

"Well, good coffee and chocolate are a lot easier to come by than good sex!" I winked at him.

"Well you just haven't found the right man yet then." Tim answered with a twinkle in his eye.

"No I haven't! Perhaps I will meet him on this journey," I said hopefully.

"Well, sorry honey, we are both married," Gary said.

"Oh, too bad!" I said with a smile. We all laughed.

"Unfortunately, I find that it is usually 90% women on these types of spiritual journeys," Vicki said.

"Yeah, well a girl can always dream!" I responded and we both smiled.

The excursion to Ollantaytambo was good, except for the fact we had to get back on the old yellow bus to get there. The ruins were okay, but for some reason didn't really pique my interest. I wasn't feeling particularly drawn to the place or the energy for that matter. I wondered why, it's really old and is supposed to have spiritual significance, so why didn't I feel anything there? It made me start to think about how many times I've been around spiritual people who feel a lot more than I do. Was there something wrong with me? Why couldn't I feel what they felt? Then I smiled. I wonder how many of them had ever had a crystal skull turn green and superimpose over their head. I had to remind myself that everyone is unique. Everyone experiences things differently. How could anyone ever really know what another person is experiencing?

Everyone gathered again in the meal hall for dinner that evening. All I wanted was something tasty and filling before I went to sleep for the night. Well, at least it turned out to be filling. My roommate was already in bed by the time I returned to the hotel room. I was starting to wonder if she was ever going to feel good enough to enjoy the tour. I thought of Toni and the way she insisted I bring all that water. I grabbed the half-used bottle and poured it on my toothbrush. Definitely, better safe than sorry. I wonder what was causing my roommate's illness. I crawled into bed and slept soundly for the first time since I had left home.

A four-hour train ride through the mountains of Peru would take us to the bottom of Machu Picchu. I loved the ride! The landscape through the Andes was spectacular. The train itself was the finest in Peru, the tour operator explained. It was old fashioned in decor, but very well kept. It was exciting to be on a train and a new experience for me altogether. It added to the adventure as we literally rocked through the Andes on our way to one of the most famous ancient cities ever discovered in South America.

As I walked down the aisle, I could hear several conversations going. Other people on the tour were talking about why they decided to come to Peru. Most of them were there because of one of the speakers, Cassandra Lee. She was a very well known channeler with lots of celebrity clients, and she'd written a couple of books that were all the rage in new age circles. Cassandra had spoken the day before, or should I say she had channeled the Star Beings the day before. I found the whole channeling thing intriguing, as I had seen a couple of people "channel" back at the Mind Body Spirit Expo. However, I did not want to sit in on Cassandra Lee's session. I had heard that she was a full trance channel, which later I found out meant that she had no conscious awareness of what was coming through her. I thought that was odd, but what did I know about channeling? I am certainly no expert on the subject. Cassandra Lee had a special group event, like an add-on workshop which was built into the tour. So those on the tour who were part of her workshop were sticking together, and if you weren't part of the group, they weren't very welcoming. Geez, it was like being back in high school.

I found my way back to Vicki, Tim and Gary. Those three were deep in conversation and barely noticed me as I slid into the seat next to them. So far, they were the only people on the tour I felt comfortable around and it made me feel almost safe. After about two hours on the train my head and butt had had enough of the bouncing and winding through the mountains. It was beautiful, but how many pictures can one person take? I had overheard bits and pieces of many conversations about this place over the last couple of days. Even without any research, I knew that Machu Picchu was an ancient sacred site and that the information available about this place barely touches on its significance and true history. Archaeologists were still unearthing sections of the ancient city even now. It was amazing to think I was going to walk around such a special spot on the planet. I closed my eyes and tried to rest. We still had about two hours before we would arrive at our destination, in the middle of the Andes, at the ancient Incan city. I probably should have done some research before I came, but I was led here by my gut instincts, and my gut had led me to a not-so-fast train in the middle of South America.

Chapter 19

Your worthiness is tested
By the Light you hold
Within your heart and consciousness
Your truth, It will be told

When initiations happen
To ignite the blessed soul
Your courage, strength and gratitude
Will determine where you go

Each soul has a contract
Long ago determined who
Would be the spiritual warrior
Bringing Light back to the world

So let your Spirit soar now
Bring in your highest Light
For you are the chosen warrior
Of Sources Pure White Light

The rocking of the train must have lulled me to sleep, as I woke up feeling like I had been running again. I remembered my dream from two nights before, running from something, but still unsure from what. My thoughts drifted back to the events at Pyramid Lake. I still couldn't get my mind around what had happened at the lake. It was such a surreal experience and so other-worldly. If Toni and Lisa had not been with me, I would have thought it all a dream. What was that crystal skull all about? It was so strange, yet I wasn't afraid. Why did I have the experience and not someone else? Why did it do a 360-degree swirl on my head and why did it ALL seem so illusive to me? When did my life start becoming so weird? The bumps of the train kept me from going into a deep sleep, each bounce and swerve bringing me back from the edge. But each time I drifted, I noticed that I had the awareness of the jaguar in my mind. A beautiful spotted jaguar, with the same amber eyes I was so used to seeing with Z. The whistle of the train signaled we had arrived at our destination. As I looked out the window, this place felt remote. REALLY remote. I felt like I had stepped into a whole other world.

Just as I was getting off of the train, I noticed her, the woman in her Hawaiian dress. That seems odd, I thought as I stepped down onto the platform. She looks so familiar, but when I looked back she was gone, nowhere to be seen. I asked Vicki if she had noticed her and she just looked at me like I was crazy.

"A woman in a Hawaiian dress? Not here honey!" she answered with a giggle. I knew I'd seen her before, but where? Was she part of the tour group? Just then I got a slight tingling in my body, but I shook it off. We were really getting up there in altitude and I was sure my body was just responding to the lack of oxygen.

The town was really basic and bustling with native Peruvians. With the arrival of the train, the locals had an opportunity to sell their goods. It was getting old, having the locals shove their goods in your face, but I guess it is all part of the experience and culture. I felt like I couldn't breathe. Too many people, too little oxygen and too much commotion for me after a four-hour train ride. I stuck close to Vicki, Gary and Tim. They seemed to sense my uneasiness.

I watched as the luggage was transferred from the train to busses.

"Where are we going from here?" I asked. Gary pointed straight up the side of the mountain.

"What? We're going up there?" I exclaimed.

"Yep!" Vicki said with a smile. They told me the hotel we were staying at was right next to the entrance of the site, at the top of the mountain.

"Yes, but not before we get some lunch in town. Come on," Gary signaled us.

It's a really strange feeling when you don't speak the local language. Luckily, Gary knew a little Spanish and could get the gist of what was on the menu. I asked him to order me something simple and not too spicy. I had a feeling my body would reject anything too unfamiliar at this point.

He laughed, "You really haven't done this much, have you? Travel in foreign countries."

"Can you tell?" I teased.

Tim replied, "Well, just stick with us, you'll be okay." I was grateful for the support and help. Gary and Tim seemed much more skilled at this foreign travel stuff than I was, and I was so grateful they didn't mind me tagging along.

"Guess it's pretty obvious this is my first time," I said with a smirk.

"Well everyone has a first time," Gary replied.

The restaurant tables were extra wobbly on the dirt floor, but the food was good and the service was friendly. It seem like the locals were happy to have the tourists come. Gary said that not every place was like that. Many places he had traveled to had hated tourists, so for him it was nice to be welcomed. A young boy came around the tables selling coca leaves. They smelled awful, but Gary said it really helped with altitude sickness and that I should tough it out and chew the leaves. I tried, but it only lasted about 45 seconds before I spit it out.

"Yuck!" I proclaimed.

He laughed. "Okay, to each their own. But remember I tried to warn you. We are going much higher and you might want to get used to the taste. You are going to need it," he warned with surety and wisdom.

After lunch, the four of us found our way back to the group where everyone was starting to gather for the bus ride up to the hotel. I grabbed a window seat, as I wanted to see where we were going. The ride was scary to say the least. There wasn't five inches from the wheel of the bus to a massive cliff drop off the road. It was crazy and thrilling all at the same time. I was hanging my head out the window watching as we circled and climbed the mountain. I've always loved roller coasters, but this wasn't at an amusement park and it didn't have safety engineers checking it out every day. I caught myself and several others squealing at times as the ground seemed to tumble off the road, plummeting down what seemed like hundreds of feet. The bus continued to climb steadily up the mountain for what seemed like at least thirty minutes before we made it to the top. The group was staying at the famous Sanctuary Lodge, situated at the entrance of the sacred site. It was quaint and rustic, with an old-world charm.

"This is a world heritage site," Gary said as we disembarked from the bus.

"It's the only place to stay when visiting Machu Picchu. That is one of the reasons we decided to come on this particular tour. And of course, for the speakers," Tim said.

"Look at the view!" Gary proclaimed, stretching his arm out at the magnificent landscape. "Wow. It's even more spectacular than I thought it would be. Come on, let's get a closer look." He started walking towards the ancient ruins.

The site was unbelievably beautiful. The high mountain peak, which was the landmark of this amazing place, was so distinctive and majestic you could feel the power of this place just by looking at it from a distance.

"I can't believe I'm here. It's awesome," I said for lack of a better adjective to describe it.

"Come on, let's get settled into our rooms so we can get busy exploring," Vicki said. I wished Vicki was my roommate on this trip. I don't think my current roommate and I had said ten words to each other. She seemed really uneasy and like she didn't feel good at all. I just kept my distance and let her have as much space as possible.

The entire tour group was to meet around three o'clock to enter the park together. That gave everyone about an hour to check in to their rooms and freshen up. With everyone gathered at the entrance to the park, the world heritage representative gave us a brief lecture about the history and significance of this place. Then the tour leader followed with a quick recap of the "spiritual" significance of Machu Picchu.

"This is considered one of the most sacred and spiritually significant sites in all the world." The tour guide gave us more facts to ensure the claim.

"We have planned this tour to provide the experience of a Sunrise Ceremony with a Peruvian Shaman, who will join us to perform this sacred rite. No one really knows what happened to the Inca people. There is much speculation, but most agree that they were a highly advanced civilization, both technologically and spiritually. We are pleased to have secured private entrance into this sacred site in the morning for this auspicious and spiritual ceremony." The tour guide continued speaking. "In the meantime, please enjoy your time today exploring this sacred site on your own. Also, it's exciting for me to share that archaeologists have just unearthed a new relic, a part of this ancient site. It is a large stone that seemed to be "placed" in the center of the courtyard. Please respect that we will have three hours in the park and then we will meet again at 6:30 for dinner in the main dining hall of the hotel. We will see you then." The tour guide handed us each our entry ticket.

I spent the next few hours exploring the ruins. I felt exhilarated walking around this ancient sacred site and was caught up in the excitement of it all. The group was scheduled to leave the park at dusk. Most had split up into small groups of four to five people and were scattered around the site. I caught up with Vicki and Gary to explore some of the higher slopes and nooks. I don't know what I had expected, but the site was so much bigger than what I had envisioned. Walking up the steep stairways, I couldn't imagine what it must have been like to live some place like this so long ago. And being at this high of an altitude was really taking its toll. What a hard life it must have been, I thought. Of course, when one really thinks about it, life was really hard for most of this earth's history. Even those currently living in the town below were living in what I would consider a primitive situation. Of course, I lived in one of the richest countries of the world. I found myself giving thanks for my life and blessings.

Chapter 20

Our soul is out of sync my friend
Within the rhythms of time
Being all illusion
So difficult to deny

Our souls will sing together
Combined within one note
To bring our promised legacy
Of liberty and hope

Throughout the spheres of space and time
The whisper has been heard
Of when the two, merge as one,
Will ignite the Sacred Soul

I t was just about time to return to the hotel when Vicki heard a couple of others from our tour talking about staying inside the park and doing ceremony around the new relic. I walked up as Gary and Vicki were discussing staying and joined in.

I knew it was forbidden, no one was allowed to stay inside the park after dark, after the gates were locked, the world heritage representative had told us earlier. But before I could think, the words "I'm in" came flying out of my mouth. Why the hell did I just say that? I didn't even think it through. Before I knew it, Vicki, Gary, Tim and I were all staying. I followed Gary back behind one of the larger rocks and waited for everyone in the park to clear out. I wasn't sure how this half-cocked plan of staying after the park closed was going to work out. Then it hit me, I didn't have a jacket, water, tissue, food. All I had with me where the clothes on my back. What the hell was I thinking? What if we got arrested? At least I knew the head of security, but his card was in my bag back at the hotel. Somehow I didn't think they would let me stop and get it as they where hauling me off to jail.

But, it was too late to back out now. I was locked into this crazy plan and in this sacred site, literally. Gary and I waited for about thirty more minutes before everyone who stayed began to gather in the center courtyard. I was in shock. There was no other plausible explanation! What in God's name made me say yes to staying? I'm sure I looked like a deer caught in headlights. I didn't have a clue what I was doing. Hell, I'd never even really camped before and here I was locked inside an ancient ruined city with no way out till morning. It was the eve of the summer solstice and the tour included a sunrise ceremony with a Peruvian Shaman, so I knew the park would open early, but that was at least twelve hours from now. I started to panic. I had to make it through the night.

"You'll be fine, kiddo. Here, take a swig of my water," Gary said as he wrapped his arm around me. I smiled sheepishly and did as he suggested. I guess several of the others had it in their minds when they entered the park that they would be staying overnight. They brought hats, jackets and toilet paper. They even brought rattles and ceremonial fare, including one who had a flute. It was exciting, dangerous and scary all at the same time. I wasn't alone, so I felt like I wasn't in any real danger, but we were NOT supposed to be there and well, as much as I am an adventurist, I don't normally break the law in foreign countries. My stomach started to turn and growl. It was going to be a long night that was for sure. I had no idea what to expect. I hadn't paid any attention to things outside at night, not that it would have mattered. We were a four-hour train ride from my last experience in Peru and several thousand feet higher in elevation. The only wildlife I had seen were the llamas on the side of one of the mountains. However, I hadn't really looked, either, and maybe I still shouldn't. That sounded like a good plan to me. Full denial about what was really lurking high in the Andes at night.

The sun was fully down and you could smell the crispness in the air. It ended up being twelve of us gathered around the newly unearthed relic in the center of the main courtyard. Twelve strangers coming together in ceremony on the eve of the summer solstice inside the ancient city of Machu Picchu. Ceremony for what, I for one didn't have a clue. I've never really done any ceremony, so I was totally unaware of what to do or how to act. I watched the others to follow their lead. We circled around the relic and sat on the earth Indian style. The man who had brought the flute pulled it out of his backpack and began to play. The sound carried across the space, and for a moment I worried that we might get caught! We heard a loud clang in the distance and the flute player went silent. All of us sat perfectly still for a minute, until we felt safe to continue. The flute player began again and the sound of the music echoed through the night sky, luring us all into a state of ease. The music brought us into a state of meditation and contemplation as we drank in the energy of this powerful ancient place. How did I get here, I wondered? I wasn't sure Toni would believe me when I told her about this!

Vicki was the first to get up and start dancing around the circle. Free flowing and graceful, she glided side to side effortlessly as the music swirled around her. Soon, several others decided to join her. The night air was getting colder and colder, as my body got more and more uncomfortable. Dancing around began to have appeal as a way to warm me up. So I joined in the dance, though I felt awkward and unsure of myself. What were we doing? What was the goal? Did there even have to be a goal?

My mind was swimming as the movement started to warm my body. Dancing seemed stupid, even silly to me. Why am I judging this? Why am I feeling like it is dumb to do? Why am I feeling so out of place? I thought to myself. I was one of twelve who took the risk of staying inside the park overnight. I had taken the leap of faith to do something completely out of my norm. So why was I feeling this way? My thoughts annoyed me and I tried to brush them from my mind. Trying to get out of my head, I focused on my feet and each time they touched the ground I could feel the surge of energy move up my body. I was dancing, high in the Andes, on sacred land where the ancient Inca civilization once thrived. But it all seemed so idiotic and I just kept getting more and more agitated at myself. Why was I fighting this so? Why couldn't I just be like the others and enjoy myself? Why, why, why? was all I could think to myself. I was so distracted and angry for missing out on the opportunity to just enjoy the experience and be in the moment. I thought too much. Just breathe, I told myself, just enjoy and receive and feel the magic. How many people get this experience? Quit fighting it, my thoughts continued. I resolved to be in the moment and continued to move with the music, letting myself go as much as possible. I tried to feel the ancientness of this space, tried to connect into whatever was available for me. We continued to dance and move around the circle for what seemed like hours. It was like everyone was trying to tap into something mystical, but I wasn't sure what.

Finally the altitude, cold and hunger got to me and I collapsed on the ground exhausted. Frustrated and confused, the tears streamed down my face. I didn't want to stay with the group. I just wanted space. I wanted to be alone. I knew I couldn't leave the park, so I decided to go back up to the Temple of the Sun, where Vicki and I had hiked to earlier in the day. I felt so drawn there and it was relatively easy to climb to. Before I left, I motioned to Vicki the general direction I was going and she nodded. I wanted someone to know where I was headed, just in case they had to send out a search and rescue team for me in the morning!

Illuminated only by the starlit night sky, I climbed up to the area known as the Temple of the Sun. That was the space I felt the most drawn to earlier and it was definitely calling me now. As I made my way up to the top where the sun disc was, I began to feel like I was not alone. I kept looking over my shoulder expecting to see someone there. My mind was really starting to play tricks on me now and I wondered if I had made a stupid decision to come up here by myself.

Just as I started to think about turning around to join the group again, I heard the familiar voice in my head.

"You're safe," Z said. "Follow your instincts. You know where to go." It was like he was watching me. "Yes, you are correct. Go lie upon the sun disc. Find the seal, Arayla," he whispered.

I stood for a moment looking around, familiarizing myself with the space. Vicki and I had hiked up here earlier, but it looked different at night. The night sky was magnificent and I realized it was the first time I had actually stopped to take in the beauty of it. I lay back on the large sun disc stone staring up at the stars. I looked for the constellations, but soon realized I was in the southern hemisphere and that all the constellations were different than the ones I would see at home. It was the most magical sky I had ever seen. I was so high up in altitude on top of the Andes there was no visible light pollution to diminish the view. There were so many stars, more than I had ever seen before with my own eyes! I just lay there soaking it all in. There I was, lying on the sun disc in the Temple of the Sun, looking at the massive sky above me, realizing how small and insignificant I really was in the scheme of things. Then for a split second, I panicked. What if a spaceship showed up? I laughed at myself and thought, what a stupid notion to have! I didn't really believe in spaceships, did I? As I lay there on the large stone, I could sense that my body temperature was starting to drop. It was cold and I began to shiver. I curled up in a ball, fetal style on the stone, closed my eyes and began to pray. Well, pray might not be the right word. I started to talk to Z.

"Please, why am I here? What am I doing here? Why have I come?" I pleaded for answers. Then my body started to have that familiar tingling feeling again. At this point I wasn't really sure if it was the cold or something else that was making my body feel this way.

"Breathe, Arayla," Z said. His voice began to swirl in my head. Those large amber eyes appeared, but this time he was not in the form of the man I was used to seeing. No, all I could see were the eyes, but they were different somehow. Primal. I could feel my heart beating faster and faster. I began to feel his pulse, not mine. I was feeling Z's heart beat. His energy was powerful and animalistic, rhythmic and seductive, primal and hypnotic. My senses sharpened as the sounds and energy around me seemed more potent and alive.

I watched as a jaguar slowly started to materialize in front of me. I knew it was not real, at least not here in the physical world. But yet at the same time, he was real. I could feel his pulse. I could feel his breath on me. I could feel his primal energy surrounding me. I was mesmerized and paralyzed at the same time, yet I had a sense of calmness and protection, more so than I had felt all night. The jaguar started to pace around me, encircling me as I lay on the ancient sun stone. His tail drew a line in the ground as Light poured out of the tip. I could feel his amber eyes upon me, penetrating me even from behind. The ground seemed to be spinning and I felt dizzy and disoriented. I felt his heart connect with mine in a powerful electrifying pulse, and the primal energy exploded throughout my body. What was happening? He could hear my thoughts, before I even thought them.

"We are ONE in the Higher Realms of Light. Feel my pulse, our pulse, the pulse of the universe move through you, Arayla. Feel the love. Feel the love as it moves through your body and soul. Feel the love, the Light as it moves throughout all space and time," Z whispered in my ear. My heartbeat quickened. I could focus on nothing but the Light that was spinning around me. Like a spider spinning a web, he was cocooning me in a pure, soft web of Light. With each circle his tail weaved another layer and the cocoon became stronger. The Light was coming from beneath me, from under the stone, encasing me fully within his Light.

"Remember who you are. Feel the knowledge feeding into your heart. You were here before, Arayla. You have walked these lands before as a Priestess of Light. You have ruled the world where magic and life intersect. You have built the bridges of Light into the outer reaches of the Universe. Remember your truth. Feel the pulse through your veins. Feel the codes flooding your soul. Remember who you are. Remember, remember..." He spoke with such power it echoed through my entire soul.

I felt as if I were going to fall off the stone, the energy was so strong. I held on for dear life, as my body felt dizzy and weak. Swirling and rocking, my body responded as his voice filled my head once again.

"It's time to rebuild you back to your true essence. Do you trust me? Will you surrender fully to me, Arayla?"

Yes, I could hear my soul crying out to him. Yes!

"Release Arayla, release your doubts, your fears, your confusion. Call back your essence. All pieces of your soul throughout all of eternity. I will rebuild you. I will bring you back into wholeness. Our hearts are as one in the higher realms of Light. Surrender to the process, Arayla. Trust me. You must trust me with everything. I am here to help you, to help you succeed," he said. While the intensity of this energy engrossed me, my mind became aware of the Crew of Light Beings standing before me.

Chapter 21

Your jaguar energy anchors me
Within this physical plane
While Lighted codes of infinity
Acquiesce my higher frames

For truth be told, you scare me
Your power beyond this realm
Yet deep within, I feel we've been
United by heaven... again

It's time to return to the beginning," one of the Crew members said. "The place and time when the Ancient Grandmothers began the cycle..."

Where am I? It always felt so surreal. I realized I was next to Z, our hands intertwined, as we stood together in front of the Crew.

"Have you gathered the knowledge?" asked the Crew member. I stood there confused, unable to answer. "Have you gathered the knowledge?" He asked again, as if I was supposed to know what he was talking about.

Z spoke up. "We are in the process of gathering it."

"Good, begin the sequence to pull the timelines. She must return to the seal. It must be anchored there. Each piece is vital. The sequencing must be precise," the Crew member directed.

"What seal? What are you talking about?" I questioned, and yet a part of me remembered standing on a seal. A round copper seal cemented in the ground with such power pulsing through it. When was that? I couldn't remember. Just then Z squeezed my hand and I zipped through space and time and found myself standing with my hands raised above my head.

Where was I? What was happening? Suddenly I was speaking in an ancient language and vocal tones were resounding from deep in my soul. My body shook and trembled as the energy poured through me. It was daylight and the sun was hot on my face. There were people around me, but I didn't seem to be able to bring them into focus. I could hear voices behind me.

"What is she doing? Ray, are you okay?" One of the onlookers was questioning me.

In a flash I was aware of the codes embedding into my matrix, into my energy fields surrounding my body. The ancient symbols lit up like fireworks pulsing throughout my body. My body was shaking and I was twirling around in a circle. As I stopped, I realized I was standing in front of the California capitol building. How did I get to Sacramento? Just as I realized where I was, everything shifted and I was floating in warm water, everything shifted again and I was aware of being with the Crew of Light Beings in no-time, no-space. Z squeezed my hand and a pulse of pure love engulfed my body.

"Is the seal prepared?" the Crew member asked.

"Yes." I responded without really knowing what I was responding to.

"Continue to rebuild her, Zaratu. We are all counting on you," the Crew member said.

In a flash the Crew of Light vanished and I was remotely aware of the solid rock beneath me. I could sense the cold around me, yet I could not actually feel it. What was happening? My awareness returned to the jaguar encircling me. The pulse of his heartbeat entrained with mine. Our hearts beating as one, as the web of Light continued to spin around me, cocooning me, protecting me. There was such immense love pouring from his heart into mine. I felt secure, I felt safe, I felt protected and I felt lost all at the same time.

"Allow me in Arayla. Release your fears. Your soul longs for this. You must trust me Arayla. You must surrender, trust me completely, allow me full access so I can expand your matrix. You must be able to hold all of the Light and knowledge." Z's words echoed in my head as the web of Light solidified around me. This energy felt loving, comforting and ancient, really ancient. I knew it was Z who was with me, but the energy surrounding me, penetrating me was so primal, so basic, so pure it was beyond what I knew as love. It was so much more, so all encompassing, so universal and so complete.

"What are you doing to me?" I asked.

"Bringing you back into wholeness," he replied.

"Why me?" I questioned.

"Because you promised to return and begin the new cycle. You promised to weave the fabric of this universe back into the purity of Love. You promised to bring back the Light to its original harmonic frequency, Arayla. It is your purpose and soul's reason for being. Remember..." Z answered.

My mind could not process all of the sensations and information flooding my fields. My thoughts just kept spinning in my head, as my awareness slipped deeper and deeper into the pulse of the jaguar...the heartbeat of the universe.

My body was getting warmer and my senses were beginning to return. My eyes could still only see light, light everywhere, but I was beginning to hear other voices in the distance. Drums, singing and chanting of some sort.

I was still focused on the jaguar, feeling the intense energy running through my body and the pure love flowing between the jaguar's heart and mine, when suddenly a fist punched through the cocoon and grabbed me, ripping me out of the Light. I gasped, as I was violently pulled back into this reality. I could feel his hand still grabbing my shirt as his eyes stared back at me with intensity and resolve. He had penetrated the web of Light the Jaguar, Z had built around me and he had pulled me back, back into this reality. Our eyes locked in a trance, while my senses returned fully and I realized where I was. I was still sitting on the rock, the Sun Disc in the Temple of the Sun. A smile crept on his face as he watched me regain my composure and then he finally released me from his grip. He had pulled me from the web of Light, never missing a beat of the drum.

"Ayha ayha ayha na." The Shaman continued as he danced around the ancient rock. It was sunrise on the summer solstice and everyone from the group was there for the ceremony at the Temple of the Sun. Vicki let out a loud gasp when she saw me materialize in front of her. She fell backwards into Gary who was standing behind her. The shock in her eyes scared me. Where did all these people come from? How had I not heard them? How did it get to be daytime? Vicki pushed her way over to me through the crowd.

Chapter 22

Starlight is our compass
Shining through the void
Expanding out the universe
Connecting Light and sound

Until the breath resends us
To change the natural flow
From expansion to contraction
Within this ALL will go

From individual expression
To united Light as One
This universal expression
Will transverse our central sun

The eons will collide then
All time and space divide
To end all things within this dream
To start again... New Time

" Oh my God! That was amazing. I can't believe that just happened. YOU, my dear, just materialized out of thin air. POOF! The Shaman was dancing around the sun stone and then suddenly you were sitting on top of it! Where have you been all night? We've been searching and searching for you. I was so afraid something had happened to you."

"Vicki, I've been right here on this rock all night," I said in my defense.

"Well I've got news for you girl, not a single person here could see you! You disappeared last night and scared the shit out of me, Ray. I was so mad at you, but now I understand. I KNEW something was different about you! Honey, you are special." Vicki spoke with a touch of awe...

The Shaman stared at us in a very commanding way, making us both stop talking, as he circled back around to where we were. The Shaman and I locked eyes and a chill moved up my spine. He took my hand and several people in the crowd gasped. I could hear them whispering... Where did she come from? I didn't think anyone was allowed on the stone. What is she doing there? How come she's so special? Why is he paying attention to her? Is she with our group? The Shaman raised his hand to silence everyone and once again made direct eye contact with me.

"Welcome Arayla. Did you receive all you came for?" The Shaman asked with gentleness.

Oh my God! How does he know my name? I wondered. I just sat there in silence not knowing how to respond. Everyone was staring at me and I felt confused and self-conscious. He squeezed my hand and the memory of the night before shot through my mind. I remembered Z doing the same thing during the night and as I remembered, the Shaman released my hand and began to chant once again.

I started to climb off the Sun Temple stone, but he put his hand out to stop me. So I closed my eyes and tried to remember what had transpired throughout the night. Images started to flash and a strange calmness moved through me. My heart started to expand and I felt whole. Standing in front of me, the Shaman grabbed both of my feet that were dangling from the rock and pulled them up to his heart. My eyes opened to see his piercing back at me, like he was looking straight into my soul. He released my feet and placed his palm directly on my heart. I didn't flinch as the blast of energy penetrated my entire body. He smiled at me once more as my body recovered, but it felt good and I felt complete. He took my hand to help me off the stone never releasing it. I stood next to him looking out at the crowd of people gathered.

There she was, out in the distance, the same woman I had seen the day before. The woman in the Hawaiian dress. She smiled, nodded and just as I was going to nod back, I started to hear rumblings again from the crowd and my attention shifted.

"Geez, who does she think she is? What was that all about? What is her name? Did you hear what the Shaman said to her?" The Shaman released me and at the same time, I noticed he placed something in my pocket.

He led us all down from the Temple of the Sun, back into the courtyard section of the city. Once there, he grabbed my hand once again, kissed it gently, released me and disappeared into the crowd.

There I was, standing alone in the crowd, trying to take in all that had happened. I started looking for Vicki or Gary for some kind of support. Where had they gone? I thought they were right next to me when we started down from the ceremony. I wanted to go back to the hotel and lie down. I spotted Vicki and started walking towards her when out of nowhere a sharp piercing pain came in through my back and went directly into my heart. I screamed in pain and bent over in agony grabbing my chest. I heard several people gasp and one directly behind me who laughed. Why would someone laugh? I thought, but then I knew. I turned quickly to see who it was, but I couldn't figure it out. I knew the laugh was female, but no one stood out that I could identify. Fear started to run through me and all my instincts went into high gear.

"Ray, are you okay? What's wrong?" Vicki asked as she tried to comfort me.

"I need to get out of here." I responded with panic in my voice.

"We can't leave now! The Shaman is not done yet." She motioned in his direction.

I realized she was right and tried to calm my fears. I was in a crowd of people. I wasn't alone anymore and it was daylight. Whatever or whoever had sent that energy into me couldn't do any real harm right now. But I knew I was wrong, even as I thought it. Whoever laughed had sent a piercing energy right through my heart. An energy that was strong enough to make me cry out loud. Whoever sent that energy could hurt me and my instincts knew that was exactly her intention. Where was Z now? He said I was safe with him. Can he protect me now? Can he protect me from someone in the physical world? I felt vulnerable and on guard as the sun rose higher in the blue sky, and I wished the Shaman would hurry up and finish.

Gary came over once the Shaman was done.

"Are you two alright? Arayla, I heard you scream out. What happened? Vicki and I were worried sick about you last night. We searched and searched for you," he continued, and you could tell he was truly concerned.

"I was right there on the sun disc all night long," I stated. He just looked and me and then at Vicki.

"We searched up there several times last night. You were nowhere to be found. Then I was watching the Shaman and bam, all of a sudden there you were sitting on the rock! What was that all about?" Gary asked.

I could tell Gary was trying to make sense of all of it, but so was I. "Honestly, I don't know Gary! I was deep in a trance I guess when all of a sudden the Shaman pulled me out."

"Out of what?" Gary cried. "You were not there, and then you were!"

"I know it sounds weird, but I was in a cocoon of Light. There was a jaguar. I was in front of a group of Light Beings. I don't know!"

"Here, drink some water," Gary handed me his water bottle. "Have you had any food or anything?"

"No! I didn't have a clue we would be staying overnight inside the park. I didn't bring any water, food, tissue, a coat. Nothing!" I was ready to burst into tears from the emotion of it all. Gary wrapped his arm around me to comfort me and offered me another drink of his water.

"You'll be okay. Don't worry. Let's get you back to the hotel. You need a good hot shower and some food!" Gary said. He was right. Tim just kept his distance as he seemed unable to comprehend what was really going on. I was grateful he wasn't questioning me too. Being out all night, in the cold and this altitude without anything was taking its toll. Maybe after some food and a shower things would start to make sense, become clearer. All I knew was that my body and senses were on complete overload.

I could still hear people talking about me behind my back all the way back to the hotel. Vicki walked close to me, like she wanted to take care of me. Thank goodness for Vicki and Gary. At least I felt somewhat safe with them. Of course, I really didn't know them either, but they were all I had. I missed Toni, now more than ever. She would have never let me go into the park and stay overnight. That was true, if Toni had been there, I wouldn't have stayed in the park and I would not have experienced what I experienced. What did I experience? My mind started spinning again with thoughts of what had happened. All I wanted was some food and a hot shower. The group was scheduled to leave in half an hour. I didn't have much time. I knew I needed more time in the park, but it wasn't going to happen today. I wondered if and when I would return, if ever.

There was no time to shower, but at least I got a few bites of papaya in me. I was starting to feel better and my head was starting to clear. My roommate was still nowhere to be found. I wondered if she had even noticed I wasn't in the room last night. I picked up my suitcase and met everyone outside as the tour was leaving.

The bus ride down the mountain was even more intense than the ride up. It scared the crap out of me and several other passengers as the twists and turns seemed even more dangerous than the day before.

"Oh my God, there is no road under the wheels!" One of the other passengers screamed as we wound our way back down to the train. Some of the young local children raced the bus down the mountain, sliding on their butts... and they won! Several tourists were giving them money for their display of courage and speed. The luggage was loaded in record time and we were back on the train to Cusco.

"So I am ready to hear...what happened to you?" Vicki finally asked as the train started to pull out of the station. Gary and Tim were sitting with us, as well as one other person I didn't recognize. I motioned toward the unfamiliar woman and gave Vicki an uneasy smile. She very blatantly asked the woman if she minded finding somewhere else to sit, as we needed to talk privately. The woman gave us an irritated look and got up and moved. Gary slid in closer.

"Come on Ray, what happened to you?" she asked again.

"The last time Vicki and I saw you, you were walking up towards the Temple of the Sun." Gary piped in. "About twenty minutes later we all heard a loud and distinct cry. We raced up there to see what was going on but no one was there. We started to look for you everywhere we had been earlier in the day. Then we would hear another cry and see large flashes of light coming from the Temple of the Sun. We ran back up, but still nothing!" Gary was agitated and sounded confused.

I sat there on the train with the rocking motion bouncing me back and forth. What did happen? I sat there silently trying to recall the events of the night. Flashes of memory where moving through my mind, and I started to question how much I really should share with Vicki, Gary and Tim. I really didn't know them, so I felt like I had to be careful with my words. Not sharing too much, yet I felt the need to voice a few things to get them clear in my own mind.

"I'm not really sure what happened." I said. "It was like I was in a lucid dream. I was on the rock, and then I was back in California, then I was in a meeting with a group of Light Beings and I was wrapped in a cocoon of Light." I was not really making any sense as the images flowed through my mind. "I was up there all night. I didn't move from that rock. I don't know why you couldn't see me when you came looking for me. I was laying right there all night!" I explained. Gary, Tim and Vicki listened intently with puzzled looks on their faces.

"I had visions of a jaguar spinning a cocoon of Light around me and the seal in the ground at the state capitol of California." I tried to recall more as they sat there staring at me. I started to go back into an altered state with flashes of light and voices in the distance. "I wish I could remember more. I didn't even know it was morning. I was shocked when you all were there with the Shaman," I said. Gary seemed upset that I wasn't recalling more details.

"Well, all I have to say was that this is definitely on my top ten list of weird life experiences. I'll be trying to figure this one out for a while! It was so weird we couldn't see you," Gary wondered.

Vicki chimed in, "Well maybe you were not really there. Maybe you were in another dimension and that might be why we couldn't see you."

Gary sighed and leaned back against the seat. Clearly he didn't know what to think, but you could tell from his questions, he thought something unusual had happened. Maybe he thought I was lying. Maybe he thought I was hiding something.

"The only thing I am sure of is the Shaman pulling me back. Back from where, I don't know, but he pulled me back and then his eyes seemed really familiar to me. I trusted him immediately," I said. Just then another person who had been in the park with us doing ceremony sat down next to Gary.

"Wow, you gave us quiet a scare last night. Glad you're okay. We were all worried about you. Where did you go?" she asked.

"That's a good question," I responded.

She just gave a weird look to Gary, shook her head and went off to sit with someone else.

"I'm just glad we didn't get caught or in trouble with the park authorities." I turned to look out the window, trying to escape the questions from Vicki and Gary, just wanting to close my eyes and rest. I had a lot of my own questions about what happened last night. I didn't remember screaming. I didn't remember hours passing. I didn't remember the sun coming up. But what I did remember is the pain I felt later when that energy pierced my heart. That was definitely real and it had happened in this dimension, of that I was sure.

I was grateful that nothing else was planned for the day, as the train arrived back in Cusco. I needed another shower and a nap. The hotel room in Cusco was nice. The bathroom was big and the shower was large and clean. I didn't know where my roommate was and I didn't care. I gathered my toiletries and started to undress.

As I pulled off my top and bra, I noticed a mark on my chest. I moved closer to the mirror to get a better look. It was right between my breasts. Right at my heart. It was larger than a half dollar, but not by much. I blinked my eyes as I looked closer. It was a symbol. I was shocked. I blinked and rubbed my eyes. Surely my mind was playing tricks on me. How did I get a symbol on my chest? I rubbed my heart and looked again. Nope, it was still there. It was real! I stared at it for a minute tracing the outline with my finger. It felt ancient. It felt sacred and I knew who had put it there. The Shaman had put it there. The Shaman had marked me with this symbol when he touched me on the disc. Then remembering he had grabbed my feet first, I slowly removed my shoes and then my socks. On the top of each foot was the same symbol. My mind started to go fuzzy as the room started to spin. I dropped to the floor and I was out, out like a light.

"Arayla, what are you doing? I need the bathroom." Her voice and the pounding on the door woke me up. My roommate had arrived and was pissed that I was taking so long in the bathroom.

"I'll be out in a minute." I stepped into the now cold shower wondering how long I had been lying on the floor to use up all the hot water. When I stepped out of the shower, I checked the mirror again and saw that the symbol was still there and so were the ones on my feet. Just as I was ready to leave, I had a strange feeling come over me. I checked my back. The exact same symbol was on my back, right behind my heart, only it was turned 180 degrees from the symbol on the front of my chest. My head got dizzy again, but I made it out of the bathroom and on to my bed. My head hit the pillow and I was gone.

Chapter 23

Within the depths of depression
Lies the Light of truth
For something deep inside you
Is screaming for review

Remembering your future
Re-creating all your past
Your soul is on a journey
For Mastery at last

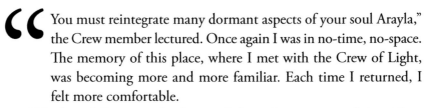 You must reintegrate many dormant aspects of your soul Arayla," the Crew member lectured. Once again I was in no-time, no-space. The memory of this place, where I met with the Crew of Light, was becoming more and more familiar. Each time I returned, I felt more comfortable.

"You have left too much of yourself throughout space and time. Your system is frayed." The Crew member continued to explain what had happened to me. "A rebuilding of your system is required. You must be able to hold all of the information and energy necessary. Zaratu designed your energy matrix. He knows exactly what your physical body is capable of in this reality. He knows how much energy can move through your body before the circuitry is blown."

"How does Zaratu know what my body can handle? Why isn't he here with me in 3D, in this reality? Where is he? I wasn't supposed to do this alone!" I exclaimed in frustration to the Crew.

"Trust the process. We are aware of what you need. There will be many to support you in your 3D reality. But you must learn to discern and keep your protection up. There are forces that do not want you to succeed," the Crew member answered. "Remember this always and travel light, my dear."

Chapter 24

The darkness is around us
Keeping tabs on all we do
Waiting for the moment
To move inside of you

Your job is clear and simple
Stay true to your own Light
Don't let the darkness fool you
Into slipping out of sight

Your work is too far reaching
Your path, far from the norm
As so much you have promised
Will change the course of life

Although you still don't see it
The impact you will have
Your soul remembers clearly
The Master that you are!

I awoke with my stomach growling. What time was it? Where was I? Then I remembered being in the hotel room in Cusco. The clock read 4:44, and my stomach growled again. I realized that I never made it to dinner the night before. I got up to use the restroom and searched my suitcase for the "emergency" food Toni had urged me to pack. I found a granola bar and proceeded to devour it. I couldn't remember the last meal I had had. I wasn't even sure what day it was. Had it only been 24 hours since I had been on the rock at the Temple of the Sun? I tried to go back to sleep but my mind was racing and I wasn't tired. I tried to retrace everything that had happened in the last couple of days.

As the sun rose, I got dressed and went down to the cafe in the hotel. I needed coffee and some real food. I pulled out the tour itinerary and found that today was a free day to explore Cusco. I wasn't sure I felt like strolling the streets of Cusco, especially alone. I seemed to have been shifting in and out of this reality, and I didn't know how safe I felt. The "episodes" came and went so suddenly. After all that had transpired, I wondered what the day would bring. All I knew now was that I wanted coffee, food and some answers. Surely someone on the trip was a skilled psychic or intuitive reader. Maybe they could help me get some answers about what had happened at the Temple of the Sun.

Then I realized, I hadn't really met many of the other tourists, so I thought I would find Vicki and see if she had run across anyone she thought might be able to help. I felt I needed help to try and understand what was going on, but I questioned if I would really be able to let anyone in to get answers. The Crew had told me to be careful to discern, that there were forces that didn't want me to succeed. I remembered the warning to keep my guard up. But I really wanted to try to figure out who the person was who sent the stabbing energy through my heart and why. I had way too many unanswered questions and felt frustrated to say the least. I decided to try and just be in the moment and enjoy the meal in front of me. At least the coffee was good and hot and the breakfast in front of me was appealing.

I was finishing about my fourth cup of coffee when Gary walked into the dining room.

"There she is. How are you feeling?" he asked with genuine concern.

"Tim and I were worried about you when you didn't show for dinner last night."

"I'm sorry you're always worried about me, Gary! I don't mean to be a pain, but I'm so glad you care."

He smiled. "It's okay. It's not every day you can worry about a woman who materializes in thin air right before your eyes. This is going to provide many hours of storytelling..." Gary said with a twinkle in his eye.

"I was planning on dinner last night, but I guess my body had other things in mind. I took a hot shower and was out like a light. I woke up this morning at 4:44, starving."

"Hmm, 4:44 you say?" Gary questioned.

"Yep, why?" I asked.

"Just curious. The numerology around 444 means the angels are surrounding you now, reassuring you of their love and help. No need to worry, as the angels are nearby. So it's a good sign that whatever happened to you was Divine." He winked.

A smile came over my face. That was the first reassurance I had received about the events from an outside source.

"That makes me feel better. It's been a wild ride to say the least." I began to relax as Gary went to get some food.

A group of women from the tour entered the restaurant, and every hair on my body stood straight up. I looked up and there was my roommate eyeing me with a very disturbing look. I flashed a phony smile back at her and looked away. Was she the one who sent the piercing energy to me yesterday? Just then Vicki came bouncing in with another group of women.

"Hey Ray, how are you? We're going shopping today, you want to join us?" she asked. I jumped at the chance to do something normal.

"Yes, I'd love to!" I said, relieved that I would have something to take my mind off of everything.

"Okay, we are out of here in thirty... be ready." She went off to get breakfast.

"It's time to head back, you ready?" Vicki yelled from across the road. I nodded and crossed the street to join her.

"Shopping in a foreign country is always an adventure, don't you think?" She lifted up all her bags of treasures she had purchased. I really hadn't done it much, but I guessed she was right. I wondered what foreign country I would be shopping in next.

"You know, I live in Oklahoma, you should come for a visit some time, Ray. I would love to have you come," Vicki said. "It's an interesting place and I have a few friends I think you should meet. It would be fun, you could stay with me and we would have a blast reminiscing about this adventure."

The offer came as a surprise. We hadn't really gotten to know each other that well and an invitation to come and stay with her seemed a little strange. It wasn't like I lived an hour or two away. It was several thousand miles and would require a flight. But she had been so helpful, so supportive during this trip, and I enjoyed her company.

"Wow, thanks for the offer, I'll think about it. We should stay in touch." I was flattered even though the whole idea seemed weird. What would I want to go to Oklahoma for? It isn't like it's a happening place. But the offer was there and I wondered what prompted her.

"You never know, you might meet Mr. Right there," she said with a smile. Mr. Right? We had not talked men at all, except that I told her I was single and still looking. That was an interesting hook and I wondered where it was coming from.

I smiled and said, "Hmm you just never know, now, do you?" Toni was going to have a good laugh over this one. Your man in Oklahoma, now that isn't somewhere I would have thought to look; I could just hear her saying it with such disbelief. My mind flashed to a dream, or was it a vision? I remembered a gorgeous man drawing a bath for me. His eyes were deep blue and dreamy. I remembered being outside. That's strange, a bath tub outside? But his eyes, oh my! I could get lost in those eyes forever. I flashed to the amber eyes I always saw when Z showed up. But these eyes were different, they were blue. Beautiful blue with a deep sensuous passion. I giggled at myself. Whew, I wanted to meet him, that is for sure!

I never did figure out if it had been my roommate who had sent the piercing energy during the sunrise ceremony. It gave me the creeps to think I was sharing a hotel room with her the entire trip. She had been so sick the whole time. Maybe that is why. Maybe making her sick was a way of protecting me. My mind raced, but I guess if I really needed to know, I would have, I thought to myself. It was another reminder of the "forces" that the Crew warned me about. I did need to keep my guard up, I did need to pay attention. I might not know if it was her who sent the piercing energy, but it was a physical reminder that not everything or everyone was good. There is darkness and opposition and I needed to be aware of it. REALLY aware.

The next day we returned to Lima. One more night in Peru and then I would head back home to California. The events of the journey were so overwhelming, all I wanted to do was sleep. Vicki, Tim and Gary had kept a close eye on me since Machu Picchu. I appreciated the concern and was so happy I had connected with them on this trip. I wondered how long it would be before I saw them all again. I sat at the airport with the group waiting for the plane that would take me home.

"Miss Weaver. There you are. You never called me so that I could show you my beautiful city!" The man I had met on the plane ride to Peru exclaimed as he took my hand and kissed it gently. "Did you enjoy your journey?" he asked with a smile.

"Yes I did. It was wonderful, thank you for asking!" I said.

"Did you receive the package from the Shaman?" I gasped and pulled my hand back from his grip.

"Please keep my card and contact me if you ever return to Peru. It was a pleasure to meet you Ms. Weaver," he said. He walked over to the attendant behind the check-in counter. They exchanged words and he looked back at me and smiled.

As I boarded the plane, the flight attendant escorted me to first class. "Compliments of the Head of Security." She smiled.

"He can do that…get me upgraded to first class on American Airlines?" I asked.

"Mama, he can do just about anything he wants to," she said with an undertone that made my skin crawl. I'm sure glad I got on his good side. He was head of security, maybe he was my protector, my own inter-dimensional security guard watching over me.

Chapter 25

She sees the world colliding
  With manufactured greed
And questions if her love can heal
  The damaged soul complete

The poles they are shifting
  The magnetic forces strong
Preparing for the final test
  Before all hell is thrown

The natural process beckons
  Of birth, of life, of death
A truly age old story
  One that's destined to commence

But all throughout the ages
  The ancients ones have taught
That with the true Light anchored
  Our souls will awaken and not be lost

Shipments, contracts, messages, meetings... Being back at work was really difficult. Everything seemed so artificial, so unimportant and so mundane since I had returned from Peru. What did any of it matter in the larger scheme of things? I didn't care one bit about the shipment of processor chips that needed to be delivered by the next week. The thousands of clients and contracts I managed on a daily basis seemed so, well stupid. What did it really matter? I was much more interested in figuring out what all my bizarre spiritual experiences were really about.

"Ray, are you ready to go to lunch?" asked my co-worker and cube mate Melissa.

"Sure, just let me send this request out to Penang...AGAIN!"

Just then the phone rang. It was the production line manager in Penang. I had been up at 2 a.m. calling him last night trying to get him to respond to my twelfth request for product to be shipped.

"It's Penang," I explained.

Melissa rolled her eyes. She knew it was not going to be a pleasant conversation. I had been upset for days because of the lack of response from him. She settled back into her chair, knowing it would be a while before we left.

"But I've been sending you requests for weeks with no response," I screamed into the receiver. "The client is furious," I continued. "No, we can't pull from another order, you were already late with that one too!"

I looked over at Melissa. She was anxious to get out of the office. I could tell by the way she was fumbling with her keys. She had a concerned look on her face, and when I motioned to her about the phone conversation, she motioned with her hands for me to calm down. She could tell I was ready to blow.

"Look, whatever it takes, get this order out today!" I demanded as I slammed down the phone. Just as the receiver hit the cradle, the power went out. At first I thought it was just in our section of the building. I slowly stood up to look out over the mass labyrinth of cubicles and saw that the whole building had lost power.

Melissa just covered her eyes in disgust.

"Ray, please let's get the hell out of here quick!" she exclaimed as she grabbed her keys and purse. "Come on. Hurry up. I don't want anyone to start yelling at you."

I knew she was right. For weeks now, I had been causing havoc with all the electronic equipment. Every time I got emotional, something would blow. The copy machine, the fax machine, my computer, now the power again.

"Ray, hurry up!" Melissa begged...

I grabbed my purse and we got out of the office as fast as we could. Even as we turned the corner to head out the door, one of our teammates looked and me and asked if I had blown the power again. I didn't respond.

Melissa took a sip of her ice tea and worried. "You know Ray, people are really starting to talk."

"Talk about what?" I tried to pretend I didn't know exactly what she was referring to.

"About how every time you get upset or angry, something electrical goes wacko." She sounded puzzled. "I know that it's keeping people away from you, and that has its own perks, but why do you think this is happening?"

"Yeah, I know it's weird," I responded quietly. "It seems to be happening a lot. I've even started to notice a pattern." I remembered the power going out for several hours last week after I got really angry, making everyone frustrated and behind schedule.

"It seems to have really started after you returned from your trip to—where the hell did you go—Peru?" Melissa questioned me. "You seem different since then. Sometimes when I look at you, you even look different." She was quiet for a moment. "It's just weird!"

"What do you mean, I look different?"

"Well, I know this might seem crazy, but sometimes you have two different colored eyes." she said in almost a whisper. "I even heard someone else in the office mention it too. They had noticed as they were talking to you, your eyes changed colors."

"My eyes haven't changed colors!" I refused to believe her.

"How would you know? You're not looking at you," Melissa insisted.

She was right. How would I know? I had seen it in the mirror myself, but figured I was just crazy. But as I looked in the mirror, I watched as one of my eyes turned blue, while the other stayed green. It was wild and as I continued to watch, I could see a reflection of the jaguar looking back at me for a split second. It was haunting. Now I had Melissa verifying that she was seeing it too. Well at least the change in eye color was the only things they were seeing and not flashes of a jaguar's face.

"Do you think the power will be back up when we return?" She took another bite of her salad.

"I don't know. I hope so. I have a lot of work to do."

"Girl, you have to figure out how to stop blowing the power. I know it's you!" Melissa tried to stay calm. "I know it sounds crazy to even say that out loud. But even our secretary is getting frustrated. Have you noticed she doesn't even want to walk into our cubicle anymore? She just stands at the entry way and waits to see if you're pissed off or not."

"Yeah, I know. I just don't know why it's happening. I am blowing all kinds of electrical things everywhere I go." I tried not to take it seriously.

"Well it's most noticeable when you are angry, so stop being angry!"

We both just looked at each other and laughed. That was so much easier said than done, especially with what we dealt with on a day-to-day basis. Trying to work with a production line halfway around the world with no real support or leadership in our office. In the last year we had had three different managers, and the organization had changed even more times than that. We were pretty much flying solo most of the time, and delays, non-responsive co-workers and more and more workload were pretty much the name of the game.

"It's a good thing we don't drink during lunch, 'cause I think a glass of wine would be in order," I said.

I really didn't want to go back and face the consequences from my

The sun was shining bright as we walked the streets of Cusco. Reds, blues, yellows, oranges, the colors were all so vibrant here and alive in this bustling city. I meandered through the shops, stopping to buy gifts and trinkets to take home. Even though I had been in Peru for almost two weeks, I still didn't feel comfortable.

"I wish I spoke the language," I said to Vicki as she was haggling over the price of a beautiful pair of earrings.

"Yes, my little bit of Spanish has helped a lot down here." She smiled as she went back in for one more round, finally settling for the price the woman was saying while throwing her hands up in the air. "They are beautiful and my sister will love them."

I'm so selfish, I hadn't thought about buying gifts for my family at all, only Toni. I had found a beautiful bracelet the shop owner swore was sterling silver and a crystal that seemed to speak to me as I passed by. I hadn't even bought anything for myself. I found a purple alpaca shawl that I really wanted, but the price was too high and I couldn't seem to get the shop owner to come down in price. I wish Vicki had been with me then, she could have gotten the price down, I'm sure of it.

A day of shopping was a nice reprieve from the events of the previous day. I felt the relief of being at a lower altitude. My body still hurt, and I was still freaked out from the new symbols that apparently were permanent on my body. How did they get there? How was that possible? I looked up to see that Vicki was signaling me from across the street.

As I started to turn, I literally bumped right into the woman I saw when I was getting off the train. "Excuse me," I said politely out of pure habit. The woman looked straight into my eyes, took my hand in hers and smiled. I didn't try and pull away. I just stood there looking back at her. She seemed so familiar. I searched my memory. Had I seen her at the train station? Had I seen her while I was still sitting on the rock? Had I seen her at Pyramid Lake? She always had on the exact same Hawaiian dress. How could this be? She squeezed my hand and gently released it, smiled and went on her way. A sense of calm and love raced through me. Who was she and why did I keep seeing her everywhere?

angry outburst. Most of my co-workers had mentioned something about it over the last few weeks since my return from Peru, and I knew I had to figure out how to control what was happening. The biggest problem is I didn't care about my work anymore. It seemed so unimportant. I couldn't seem to get engaged and it was starting to show in my performance. I was headed for trouble and I knew it. But somehow I just didn't care.

Chapter 26

The wisdom and the courage
To break the patterns free
Will not be enough to shatter
Your hologram complete

Your heart will need to surrender
Your soul will need to grieve
For things which you've done
Your Akashic Records will be sung
Then cleared for all eternity

The electrical malfunctions continued until it seemed to become "normal." I had even started to go through tons of batteries for my remotes and upon occasion, the television would just turn on as I walked by. It was strange, but what was even stranger is I didn't feel anything when it happened. No surge of electricity, no tingling in my body, nothing!

"So, why are you going to Oklahoma again?" Toni asked as she bit into another piece of pizza.

Toni knew about all the craziness around the electronics, and she also knew that I had my mind set on going to Oklahoma next. It had been five months since my return from Peru and the events of that journey still were unclear to me. I was frustrated to say the least. I so wanted to understand all the "spiritual" stuff that had happened, but I also wanted my life to be normal again. The spiritual things didn't seem to be making much difference in my life. And other than being able to share it with Toni, no one else except whoever was present at the "occurrences" was even aware that anything strange or out of the ordinary was happening with me. Well that wasn't entirely true, the people at my office knew something about me had changed. I was still blowing out the computer systems, fax and copy machines and my secretary still cringed every time she saw me. A look of panic would come over her face if I was the least bit angry, and she'd stop dead in her tracks just waiting for the other shoe to fall.

"Why not? Vicki's invited me and well, you never know. Maybe my man is in Oklahoma." We both looked at each other and laughed.

"But over Thanksgiving? Why right now?" Toni asked. "Don't you want to be with your family over the holiday?" Toni already knew the answer.

"I got a cheap flight. I guess very few people actually fly on Thanksgiving Day. Most fly the day before, so I got a great price. Thanksgiving isn't really a very popular holiday for my family. We eat early and then sleep. That's about it, so I'm not really missing anything. Besides, you know I hate football," I said.

Toni giggled. She loves the game and has tried countless times to get me to like it over the years. I can't stand it. It's too slow for me. Now basketball I can get excited about, but football, not so much.

"Vicki seemed excited I was coming, and I don't know that she has any family to spend the holiday with. Besides, I don't have to take any extra vacation time, so it seemed like a good time to go."

"Do you have a ride to the airport?" Toni asked as she took another piece of pizza.

"Nope, you game?" I replied with as cute a smile as I could muster.

"What time is your flight? Is it going to be right in the middle of the game?"

"Probably, but they last for hours, so you won't really miss anything." I tried to convince her to give me a ride. She threw her dirty napkin at me across the table and laughed.

"Call me so I can put it on my calendar," she said. As long as I was on the calendar, I had nothing to worry about. Toni lived by her calendar. At the beginning of each month she would send me a copy of the upcoming schedule. She was nothing if not organized. Me, everything was in my head. I think I had a wall calendar somewhere, but I never managed to put it up. It was November already, so I guess it was too late to hang it now.

We were all gathered around the Thanksgiving table. My brother Bob, his wife Kathy, their son Josh and his current girlfriend, my mom, my nephew Joel and his wife Terri who had driven up from the Bay Area to be with family for the holiday, and me. It seemed I was always the odd one out. I can't remember the last time I had brought a man to Thanksgiving dinner. Maybe next year would be different, I thought.

My family never had the "Martha Stewart" touch even though both my sister-in-law and I try to bring some sense of elegance to make things special. Even for a holiday dinner, we all dressed in jeans and casual clothing. Comfort over fashion in my family.

We prepared the traditional holiday menu; turkey with homemade stuffing, mash potatoes and gravy, green beans, cranberry sauce and several varieties of pie. The food was always good but the essence of the holiday seemed to be missing. Yes, it was about gathering with family, but we never really focused on what we were thankful for. After my experience of being in Peru months earlier, my appreciation for my life and all of my blessings seemed more pronounced and important than in years past. I realized how much I had taken for granted as I reminisced about the children begging on the streets of Cusco.

I was deep in thought when my brother blurted out, "What is wrong with your eyes? Did you get colored contacts?"

I rolled my eyes and did not respond. He had a knack for asking the blunt questions. He was smart, confident and somewhat opinionated and although we loved each other, we had very different life styles. Sometimes he could really make me feel uncomfortable and today was no exception. It seems like all the way through dinner, the questions continued. "Oklahoma? Why are you going there?" my brother asked.

"To see a friend of mine I met in Peru," I answered.

"Oh, one of those woo-woo, spiritual types," he said condescendingly.

"Geez, thanks a lot bro." My brother thought my interest in spiritual things was all a bunch of hogwash and reminded me every chance he got. He's an engineer and doesn't believe in anything he can't see or prove. So sharing anything about what was happening with me was not an option and I knew it.

"I'm sure she is a nice friend. Why shouldn't she go and visit?" My sister-in-law Kathy tried to change the subject. "It's good to see new places."

"Oklahoma, that's just a lousy place to visit. Now if she lived in Hawaii or somewhere beautiful, then..." my brother continued. Kathy slugged him in the arm and got up to start clearing the table.

"Well it's better than sitting around here all weekend doing the same old thing," I explained as I joined her in the kitchen.

"He loves you, you know that, right?" Kathy reminded me. We started to load the dishwasher. "He just doesn't understand you and your interest in those kinds of things." I shrugged at her comment. "He went on and on about how dangerous and crazy it was for you to go by yourself to Peru."

"I wasn't by myself. I was with eighty other people on an escorted tour," I answered back.

"I know, but he thinks that was weird and doesn't understand why you would want to do a trip with eighty people you don't know anyway."

"Well, who else am I going to travel with? It's not like I have a partner to go and have fun with." Now I was defensive.

"I know, Ray. I know. Your brother just worries about you. He doesn't understand why you haven't found anyone."

"I don't either. I wish he would show up. I'm so tired of being alone. I guess that is one of the OTHER reasons why I'm going to Oklahoma," I replied as Kathy gave me a strange look. I added with as much hope in my voice as I could manage, "Well he doesn't seem to be here in Sacramento, so I guess I better start doing something different. Maybe he is in Oklahoma."

Kathy rolled her eyes, and just then my mom walked into the room.

"What are you two talking about in here?" Mom asked.

"Men, or the lack thereof," I responded and that stopped her questioning quickly and she went back into the living room. Kathy and I just rolled our eyes and smiled.

"Would you like me to fix you a turkey sandwich for the plane?" Kathy asked. "We always eat early on Thanksgiving. You'll be starving by the time you land."

She fixed me a meal between two pieces of bread. Stuffing, turkey, cranberry sauce and even a little gravy instead of mayo on the bread. It was going to be messy to eat, but I was sure it would taste awesome.

Chapter 27

People come and go in life
  Who somehow make the choice
To bring into your awareness
  The lessons for your growth

Remember they are mirrors
  Reflecting your true self
Or perhaps you are the mirror
  Reflecting back for them too

The trick is knowing somehow
  That all is done in love
Without the disillusion
  That comes with such tough love

You ready to go?" Toni asked as she stood behind her trunk waiting to load my suitcase.

"Yep. I wonder why I'm going actually. I don't really know her very well." I was kind of regretting my decision.

"Come on Ray. Do you really think there might not be another 'adventure' for you there?"

"I don't know. I was guided to keep in touch with her and take her up on her offer to visit. I guess I'm just tired of not getting more information. It's just always so cryptic, just a piece here and hint there. And always being told to remember. Remember what? They haven't told me anything!" I said referring to Z and the Crew of Light. "I just get frustrated, you know."

"Yes, but you know this has to be leading to something. Too much has happened not to know that. You've always been good at following your gut. Now is not the time to stop."

I knew she was right. Time would tell…

It was late by the time my flight landed in Tulsa. Vicki was waiting curbside in her Toyota Camry, which looked like it had seen a few brawls. She ran around the car to give me a hug and help me with my luggage.

"Is this all you brought?" she asked as she quickly threw it into the trunk.

"Yep, I'm learning to travel light!"

"Yes, I guess you are!"

"I'm only here for a couple of nights. I don't need much." She asked how the flight was and if I had eaten Thanksgiving dinner with my family before I left. It was a quick drive back to her place. She had a sweet house. It was a two-bedroom, one bath older home and it was decorated with a shabby chic flare. The room I was staying in had a twin bed and small dresser painted white with sarongs draped from the ceiling creating a canopy effect. Vicki had placed cut flowers in a cute pitcher of water on the nightstand. The room was cozy and smelled of lavender. She had made it so inviting. She put my luggage down and showed me the bathroom where she had placed fresh towels and a washcloth for me to use.

"Let me get us something to snack on. Do you like wine?" she asked.

"Yes, what kind do you have?"

"A cheap bottle of white," she responded with a laugh.

"Is it dry or sweet?"

"Sweet."

"Perfect!" I answered as I found a spot on the well-worn love seat. She came in with a plate of crackers, cheese and a tangerine all sectioned out. I couldn't believe it. I was actually hungry, but I guess it had been hours since the Thanksgiving feast with my family. I thought of the sandwich Kathy had made, which was now squished somewhere at the bottom of my purse.

"Ray, I'm so glad you are here," Vicki said as she poured me a glass of wine.

"Me, too," I answered.

"I don't quite know how to tell you this..." she started.

My heart sank at the seriousness of her tone.

"I have a wedding to go to tomorrow and well, it isn't really appropriate that you come with me," she explained.

I'm sure the expression on my face was less than pleasant. "Oh," was all I could say. The electricity went out. Whoops, I thought I was getting better at controlling the energetic disturbances...

"That's weird." Vicki said. "We aren't having storms...wonder what's up with the power."

I calmed down and the power returned. I wondered why she had not told me this before I got on a plane and flew halfway across the country to visit her. What the hell was I going to do sitting in her house in Oklahoma all day while she was at a wedding for heaven's sake? I'm sure she could see the frustration on my face as I was trying to process what she had just told me.

"It's a very close friend and they are only having a few people at the ceremony. I would invite you, but it really isn't appropriate," she explained again.

"Sure, I understand."

"My best friend and her husband have offered to take you with them tomorrow," she added. Great, I was getting handed off to a couple I didn't even know. What was I doing here? Who came up with this great idea to come to Oklahoma?

"Okay," I responded, less than enthusiastic.

"I'm sorry Ray. I should have told you, but I really wanted you to come and I didn't realize the wedding was this weekend until you had already bought your tickets. I was afraid to tell you before you got here. You'll have fun with my friends. I promise," Vicki insisted.

She tried to make small talk, but I was too tired and frustrated. Within a few minutes she gave up and suggested we get some rest. "They will be here to pick you up around nine in the morning."

I crawled into bed with two choices going through my head. I could be mad and ruin the visit or I could go with the flow and try and enjoy myself. I didn't take long to make the choice. Vicki knocked on my door to see if I had everything I needed.

"I'm sorry Vicki. I didn't mean to respond the way I did. It just came as a surprise. I'm sure I will have a good time with your friends. I'm grateful they are willing to entertain me."

"They are good people and I know you will have a nice time whatever you do," she said and closed the door behind her. I laid there awake for what seemed like forever. This was crazy. Here I was sleeping in a strange bed, in a strange house, in a strange place, visiting someone I barely knew over Thanksgiving weekend. I drifted off to sleep wondering what her friends would be like.

I woke the next morning to the smell of fresh brewed coffee and music playing in the background. I love the smell of coffee in the morning. It took me a minute to remember I was at Vicki's getting ready to spend the day with her friends doing God knows what. I headed out to get a cup of hot joe.

"Cream?" she asked.

"Yes, please and sugar if you have it," I answered.

"Hmm, I don't use sugar, how about honey?" she replied.

My heart sank. Honey? I hate honey in coffee, I thought to myself.

"Sure that will do." I answered trying to hide my disappointment. Geez, just when I thought the day was getting off to a good start. I'm a lousy guest, quit being such a bitch Arayla, I thought to myself.

"I'm going to jump in the shower. There is toast and juice for breakfast if you like." Vicki walked out of the kitchen. Well the honey would go well on the toast, I thought as I pulled out two pieces of bread and placed them in the old fashioned toaster sitting on the small block table she used to extend her counter space. She really did have a lot of cute ideas to maximize her space. I would have to pay closer attention. I liked her style. The toaster made a loud noise as the bread flew up out of the sockets. The sound made me jump a mile. Her dishes were all mix and match and the glasses she had on the counter for the juice were actually Mexican margarita glasses. Cute and multi-functional!

"The shower's free!" she yelled just as I was pouring my second cup of coffee. Why oh why had I not pocketed a few of the sweetener packets at the airport? I never thought that she wouldn't have any sugar in the house. I made a mental note to pick some up today if we stopped anywhere that had some. Then I flashed back to the first time Toni came to my apartment. She was flabbergasted that I didn't have regular sugar, flour, canned goods or extra toilet paper stocked up. What would I need real sugar for? I didn't bake for hell's sake. I laughed... why would Vicki need real sugar either? Touché I thought as I took my coffee with me into the bathroom...

Vicki jumped up with excitement to answer the door. She hugged her friend and motioned for her to come inside.

"Sandra this is Arayla, Arayla, this is my good friend Sandra." She made introductions as Sandra stood there with a slight smile on her face. "I know you two are going to get along just great!" Vicki proclaimed as Sandra put out her hand in formal introduction.

"I'm sure we will." I said quickly to try and calm the situation.

"Arayla, my husband and I are glad you will be joining us today," Sandra said as Vicki asked where Tom was. "He is waiting in the car."

"He didn't want to come in?" Vicki asked looking worried.

"We have a long drive and he is anxious to get on the road," Sandra replied with a weak smile. A long drive, shit, where are we going, I thought to myself. "You better use the restroom before we leave. There aren't many places to stop," Sandra suggested.

I quickly regretted the fourth cup of coffee I had just consumed. I headed off to the bathroom to try and squeeze everything I could out of my bladder. My body was off from the time zone difference and well, I wasn't sure how I would react to a long drive and coffee with honey in it.

"It's going to be fine, Sandra. She's a nice person and you will enjoy her company. She is very spiritual and she has a great sense of humor." Vicki reassured her as I was coming back into the room. "Get your coat, you never know about the weather here," Vicki added.

I swung back into my room and picked up my coat and the book I had brought to read on the plane. It was an erotic novel by Erica Jong, *The Fear of Flying*. I thought briefly about what they would think of me for reading it, but quickly disregarded the thought. Heck, what did I care what these people thought of me? I blushed quickly and thought about what most people would think about someone reading this book. I shoved it in my oversized purse and decided to bring it anyways. She said we would have a long drive to wherever we were going. How did I get myself into this? I wondered as I climbed into the back seat of a Cadillac Seville. At least it would be a comfortable ride.

"Arayla, I would like you to meet my husband Tom. Tom, this is Arayla," Sandra said with a smile.

"Bet this was the last thing you expected when you landed last night." Tom smiled at me. Sandra hit him gently on the arm.

"What I think my husband meant to say is that we are glad you will be joining us today," Sandra insisted. He backed out of the driveway and we were off.

"So have you ever been to Oklahoma, Arayla?" Tom asked as he sailed down the street in his oversized toy.

"No, this is my first time," I answered.

"Honey, can we stop for coffee?" Sandra pleaded.

"Of course, do you like coffee, Arayla?"

Boy, do I like coffee, good coffee that is. "Yes I do!"

"Then you are going to love this place," he said. It was about 15 minutes before we pulled off the highway into the parking lot of an old diner.

"I know it doesn't look like much, but the coffee is good and they have an espresso machine. Do you like mochas?" Tom asked with a twinkle in his eye.

"Do I like mochas? That is like asking if Harleys like the open road," I responded and laughed at the analogy. Where the hell did that come from? I wondered as we all piled out of the car.

"I'm going to use the rest room again. Sandra said it was a long ride to wherever we are going."

"Yes, good idea. Would you like me to order you a mocha?" Tom responded.

"Yes, please…the largest they have," I asked as Tom smiled.

"May I ask where we are going?" I finally said as we slid back onto the highway headed west, I think.

"Oh, I'm sorry, I never told you, did I?" Sandra apologized. "Tom is a lawyer. He represents one of the biggest Indian tribes in Oklahoma, the Choctaw Nation. They have invited him out to speak with the chief and medicine man. He called yesterday to make sure it was alright to bring a guest. And they said it was okay. So we are headed out to one of their bunkers," Sandra explained.

"What? We are going out to meet the chief of one of the Indian tribes?" I asked in complete shock.

"Yes, it's still about a two-hour drive from here," she said.

"Oh, no wonder you didn't get what I was saying when you first got in. You didn't even know," Tom said with a smirk. "Yes, I am taking you deep into Indian territory!" He smiled like I should be scared or something.

Should I be concerned, I thought to myself? I was riding hours into the middle of nowhere to meet with real live Indians, taken there by people I didn't know. I seemed to be in good company, so how much trouble could I get into really? Real live Indians, I didn't see that one coming.

The Oklahoma landscape was deserted and desolate and not very interesting to look at. I decided to pull out my book and tried not to gasp or blush too much as I read.

"What are you reading?" Sandra asked from the front seat.

"Oh just a novel," I replied.

"Any good?" Sandra asked.

"Well that depends upon what you consider good." I replied. "It's not the kind I would lend to my mother," I said as Tom laughed out loud.

"That good, ay?" Tom replied.

"Yes, that good..."

"Sandra, you should get a copy then." Tom said and laughed out loud again. We all settled back into the groove of the ride; apparently we still had at least an hour to go...

"We're here," Tom exclaimed. I looked out the window and saw what looked like an airplane hangar. It was large, plain and tan in color.

"Are you sure this is it?" Sandra was concerned. "It doesn't look like a meeting place for the Indian chief."

"What does the meeting place for the Indian chief normally look like?" Tom asked.

None of us had a clue what it "should" look like. We were all just surprised and a little confused, or perhaps disappointed. It didn't look like much, especially after the long drive. There were a few old cars parked around and even more motorcycles. All of which looked like they had seen better days.

It was hot, even though it was the end of November. Dust was flying everywhere and the pavement was glaring. Tom motioned for us to follow him into the bunker. As we entered, it was dark and cooler, a stark contrast to the sunlight outside. It took a moment for our eyes to adjust, but you could hear the bustle of excitement building on the other side of the structure. Tom paused to look around and spotted the chief, the man who had asked him to come.

"There he is," Tom said and motioned for us to follow him.

"Tom, it's so nice to see you," the chief said as they shook hands in formal welcome. Both Sandra and I stood back slightly to allow for the formality of the greeting to take place. The chief was in full formal Indian attire. It was what you would expect if you were going to see a tribal ceremony or dance. But what did I know about Indian ceremony? Another man with a huge headdress and costume followed the chief to greet Tom. He stood next to the chief in silence, looking at Tom, Sandra and me. Tom motioned for Sandra and me to stand next to him.

"Chief, this is my wife Sandra and a new friend of ours, Arayla, who is visiting." The chief extended his hand for a formal handshake. He then motioned for the man standing next to him to be formally introduced.

"Tom, this our medicine man, Soft Feather." Soft Feather took Tom's hand and shook it. Then he turned to Sandra and took her hand smiling. "It's nice to meet you Sandra." He reached for my hand, "Arayla, is that your real name?" he asked. What a strange question I thought. I nodded my head.

"Yes," I said in response, still wondering why he would ask something like that.

"Are you the one from California?" he asked. I nodded my head in agreement while a feeling of shock ran through my mind.

"Yes," I answered.

"We've been expecting you," he continued. My mouth dropped open as did Tom's and Sandra's. The chief just stood there smiling.

"Come with me." Soft Feather said, and I did as I was asked. How did this man know I was from California? Did Tom tell him? Did Tom tell the chief he had someone from California coming with him? That would have been a strange thing to mention. And why would that be important? I turned back to look at Sandra and Tom as the medicine man led me to the other side of the bunker. They've been expecting me? Why would they have been expecting me? What was going on? My mind was trying to process the words Soft Feather had said as the knots in my stomach began to build.

The medicine man asked me to sit down on a wooden bleacher, the kind you would find at a football stadium at a high school. The bench was in the middle of the bunker, and several other members of the tribe were already sitting there. I did as I was told, wondering what was happening. Small children in ceremonial attire were dancing around, mothers with babies at their breasts suckling, men talking in small groups and the medicine man speaking with several of the elder members of the tribe in the center of the bunker. After what seemed like an eternity, Soft Feather walked back over to me. His hands were behind his back and when he brought his hands forward he revealed a single feather. A long green feather, like a peacock's.

"Are you ready to take flight?" he asked me.

"Are you talking about in one of those old planes?" I responded, not understanding what was going on.

Chapter 28

To walk the path of sacredness
Opens up the portal doors
Of pathways and connection
Between the inner worlds

So much more is happening
Than your conscious mind can see
As ancient codes and promises
Resurface to fulfill

The legends and the prophecies
Whispered between the clans
To bring about the sacred ways
To the world, once again

"Come Arayla, it's time to fly!" Soft Feather took my hand and pulled me up. We walked into the center of the space. He motioned for me to sit down opposite him, so I did. He touched the floor with the feather and then made a circle around me three times in a counterclockwise direction. Then he sat down facing me.

Several members of the tribe silently took their positions in a circle around us. I just sat there in silence wondering what was happening, wondering what I was supposed to do, wondering how I had gotten in the middle of the circle. Soft Feather just smiled at me. My thoughts were racing and I began to get lightheaded. He stood up and walked over to the chief. The chief then walked into the center of the circle to join us. They both sat down again so that the three of us were in a triangle formation, so close that our knees were almost touching. The chief took out a pipe from a pouch he had slung across his back. He loaded the pipe with tobacco and began to offer a prayer.

Slowly the members of the tribe began to move around us. They began chanting soft and low. The rhythm of the dance added to the swirling of my mind. With raised hands the chief finished his prayer. He lowered the pipe and handed it to the medicine man. Soft Feather then raised it as well, offering another prayer. Lowering the pipe, he placed it between his lips and lit it. He inhaled with several short breathes. Then he let out a long spiral of white smoke that swirled around me. The smell was sweet and overwhelming as it filled my senses. The smoke seemed to dance around my head as he inhaled and released another ring around me.

My vision blurred slowly and I began to feel the same familiar sensation in my body. I heard an eagle squawk above my head, at least I thought it was an eagle. But I'm inside, there are no eagles flying over my head, I thought. My surroundings disintegrated, but I could still hear the chanting and dancing that was happening around me. My awareness moved swiftly through space and time. It was like I was going through a dark tunnel coming out somewhere else. I knew I was still sitting Indian style in the middle of a tribal dance, but I was fully aware that I was NOT there. As I looked around I could feel the warmth of the sun on my face. I was high above the ground in the air looking far out into the distance. The sky was blue and the earth was barren. I could feel the eagle flying next to me. Is it an eagle? Am I flying? I looked below me and there were these strange lines etched in the earth. Lines that seem to go on forever. There were several groups of them, and as I looked closer, each group seemed to have visible form. I was flying high above the earth and as I looked down, the lines began to expand.

What is this? Where am I? From high above the ground the lines seemed to form shapes. Strange shapes of birds or planes, people or maybe animals. I wasn't sure. My senses were heightened significantly. I could feel the eagle as if he were a part of me, inside me. As I looked down at the strange visual formations, my focus shifted and somehow, someway I was becoming the lines. I could feel myself—I have become the lines in the ground that extend for miles. How can this be? What is happening to me? The lines are energy. Distinct frequencies of energy. How do I know this? I realized I was becoming one with the lines, one with the frequencies. Something deep inside me understood, even though my conscious mind couldn't comprehend any of this. I was trying to release my understanding of reality and embrace what was happening to me. Deep within my soul I knew that infused into this landscape was sacred knowledge, secret knowledge that had been locked in the energy, the Earth since the beginning of time. My mind shifted back into the hangar and the tribal ceremony that was happening around me and then back again into being completely immersed in the lines below me. There was no logic to what was happening. There was no understanding from the human perspective. Yet I knew where I was. I recognized that place. What is this shape? What is the significance of these particular lines?

The beloved voice I've come to know as Z spoke to me loud and clear. It seemed like it has been a long time since I'd heard him and a sense of relief filled me.

"Merge with the line of wisdom, Arayla. You ARE the wisdom. You ARE ..." I could not understand the last word he said.

"Where am I?" I asked.

"You know this place well. You are above the Nazca lines in South America." He answered. My head was swimming and my senses were fully alive—I was in Oklahoma and I was in South America, both places simultaneously. I was actually becoming the lines of the hummingbird figure. I could feel myself in the Earth. I was becoming the entire pattern of Light. How was this possible? I was moving from inside the lines on the surface below, to flying high above in the sky as the figure of the hummingbird.

"Become the hummingbird. That's right! Drink the nectar of the Gods, Arayla," Z said. I could hear the excitement in his voice. He was proud of me and I knew it.

Looking at myself, my body had become a living grid. No more a human body, no skin or bones. There was only Light in the exact same pattern of the hummingbird I saw below me on the ground. Bright golden Light streaming and moving in what I knew was my body, my vehicle, but with no resemblance to a human form.

"Arayla! You are a Master shape-shifter. Remember! Be the humming-bird and fly." I heard Z as if he were gliding right beside me.

What is happening? My mind was trying to focus on the drumming and chanting I was hearing in the physical, but my senses were fully fix-ated on the energy that was ripping through me. I was the Light! A grid of massive Light in the shape of a hummingbird, flying high above the earth, above the Nazca lines in Peru. It was magical and I could almost hear the information locking into my matrix. Clicking, like the sound you hear when a combination lock is opened. The information was streaming into me from deep inside the Earth, moving through the lines of Light as if a cable had been hooked up to a computer. Flying high and free above the Earth, I shifted once again, only this time into a living ship or aircraft of some type. I expanded larger, much larger than the hummingbird. The feeling was much more solid and there was so much more going on "inside" me. What is happening? I thought. I really didn't know.

"There will always be someone or something that is trying to keep you from completing your mission," the Crew member stated. "You must be able to detect and self-monitor your systems."

"We have put safeguards in for you, but there are always others, those with as much power as you, that want access to your knowledge," said another Crew member.

"Being of the Light is not enough when you are in such density as your physical world. The rules of engagement and the laws of physics do not protect you like in other systems. There are forces that do not want you to succeed. Forces that would do anything to erase your hard drive and sever your connection to the source of creation. You must be stronger, Arayla. You must keep yourself hidden. You must continue to be diligent in your protection, for each day of each hour, the dark will be waiting," the second Crew member continued with a tone that made me squirm.

Z was standing with me in front of the Crew once again. He took my hand and squeezed it. "But I have built the most sophisticated energy system known on earth! Surely she should be protected," he pleaded with the Crew.

"The technology is only as good as the next advancement. Her system must be upgraded continuously to be safe and will only be if your knowledge is superior to those working for the dark. You must work together to keep one step ahead of what is opposing you." He instructed, "You must keep her safe."

"Why aren't you physically with me?" I turned and asked Z directly. He did not respond.

I turned back to the Crew and pleaded again, "Why isn't Z with me in the physical world? I need him beside me, protecting me on earth. Can he protect me from here?" I said, almost screaming the words.

I found myself looking deep inside myself. Deep into the ship of Light that I had become. It was foreign and confusing as I tried to make sense of what I was seeing. It looked like the inside of a computer. It was three dimensional and I moved through it like I was floating inside of a computer game. But it is me, or is it? How can I tell what is real?

"Go deep inside." I heard Z say. "Search and remove all that is not divine Light. Delete the viruses. Delete the false programming. Banish the darkness that has found its way inside. You must be clear. You must be pure."

A rush of knowing entered my awareness. I began to search my vehicle, my ship, my body for everything that did not belong. I had to know what was supposed to be there and what was foreign and unwanted. With absolute clarity, I searched each section of the ship, my body, my matrix looking for all that did not belong. I knew the dark energy would try to hide from me, from my Light. Systematically I searched and checked each layer, each program, each energy, making it stand in the Light of truth, the Light of source.

When the energies, or in some cases entities, tried to run and hide, I flooded them with brilliant pure white Light, and they disappeared right before my eyes. With each section clear, my ship, my matrix, my body grew brighter. I scanned my vehicle again and again until I felt complete. A feeling of such clarity and power came over me. I watched as I transformed back into the shape of the hummingbird. I was experiencing such love, such joy, such happiness but at the same time feeling fiercely protective of my surroundings, my body, my matrix. There was no fear, no hesitation, only a feeling of being confident and in control.

I was floating high above the earth, feeling free and soaring. My awareness shifted back to the portal, the same portal that had brought me here, high above the Nazca lines. I watched as the medicine man, Soft Feather, appeared in front of me. Our eyes met and he smiled. His hand gently rose up and lifted my chin. Am I human or am I still a hummingbird? I couldn't tell. I only felt the touch of his hand on my chin. His smile so warm and reassuring. His eyes so filled with wisdom and compassion. Then suddenly he reached his hand in, tore out my larynx and replaced it with a ruby crystal. It happened so fast, I didn't even have time to flinch.

I was so confused and disoriented as a woman looked down at me and extended her hand to help me up and escort me back to Tom and Sandra. The drumming had stopped. The ceremony was over. I reached up to feel my throat, half expecting to feel blood from my larynx being ripped out. Is my throat still there? Do I still have a throat at all? Can I feel the crystal? As I did this, the medicine man smiled at me in recognition. He reached out and took my hand, helping me to my feet. When he removed his hand, a glass vial, filled with what looked like sand, was in mine. As I looked at it, he took it and placed it around my neck. He then held it in his hand and with his eyes closed, proceeded to bless it. He opened his eyes and for a moment they changed colors from blue to amber to brown.

"Remember this moment, Arayla. Keep this with you always," Soft Feather said, as if I could ever forget.

He smiled and motioned for me to go with this other woman. She looked so familiar, but I couldn't place her. She had dark skin, but she didn't look Native America. She looked more Hawaiian to me and she was dressed funny. Different than the rest of the women. I took her hand. She was solid and steady and I needed that, as my body was shaking and I felt really weak. Then I remembered seeing her in Peru and at Pyramid Lake. She took me back to Tom and Sandra without saying a word. They helped me out to the car. I crawled into the back seat without saying a word and was out like a light...

Chapter 29

Illusion as a platform
Illusion as a guise
Deep within the chambers
Our true splendor will arise

Memories and lightening
The power and our truth
Deep within our chambers
Resides our hidden fruit

Hey beautiful, are you okay in there?" The bath water is starting to cool down, but the wind still gently moves through the open space. I start to come back to my senses.

"I'm waiting for you, my love." I hear him say as my mind tries to formulate where I am. His voice is so familiar. Suddenly, the events of the day flood back into my mind and a warm sensation comes over my body. I'm ready to feel him inside me, deep inside me. We have waited so long to be together. His voice has such desire and longing. Oh, what he does to my soul. He's been so patient with me, so honoring, so loving. I take another breath... What a beautiful ceremony it had been. So absolutely perfect. I think of our first kiss as husband and wife and my mind flashed... But who was that woman? Just as I see her face in my mind, a hummingbird feather, floating on the wind, lands in the bath water.

Chapter 30

Within the blood reside the codes
Of evolution's way
To change the sequence of the pulse
And chemical displays

Creating a reaction
Which restores the hidden truths
Of DNA perfection
And spiritual pursuits

For when the blueprint fires
Restoring all the codes
Your memory will surface
Bringing back your Divine soul

I've never seen water so turquoise. It almost feels like silk on your skin. Get in, it's warm!" I said to Vicki, Gary, and Tim. "It feels amazing, you're gonna love it."

I was so glad that Gary and Tim had stayed in touch after Machu Picchu. They wanted to keep Vicki and me in the loop about upcoming adventures. I was happy to have people to travel with that I knew and somewhat trusted. My "episodes" were becoming easier to manage, but you just never know…

Vicki lives for the water and playfully ran, diving head first into the clear Caribbean Sea. Tim just laughed.

"How many times have we watched her dive into water now? Now I know that it just doesn't matter. If the water is dark, murky, ice cold, in the form of lakes, rivers, streams, pools, the Pacific, the Atlantic… if it's water, Vicki will love it," Gary said.

"Whew. It's amazing," Vicki exclaimed with a wild smile on her face. Gary moved gently into the warm water.

"Wow, this is nice!" he agreed. "So much better than the last water we went into."

"Sounds like I've missed a few adventures," I said disappointingly.

"Yes, but as far as water goes, this is by far the most beautiful and nurturing EVER," Vicki claimed and she was clearly the expert on water.

We were swirling around like four playful dolphins. What a treat to be together again in such a beautiful place. It was paradise!

Bimini was the first Caribbean island I had ever stayed on. I'd done day visits to several islands while on cruises, but staying here—this was a real joy. No timelines, no schedules to adhere to, no crowds. Just swimming with my friends without a care in the world. Vacation. This was the first real vacation I had taken in years. The resort was beautiful, but I wasn't feeling real comfortable with the rest of the island.

"Don't you just love all the bright colors? It makes it feel so alive," I beamed as Vicki floated close to me.

"Yep. Really is pretty, but oh, this water is so nice. As far as I am concerned, we should just get our meals delivered here." She laughed.

"We really should get out and shower. I'm starving, and apparently there is only one restaurant open tonight," Gary told us. "I hope there is something good on the menu."

We were all feeling the effects of the travel. We had flown in from different parts of the country to vacation together. My trip from the west coast had been the longest. Connecticut and Oklahoma were closer, but still we were all tired.

"I'm going to sleep well tonight," I insisted as we dragged our tired and waterlogged bodies through the resort to our rooms.

The rooms were nice and bright. They had high ceilings with fans in every section. Large oversized beds with brightly colored bedspreads and pillows were perfectly laid out for the full paradise affect. Blues, pinks, corals, all the colors of the Caribbean. There were cheap mass production pictures of beach chairs and oceans on the walls, but it didn't matter. We were in paradise. The rooms all had a little kitchenette with a mini fridge, coffeemaker with packets of what I was sure would be pretend coffee by my standards and a few plates, utensils and a blender.

"Look here." Vicki said with a giggle. "Ray, do you want me to make you a pot of coffee?" She laughed. Vicki knew my passion for good coffee.

"Good thing I brought my own," I proclaimed.

"Jesus, lord help this island if you had to live without your 'special' coffee." Vicki giggled, remembering my disappointment when I had visited and she had only had regular coffee and honey, heaven forbid!

I walked over to my suitcase and pulled out my own coffeemaker.

"Oh God! Are you kidding me? You actually brought your own coffeemaker? I thought you were learning to travel light?" Vicki rolled her eyes and pretended to be disgusted.

"Girl, I knew you liked good coffee, but this is a little over the top, don't you think?" Gary chuckled.

"Well, actually it's an espresso maker and I even brought a steamer for the milk!" I said proudly as I took it over and placed it prominently on the counter. I picked up the coffeemaker that was there and quickly shoved it under the sink.

Vicki just kept laughing. "Well at least we know you will be pleasant this trip," indicating she knew full well what I was like without my coffee fix in the morning.

"I'm going to my and Tim's room and jumping in the shower. Don't take long, you two, I'm starving!" Gary said, then grabbed his beach bag and headed out the door to his room. We had booked rooms right next to each other hoping there would be a connecting door, but that was not the way this resort was built. Each was a standalone condo or suite.

"I can't believe you ordered lamb chops," Gary said as we all relaxed on the patio of the restaurant. "We are on a Caribbean island and you order lamb chops?"

"I know, I know but I didn't want fried shrimp or conch," I said.

The setting was beautiful. We were outside on the patio overlooking one of the two pools at the resort. The sky was starting to change colors. Pink clouds surrounded by blue sky. The sun was beginning to set and the "show" was beautiful. There were only a few other tables occupied around us. Someone lit up a cigarette.

"Damn I hate that! Such a beautiful setting and someone has to ruin it with that disgusting smell!" I said.

"Just enjoy the setting Arayla...we're in paradise, remember?" Just then, as if right on cue, the fountain started to flow with pulsing colored lights, making it look like the water was actually dancing. "See, paradise!" Vicki laughed.

"Yes, a few days in paradise. Just what the doctor ordered. What is on the agenda for tomorrow?" I asked.

"Snorkeling with the dolphins. I hope we see dolphins. It's always a hit or miss, you know. Bimini is known for dolphin swims, so hopefully there will be a lot of them," Gary said.

"What time?" I asked.

"Don't worry Arayla, we booked an afternoon swim. This time it really is vacation rather than a grueling spiritual journey," Tim added.

"How are the salads?" the waiter asked while refilling our water glasses. "Your main course should be out shortly. Is this your first time to the island?"

"Yes, it is," I replied.

"Well, welcome to our little piece of paradise. Are you doing anything special while you're here?"

"We planned a dolphin swim and snorkeling over Bimini Road," Tim said.

"Ah, the famous Bimini Road. The road that leads to Atlantis! Be careful that you don't disappear!" The waiter winked.

"Yes, Arayla, there will be no disappearing into thin air this trip!" Gary said with robust authority. We all just laughed but I could tell they weren't too sure.

"Did you ever figure out what happened in Peru, Arayla?" Tim asked.

"I think I really did go into another dimension. That is why you couldn't see me."

"What does that mean?" He sounded a bit irritated.

"Well I'm not totally sure, but I think it has to do with quantum physics and frequency," I explained as Vicki nodded her head in agreement.

"Hmm," he said as the waiter came back with our entrees.

Bimini Road. I wonder what it will be like? My thoughts swirled as I watched the sunset. The sky was changing again and the reflection of the light on the water was spectacular. Bimini and the road to Atlantis... My mind started to drift as images of Atlantis started coming into my awareness. Large open-aired structures with marble pillars. Huge crystals beaming different colored rays of healing Light, both as laser pinpoint beams and soft waves, like the waves from a gentle surf. It was so nurturing, like the water I had been in earlier. I felt calm and peaceful.

"It's going to be interesting to swim over the road to Atlantis," Vicki said. "Wonder what it will be like? Do you think we will be able to see it clearly?"

"Hopefully. Especially if the water is as beautiful as it was today," Gary answered.

"Hey, why didn't your wives want to come to Bimini? It sure seems like their kind of trip," I asked.

"They're attending some kind of women's conference together, so Gary and I were free!" Tim exclaimed with a little too much enthusiasm.

"And they don't mind you traveling with two single women?" I asked.

"We both have very solid relationships. It is rare and we both know it," Gary said with pride.

Later, I crawled into the oversized king bed with images of Atlantis dancing through my head. I wondered what it was like… Was it real? Of course I just knew it was real, but I had not really thought too much about it. I didn't even know Bimini was said to be part of the legendary Atlantis or that there was anything called Bimini Road prior to a couple of weeks ago when I got the notion to go to the Caribbean on vacation. So when Vicki called and said Gary and Tim were going to Bimini and asked us to join, I knew I had to be there. A long weekend with friends, friends I had traveled with before, who had witnessed some of my "bizarre episodes" first hand and that I felt comfortable with. It was obviously meant to be and sounded fun.

I didn't even know exactly where Bimini was. Now, I'd heard of Bermuda. Everyone's heard of Bermuda and the Bermuda triangle. Boy I hope that was not part of the Bimini road. My thoughts drifted back to the images of the marble pillars and the light show cascading through it. Atlantis…

"Okay everyone, we're here. Bimini Road is just below." The boat captain pointed just over the side of the fourteen-passenger boat. It had taken much longer than I had anticipated. You have to travel all the way around the island to get there. Apparently the water is too shallow to go directly from the resort to this spot, although we could see it from the balcony of our room.

"The three sisters are just there," he motioned, pointing directly behind the boat at the large rock formations jutting out of the sea. "Now if you would please get your snorkel gear on."

"This is so exciting. Look, you can see the Bimini Road from here," Vicki exclaimed as she was fastening her goggles.

"I know, it's cool. The water is so clear!" I said as I was still trying to get my flippers on.

"I hate using rented equipment," Tim complained. "I hope it stays secure. I don't want to lose my contacts. I want to see this thing!" he said as he bent down to pick up the snorkel mask.

"It's going to be great! Hurry up you guys," Vicki yelled. She was always the first one in the water, always! She jumped from the platform of the boat and started to swim away.

"Okay! Me next," I squealed. I put the snorkel mask on, put the flute in my mouth and jumped. I swam back around and motioned for the others to follow.

This was so cool! The water was absolutely crystal clear. You could see the road easily below us. It was very distinct. Large blocks of rock, flat and square. It was obvious it was not natural. These blocks had been deliberately placed there. It was just like the pictures, I thought. The photos hadn't been doctored as they say. Bimini Road was undeniably real and we were swimming directly over it.

Vicki motioned for me to follow her closer and I did. We dove as deep as we could. I haven't mastered the art of diving with a snorkel mask, but Vicki was rather skilled. She kept going deeper and deeper pointing at different things she was seeing. There was very little else swimming around with us, and I thought that was odd. There were no fish or anything. I guess I expected a snorkel trip to have fish. Not this snorkel, not the snorkel to Bimini Road. The large blocks of rocks below were the entire show. We swam around for about twenty minutes before Gary decided he had had enough. I swam back up to the boat with him to hear what he had to say.

"Isn't it cool!" he said. "You can really see where it led and it is obviously not natural. This was put here!"

"I know, you just don't really believe it until you swim above it, do you?" I said.

"Nope. I'm pooped. You ready to get back in the boat?"

"Nope, I want to swim some more." I insisted as I turned and headed back out over the stones.

It was lovely to just float above it, the road to Atlantis directly below me. I wondered if in a past life I had actually been there?

"Of course you were." I heard the familiar voice. "We were here together. You are an Atlantean Master healer and part of the ancient ones called Atla-Ra. You are part of the Law of One, Arayla. Remember this place," Z said.

My mind started to drift and the next thing I knew, Vicki was shaking me. She scared the heck out of me. I don't know how long I had been floating there. I looked up at her and she looked panicked, really panicked. I went vertical in the water and removed my mask.

"What is wrong?" I asked.

"Geez Ray! We could not find you," she yelled.

"What do you mean you couldn't find me?" Vicki just started to pull me back towards the boat. I swam with her and made my way back up to the platform. We just sat there for a minute before she started yelling at me.

"You disappeared again. Just like at Machu Picchu!"

"What are you talking about? That's not true. I was here all the time. I've just been floating over the rocks!"

"No you haven't. Gary was watching you from the boat. He didn't take his eyes off you. Then, suddenly you were gone. Nowhere to be found. POOF! You vanished and we have all been searching for you for the last twenty minutes." She continued to yell at me.

"I can't believe she did it again!" Tim shook his head in disbelief as he sat beside Gary in the boat.

"I don't understand…I never left. I was just floating," I said, but I knew full well what had happened. I had slipped into another dimension again.

The captain of the boat came over to make sure I was okay.

"You gave us quiet a scare young lady." He reached for my hand to pull me onto the boat.

"I was beginning to think I had witnessed an actual disappearance. I'll admit that I've seen some strange things happen here. But I've never lost a passenger and I plan to keep it that way. Back to the boat, missy! You'll be staying topside," the captain said with a rather authoritative but playful tone.

"Look Ray, I don't know what just happened, but I had my eyes on you, watching you and all of a sudden you were gone. Poof! The girl is gone! Nowhere to be seen. I could see sixty feet down into this water. It's crystal clear. You were not there. You were just gone!" Gary was furious.

"Okay, I hear you," I agreed, trying to give him some acknowledgment that yes, I might have just disappeared again right before his eyes.

"Okay everyone please take your seats and hold on," the captain ordered. "We are running late and need to get back to the dock."

The motor came on with a loud roar and the boat took off towards the island. The sound of the motor was too loud for us to talk, so I just sat there trying to assimilate what my friends had just told me. I had disappeared, again! How could I just disappear? I had lost my sense of being in the water. I had to admit that to myself. It was like I had been jerked awake when she started to shake me. I couldn't have fallen asleep while floating there, surely and I do remember Z talking to me. I looked over to Vicki, Tim and Gary. They were calm now and I was grateful they were with me.

The ride back to the dock was bumpy and felt like it took twice as long as the ride out. Everyone seemed exhausted. As we left, several of the other people who had been on the boat looked at me like I was totally weird. Geez, what is it with them? I thought, knowing full well why they were looking at me funny.

Vicki noticed my reaction and just shook her head and motioned for me to get off the boat. "Yep, they are all pissed at you for disappearing. It made everyone late," she explained.

"Just forget about them Ray, and let's go back to the room, get a shower and some food," Gary said. He was right, why did I care about what they thought? I didn't even know them. Tim wasn't saying much at this point. You could tell he was just stupefied by the whole experience.

Back at the room, as the door closed behind me, I dropped everything and laid down on the bed. My head was swimming, but I wasn't sure with what. Nothing was coming into full images. I just felt weird and like I had really spaced out. A nice shower will make me feel better, I thought. I walked into the bathroom to start the water and looked into the mirror. All I saw stare back at me was a beautiful pair of green eyes larger than my head. I shook my head to try and clear my sight. As I looked again, the eyes winked at me and faded. What the hell? I'm going to need a drink tonight. I stripped out of my wet bathing suit and cover-up and stepped into the soothing shower. I winced as the hot water ran over my sunburn. I guess I really had been out in the water longer than I had thought.

"Well, hello again!" The same waiter ushered us back to the same table we were at the night before. "You all look like you got some island sun today."

"Yes we did!" I said with a smile.

"Well it looks good on you," he said as he placed the menus down in front of us. "Can I start you off with a cocktail this evening?"

"Yes," I quickly answered as Vicki gave me a sharp and disapproving look.

"I think we better keep our wits about us this evening, but thank you," she quickly replied for both of us. "I think I would like a Coke. How about you, Ray?"

"Yeah, no wait, make mine a Sprite please." After the waiter left I said, "Whew, my head is spinning."

"A perfectly logical reason why you shouldn't have any alcohol, Ray. Geez girl, it's going to be a long night, I can tell already," Vicki said with a roll of her eyes.

Chapter 31

The world around us shatters, beneath the veil of lies
That disengage our memory, of the simple truth of life

So much is left untapped now, our potential still unseen
Behind the web of mistruths, the masses now believe

So much controlled by media, so little left to chance
As people fear the chaos, misguided happenstance

As humans we resign to, misconception that we see
Until we move our consciousness, beyond the daily dream

Open up your true heart, feel your way back home
To the connections deep inside you, forgotten for so long

Your higher mind reveals now, the wisdom of your soul
To reunite the knowing, to find your way back home

"Okay, so what happened?" Gary asked as soon as the waiter left with our dinner orders. "Was it just like at Machu Picchu?"

"Well, sort of, there was no shaman doing ceremony that was for sure. I'm not sure what happened. You guys say I disappeared and all I remember was floating above the stones. I don't know why you guys thought I was gone."

"Well I KNOW you were gone because I was looking straight at you and then you were nowhere to be seen. That's gone!" Gary said.

"That is so weird. I know I felt like I had kind of zoned for a few, like I was in a deep meditation. And then was brought back when Vicki touched me."

"Think Arayla, go back and feel into what happened," Vicki pleaded.

I sat there looking out over the sunset again. I closed my eyes and went back to that space. Floating over the stones, over the road to Atlantis. Suddenly I began to see flashes of Light energy and dolphins swimming around me. I spoke out loud...

"Did you guys see the dolphins swimming around me?" I asked with my eyes still closed.

"There were no dolphins Arayla," Vicki answered.

"I didn't see any dolphins either," Tim proclaimed. "Weren't there supposed to be dolphins?"

"Well, I saw dolphins swimming around me and flashes of light moving through the water. Z was with me and I saw several huge pillars of stone."

"Who is Z?" Gary asked.

"I really don't know who he is, exactly. But I have seen him before many times, in my dreams and visions. Remember when I said there was a jaguar with me in Peru? Well, that was Z, or some part of him. But he normally shows up like a normal man, well not quiet solid." I still wasn't sure how much I was ready to share with them.

"Go on," Gary asked for more.

"Anyway, I wasn't really in the water anymore. The space was huge and open, really spacious. I could hear music playing. Actually, it was more like tones or just frequencies. Z and I were 'walking' around." He was showing the crystals to me and telling me how powerful they are. How I actually held the knowledge to work with the crystals, how to harness their power to heal."

I paused, searching my memory. "He told me that I have the ancient knowledge of the Atla-Ra and the Law of One inside me, inside my matrix. He told me to remember who else was with me in Atlantis. That I needed to remember who else had access to the ancient knowledge. It was important for me to remember who they were."

Just then the waiter returned with our salads. I opened my eyes and looked out at the sunset trying to recall what else had transpired. Tim started in on the bread and butter.

"I wonder who else you're supposed to remember?" he said curiously.

I was amazed at how much I was remembering. It was easy to tap into, to remember this time. It all seemed so clear to me. "My body feels funny," I said.

"Oh shit, here we go. Hurry up and eat your salad. We need to get food in you, Arayla. Eat!" Vicki urged. "It will help ground you." Vicki was starting to know me well. Between the experiences in Peru and what she had heard from my experience in Oklahoma from her friends, she recognized when something was about to happen.

We sat there for a while in silence, each of us trying to process what I had just said. Gary and Tim seemed perplexed, but Vicki, well I could see her mind going a mile a minute.

"I think you went into another dimension, Ray. I think you were actually still floating in the water, but that you were in another dimension and that is why we couldn't see you. I don't understand why it happens… it's like something in you has been "activated" so you can pass through into other dimensions. I'm sure that is what happened to you in Peru as well. The big question is why? What is the reason you move between the dimensions? Why do you have this skill and not us?" Vicki asked.

"I wish I knew..." I said.

We sat there together, everyone deep into their own thoughts as we finished our meals and watched the magnificent sunset across the water. This place really was paradise. The walk back to the room helped ground me. Or at least that is what I wanted to tell myself.

"Vicki, do you feel the room spinning?" I asked as I sat on the edge of the bed.

"Yes, I've felt the entire island spinning all day. Don't worry. I will stay awake and watch over you tonight," she insisted, as if it was her sworn duty or something.

Vicki tried to stand up and as she did, slipped right back down onto the couch. "Whoa. I don't think I can move right now. Arayla, please make the floor stop moving," she pleaded.

"I'm trying, I'm trying," I cried, like I had any conscious control over anything that was happening.

"The energy is really intense and just flowing through me in waves."

Vicki rubbed her head. "You aren't kidding. Did I tell you the guy on the boat, the helper, he asked me what you were doing to his island. I just stared at him. He pointed to you out in the water, before you disappeared and said, 'That girl is spinning this island.' Then he grabbed something hanging around his neck like a talisman and brought it up to his lips and kissed it. 'The ancestors told me she would be coming and to allow her access," he said. I just stared at him in shock. Then he smiled and went back to taking care of business.

"What? Why didn't you tell this to me earlier?" I pleaded.

"I just remembered," she answered. "Well, he seemed happy you were here. And he said that the ancestors were happy, so I guess I didn't worry about it." She acted as if it was an everyday occurrence.

"Yes, but it would have been nice to know," I insisted.

"Well you know now!" She stood up again and held onto the wall as she walked over to the closet.

"I don't know what's happening, but I have got to lie down," I said as the room started to disappear around me. "Oh God, I am divine light, I am divine light, I am divine light," I stated over and over again, trying to convince myself I was alright. Just as my head hit the bed, Z appeared.

I was standing with him in what seemed like a concert stadium. There was a long line of Beings waiting to take their places. There was a reception table right by the doorway, where each group was signing in and getting their access or passes. Each group would then present their pass to Z and he would walk them over and introduce them to me. It was all very formal, each group leader announcing their "specialty" or area of expertise and then leaving to take their place in what I now realized was a huge control room. It was like being at NASA or something. The line continued to grow and Z kept presenting the groups and their areas of expertise, along with where they were from in the universe. Each group looked different, yet I could see the Light emanating from them. As they walked up to me, they bowed. It was unnerving, yet it seemed appropriate somehow. Like an acknowledgment or way to show respect.

"Director, we are from what will be known as P5, a moon system around Pluto that earth scientists have not yet discovered. Our specialty is gravitational forces within the magnetic spectrum of photon light. It is our honor to be here in service to you and all of humanity." The human-like being bowed and waited for my acknowledgement. Did he just call me Director?

"Your service is vital, thank you," I said as I motioned for him to be led to his position within the command center.

Z smiled at me and winked. I nodded and continued as at least a hundred teams entered the stadium, all bringing specialists highly skilled within their area of expertise. There was a delay in the line so Z walked over to the reception desk. "What's the issue here?" I heard him say.

"Well sir, this group isn't on my list. They don't seem to have a specialty. They said they received special permission to be here," the Being behind the reception desk reported. "They said the Director told them they could come and watch. They said you promised you would remember them when this day came." Z looked at her and then at the Being who was obviously negotiating for the group.

"Sir, you promised you would remember. See, we have the same birthmark." the Being said as he pointed down to his left forearm. It had a very distinct dark ruby marking. Z looked down at his own forearm and the mark looked the same.

"You did that so you would remember your promise, sir," the Being reminded him. "We just want to watch. We will not get in the way. The Director told us when the time came, we could watch and learn."

Z looked at me and shrugged his shoulders. The Being behind reception gave them a pass and motioned to Z to lead them in. "Oh sir, this is such an honor. This is such an honor. How can we ever repay you?" the Being replied with joy.

Z just motioned to have them follow. "Director, these Beings are here only to observe. They are not part of the specialists you have called in," he said to me. He looked over to the group and they were ten paces behind him and would not look up from the floor. Z stopped and waited for them to approach. Their eyes still turned towards the ground.

"Sir, we cannot." The leader of the group said shyly.

"Of course you can," Z replied. "She's loving and kind."

"Of course, we only meant it was too high an honor to be received by her," the group leader explained.

"Ridiculous! She knows we are all one. She will respect you more if you look her in the eye," Z said.

Slowly he raised his eyes to meet me, then quickly lowered his head and body in a bow.

"We are at your service in any way we are capable." His voice was respectful and honoring.

"Thank you for coming," I replied. Z then quickly motioned for them to find their seats. Turning back to me, he smiled again and winked as the next group made their specialty known.

When the stadium was full, Z began to address the whole group.

"I want to thank you all for coming. This has been a massive joint effort, and your expertise and technical assistance in this endeavor has been greatly appreciated." Z continued to speak:

"As you are all well aware, the great galactic experiment has been one of the most critical opportunities we have had to collectively repair the multi-dimensional damages from frays in the grids that developed after the energetic disturbances which resulted from mass conflicts on earth. We all know that many humans have also compounded this problem. In their ignorance and arrogance, they contaminated the frequencies, creating more havoc and chaos in this dimension and beyond. We have waited for the trainings, testing and initiations to be completed and NOW IS THE TIME to finish the repairs and finally recalibrate the frequencies. We will return Earth to its original divine frequency, thus bringing each dimension back into perfect harmonic alignment!"

The human part of me expected the Beings in the stadium to cheer. They did not. Not a sound. No one flinched. Complete silence. Every being was focused totally on ME.

Z looked at me with his big amber eyes, took a long deep breath and smiled. Our eyes locked and our hearts began to beat as one. He took another long deep breath and as he did, he touched my heart and the symbol fired. He touched my throat and the ruby inside started to hum. He touched the temple to the right of my eye and the crystal skull rose above me. He touched my sacral and....

"Arayla, Arayla honey...are you in there?" Vicki whispered.

Vicki was speaking to me, very softly, very cautiously. My awareness started to come back into the hotel room. I sat up straight, looked her in the eyes and fell back onto the pillow.

As my eyes began to adjust, I could tell it was daylight. I felt like I had been hit by a Mack truck. My body hurt everywhere and my eyes felt like they had been open for forty-eight hours straight. They were burning from the inside out. I slowly sat up and rubbed my head. Oh wow, my neck hurt!

Vicki whispered again, "Are you back with us? Ray, are you back?"

I smiled. "I think so." Then the realization hit. "Oh my God, Oh my God, it didn't work. Holy shit, it didn't fire." I yelled as I went into a complete panic. My head was pounding and waves of nausea were moving through me. "Oh my God, I failed. It didn't fire." With my head in my hands, I started to sob. Vicki tried to console me.

"Oh my God! What am I going to do?" I sobbed even harder.

"Breathe, Ray, breathe," Vicki insisted.

I took a couple of deep breaths and tried to get a grip.

"What happened?" she asked.

"We tried to repair the damages and fire the grid. So much preparation and I couldn't make it work," I screamed, still not really understanding what had happened. I just had a feeling deep in the pit of my stomach that I had failed. And I had failed BIG!

I heard Z and the Crew members, "Arayla, it was just a test run. It was only a test run. You did not fail. It was a test." I tried to focus on what they were saying. And then it hit me...

"A test run!" I screamed. "All this for a test run?" I couldn't believe what I was hearing. I was suddenly back in front of the Crew.

"Yes, this was a test run. Of course we needed to do a test to see if the system was operational. We can't fire a grid of this magnitude without performing our due diligence. We were able to identify several areas where the grids have been distorted, even tampered with. This was invaluable and necessary step," the head Crew member reassured me.

"But what if it had worked?" I asked confused and a little put off.

"Well then, we would have fired the grid," the Crew member noted without emotion.

"Are we ready? Could it have fired?" I demanded.

"That is why we were testing the system. If it had been ready, fully operational, we would have gone live. Now we know what needs to be repaired and where the problems are. Good work, you two." The Crew member faded from my awareness.

Just when I think I'm actually going on vacation for a change, there is always something, always a higher reason for going somewhere. Z had told me I needed to go to the Caribbean, and within a week, I had an invitation to go with friends. Now, I come here and get put through a "trial run." It was insane! Yet, I knew I had been working towards completing my "role," but I still didn't know what that role actually was. I always get just enough. Enough to get me to the next place, the next set of circumstances that gets me one step closer. I know that in the higher realms I am confident, in control and aware of the "big picture" so to speak, but in 3D I wish I knew more. Trust, intuition and my guidance are all I can go by as each piece, each part of the puzzle is only revealed as needed. Clearly my role involved working with Light Beings from all over the universe. It was connected to the Galactic Alignment and it had far reaching effects. Really far reaching.

Chapter 32

Unbridled passion enlivens
Within all sacred life
Light and Love's expansion
Within the space so ripe

As rhythmic movement ushers
A feeling so surreal
Our hearts and soul advancement
Will forever be fulfilled

Man, it's cold in here. Why is it always so bright? I wish they would turn down the television. How is a girl supposed to sleep around here?

I open my eyes to see where I am. Oh god, how I love those beautiful blue eyes. I just smile as he stares lovingly at me while stroking my cheek.

"Hello Beautiful! How are you feeling?" he asks as he takes my hand in his. Oh, how was I so lucky? This man, with the gorgeous blue eyes, loves me. He loves ME. I wish we would just come back to bed and snuggle with me. I'm so cold...

Chapter 33

Our eyes are only capable
  Of seeing frequencies
Within the Light wave measurements
  Of what we now perceive

That spectrum is a fraction
  Of what is truly there
Within our magnificent universe
  Expanding constantly

Our perception, it is changing
  To see the other realms
Of Light, matter and consciousness
  Beyond our current dwell

So open up your mind
  To recognize the truth
That each of us is changing
  It's evolution, it is truth

Vicki handed me a cup of coffee. "I know this isn't your special stuff, but it will have to do," she said with a smile. I took the warm cup of liquid from her and took a long slow sip.

"Drink, you need to ground yourself back into this reality," she ordered. I took another long drink and started to stand up to go to the restroom. "Whoa, where do you think you're going?" Vicki asked as I stumbled back onto the bed.

"I need to pee," I said.

"Okay, let me help you." Vickie stood up and took my arm. "Easy does it," she instructed. "One foot in front of the other." I just looked at her like she was crazy. She laughed. "Well you should have seen yourself last night, missy. You would not be looking at me so crazy if you had."

After getting a real espresso latte from my special machine, I sat back on the now made bed. I realized how worn and wiped out Vicki looked.

"You look like I feel," I said.

"Girl you have no idea what you put me through last night. You were screaming in pain and jolting up. You would sit up straight in the bed and start speaking in a funny language. At one point you toned for so long I couldn't figure out how you were even breathing. You never once took a breath. You thrashed all over the bed and the whole time the walls and floor were moving and swaying. I tried to call Gary and Tim for help and I couldn't reach the phone, so I just sat here holding on for dear life," Vicki explained. I just looked at her with a blank stare and started laughing.

"Don't laugh at me! I'm telling you, you were moving me through the dimensions, Arayla. You disappeared and reappeared, I can't tell you how many times. The energy was beyond anything I have EVER experienced. And I've experienced a lot. I'm just glad we are all okay. At one point, I was afraid you were going to just explode and take the whole damn island with you," she almost shouted while flinging her arms in the air.

"What do you remember?" she asked.

I shared with her what I remembered about the groups of experts showing up and Z starting out with the speech. I didn't remember much of anything else after that until I started panicking that I had failed. And then having the Crew member explain to me that it wasn't something I did, that it was just a test run.

"Of course, that makes sense. You can't just expect a system to work the first time you flip the switch. You have to test it, you have to run system checks. Of course, that makes perfect sense," Vicki admitted as if she were an expert herself.

The realization that this was true sank in deeper. "We would be idiots to think we could just expect it to run perfectly without testing it out. Any computer programmer will tell you that," I said, trying to regain my confidence.

After we got some real food, Vicki and I decided to spend the day back in the water. It sounded like good therapy to me. I love the water, almost as much as Vicki does.

"I'd love to go back to the three sisters," Vicki said. "I think I can swim there faster than taking the boat." She laughed. "The captain said there was a tunnel you can swim through if you can hold your breath long enough to get to the other side."

We were floating and swimming around in the beautiful warm turquoise water. "God, I love this water," I moaned with pleasure as Vicki floated by me. "The boys are missing out. I'm sure they're having fun wherever they are."

"Yes, this I could do again, but forget last night. That was too much, Ray. How the hell did I get involved with this "multi-dimensional" work?" she asked, smiling.

"Just lucky I guess," I replied. I laid back and allowed my body to fully surrender to the water. I floated effortlessly, rocking slowly and feeling the warmth of the sun hitting my face. My body was still aching from last night. My muscles were throbbing and the water soothed me. My mind replayed the events of the last couple of days.

Director. They had actually called me Director. Was I in charge? It seemed like I was in charge. The idea made me worry. What was the Atla-Ra and the Law of One? I will have to google it when I get back to the room. I bet there will be something floating around the internet that will give me a good idea of what it is. But then again, I have googled things like this before and been so disappointed with the results. Sometimes they are so far removed from what I am experiencing or know to be true. But still, it is fun to see if the terms actually do exist.

I know in my soul I really am directing this. How can that be? How do I know what I am doing? Clearly I am skilled in the higher realms or what does Vicki always call it, the other dimensions. But in charge? Wow, now that is a lot to own. Where did all those specialists come from? How did they know to come right now? What was special about this time? How did I know to be on Bimini? How did the guy from the boat know I was coming? The ancestors told him. Oh right, I thought to myself, but it did make logical sense. Were his ancestors connected to Atlantis? Surely there would be those living here who were connected to the energies, who knew about this place. My mind was still trying to process all the information I had received over the last twenty-four hours. It had been so real being in that control station. And all the groups being presented to me with their areas of expertise and by Z, no less. How did I get to be in charge? I realized how in control and focused I had been during the test run. In my "human" life I am not like that at all. Of course, I probably have a few friends that would argue that. In the higher dimensions, I have confidence. I was clearly very comfortable in that role, the role of Director.

A test run of the grid. Wow, that was a lot to get my head around. Anyone who was spiritual had heard of the 144 crystalline grid system. It was part of an informational grid, designed to bring the Atlantean knowledge of advanced spiritual law back onto the planet. A lot of spiritual "teachers" were talking about it. Apparently, the entire Atlantean "group" was back on the planet to help bring this knowledge to humanity. But if there were so many, how come it was up to me to be here on Bimini running the test? Where the hell was everyone else? Why weren't those teachers and spiritual leaders here helping out? As I continued to ponder the situation, it made sense that the control station for an Atlantean grid structure would be facilitated on Bimini. I wonder if I did go into other dimensions yesterday while floating over the ancient stones. Of course I did!! I was there to get the knowledge and information I needed for last night. That made perfect sense.

"Hey Ray, the island is starting to spin again," Vicki yelled from across the water. "We better get back to the beach."

"You're right, I'm right behind you." As I sat down on the towel and lay back, the island disappeared and I was back with the Crew.

"You must go to Bolivia NOW! You must protect the wisdom and knowledge. Retrieve the codes before the opposition. Do not let the codes be corrupted. The opposition is trying to get the codes from the Ancient Grandmothers of Mu. There is so much that will be lost forever if they succeed. Go! You must travel back in the timeline to protect the codes. Go back to Bolivia! You must go NOW!" The Crew member instructed me as I desperately looked for Z. He was nowhere to be found.

"But wait, where is Zaratu? Don't send me there alone," I pleaded.

"Don't worry Arayla. You will always have the help you need," the Crew member reassured me.

Chapter 34

What drives the inner passion
What determines your next move
Is it greed or lust or illusion
Of an outcome you pursue

Or is it truly service
To humanity or a friend
Which gives you satisfaction
A deep knowing within your soul

So what's the satisfaction
Is it ego or is it truth
For true untainted service
Only serves the higher good

Jazmin and I had met a couple of years before at a spiritual lecture. I knew her the minute I laid eyes on her. It was just one of those things where you just instantaneously like someone. She felt it too. We sat down next to each other and that was it. We had been friends ever since. I had shared just about everything I had experienced over the last few years. Next to Toni, she was my closest and dearest friend. Although she lived in another state and was married, we have kept close over the years. We talked at least once a week, but really had not spent much time together in the physical. So when we talked she told me she was going on this spiritual pilgrimage to Bolivia with a woman who she admired, and it dawned on me that it was the same journey I had just received the email about earlier that week. She knew I had gone to Peru and thought I might be interested in going with her to Bolivia. My first reaction was, no way! I didn't want to travel to South America again.

"Oh Ray, it will be great! We can travel together and be roommates. It will be awesome! You will love the woman who is facilitating it and I'm sure we will meet a lot of like-minded soul family," she said as she tried to convince me to join her.

But even as my mind was screaming no, I told her yes! I knew I would go, there was no use fighting it. Even as much as I didn't want to do it, I felt it deep in my core. It was just like when I went to Peru, it was undeniable. I was supposed to go to Bolivia. But why?

"Did you just say yes?" she squealed.

I was in shock. I had just said yes, when everything in my personality was saying no. "Yes, Jazmin, I did," I said slowly and very controlled. I could already hear Toni laughing…

The airport was busy as I stood waiting for Jazmin to arrive at baggage claim.

"Ray, Ray!" she squealed as she dropped her bags and gave me a great big hug. She was too cute for words, dressed like a little pixie. She was all of five feet tall and tiny, maybe hundred pounds if she was soaking wet. I swear, I could carry her. She had cut her hair and highlighted it since the last time I had seen her. That had been over a year ago.

"You look so cute, Jazmin!" I said. With a name like Jazmin, what else would you expect? She was in a colorful tunic that flowed below her butt, black leggings, a colorful scarf around her neck that somehow did not clash with the tunic, a hat that only she could pull off and adorable suede-like flat boots. She twirled around to show me all angles. I laughed. I was in blue jeans and a plain cotton shirt. I did have a plain colored scarf around my neck, but that was about as flashy as I got. Oh wait, I did have earrings and a couple of silver bracelets too. I wasn't too fashionably flawed. But Jazmin's style matched the unique spelling and sound of her name. She was one of eight siblings, all of whom had been given boring biblical names. She had decided to officially change hers back in her twenties to better reflect the free-spirited nature she had. She was an artist and dreamer at heart.

"Let's go get your suitcases," I said as I started to head off towards the carousel.

"What suitcases?" she asked.

"What?" I asked. She pointed to her backpack and a small carry-on she had at her feet. "You mean to tell me that is all you have for two weeks in Bolivia?" I questioned.

Yep!" she smiled.

"You have got to be kidding!" I exclaimed. I was in shock, literally in shock. How in the hell could she pack for two weeks in those tiny bags? I couldn't even think about two days worth of clothes in those, let alone two weeks.

"I told you I travel light," she said with a smile. "I'm starving. Can we stop and get something to eat?" she asked as she started towards the exit.

"Of course, but I'm still in shock over your luggage." I took the handle of her carry-on. "I'm parked over here, just follow me. It's a small airport."

"Not as small as the one I just left this morning." Jazmin laughed.

"What do you want to eat? We can stop anywhere you'd like."

"Well, how about a steak?" she asked looking at me. For a week prior to the trip we had both been commenting on how much meat we had been eating. We both could not get enough, we were just craving it.

I laughed. "I'm so glad you said that. I'm starving too."

"So can you believe we leave for Bolivia in the morning Ray?" She took another sip of wine. "Um, this is good," she commented. "You want a sip?" she asked as she handed me the glass.

"Yes, it is good. Maybe I'll order a glass."

"Yeah, I can't believe we are actually going. I wish I was more excited. I mean, I'm excited, but why didn't you call and say let's go to Spain or Italy?" I said, laughing. I'd been complaining about going to Bolivia since I had said yes. Jazmin had gotten used to it, but I'm sure she was tired of hearing it.

"So how is your husband with you traipsing around the world with someone besides him?" I asked to change the subject. I was tired of being defiant about going myself. I had made the decision to go because my intuition had not let up. I knew I was supposed to be there for some reason. I remembered the Crew member telling me I had to go to Bolivia. Then Jazmin asked if I wanted to go with her... and so tomorrow we would jump on a plane to South America. I was learning to just roll with the punches.

Besides, maybe I would meet my true love on this trip. Of course, he would have to be a participant! I wasn't about to fall in love with a Bolivian! I was ready for my true love to show up in the 3D world. My last relationship had lasted only six months before my desire had waned. He was a nice enough guy, the sexual heat had been there for sure, but something was missing. I wanted more. I wanted that deep connection I felt with Z, but Z wasn't real. At least not in this reality and our connection was different. It wasn't the passion or the desire you have with a lover. I wanted more, much more and here in the physical! I wanted the man I kept seeing with the beautiful blue eyes. Was he real? I wondered.

"Arayla!" Jazmin shouted. "Where did you go?" she asked as she took another sip of wine.

"Sorry, I was just thinking about finding my true love," I said with a smile. Jazmin rolled her eyes and picked up another bread roll.

"I know, I know." The waiter returned with our steaks. "God, this looks so good!" I said as we both picked up our forks and dived in.

"Maybe we can make it through the night without anything else." We both knew that would never happen. The energy that was coming through had made it so we both were eating about every two hours. It was crazy! I've found when I run a lot of energy through my body, I have to eat a lot more. I seem to burn through it fast. Especially protein. It's always a really good indicator that something is about to happen.

"Enjoy!" I raised my glass of wine in a toast. "To two friends going on a spiritual adventure to the ancient land of Mu."

With only a one bedroom apartment and a couch that was anything but comfortable to sleep on, Jazmin decided to share my bed. She had flown into Sacramento so we could travel together from here. Hopefully, we wouldn't have to share a bed too often during this trip. I remembered my last trip to South America, the accommodations had been sparse, but at least I never had to share a bed for heaven's sake.

"Shoot, I can't sleep!" Jazmin said as she rolled over and adjusted her pillow for the hundredth time. I looked at the clock. It read 4:44 a.m. Hmm, it reminded me of Peru.

"Don't you like sleeping with me?" I giggled. She shoved me gently and laughed.

"At least you don't snore as loud as my husband does."

"Sorry I don't have a spare bedroom to offer you. Hopefully we won't have to actually share a bed on this trip." I said. I'm glad Toni reminded me to pack earplugs because Jazmin snores too.

"This is going to be a great adventure," Jazmin mumbled as she turned again.

"Do you think he's going to be there?" I asked.

"Who?" She sighed and I laughed.

"Who else, my soul mate, partner, lover!" I said trying not to sound too desperate. "I hope to God that is why spirit is pushing me to go back to South America."

"Maybe, I knew from the minute I heard about this trip that you and I would be going together," she said as her voice faded.

I lay there thinking about what he would be like. I felt like I already knew him. He's going to have blue eyes, that I know for sure. I've seen them several times or at least I have in my dreams. I tossed and turned trying to make sense of it all. Tomorrow Jazmin and I would leave for Bolivia. I couldn't believe I was actually going back to South America. The journey to Peru years ago was still somewhat of a mystery. So much had happened, yet the true meaning about all the "other worldly" events still seemed to make little logical sense or have any real tangible impact on my life. I knew what was happening was important, I knew it in my soul.

I began to wonder what is in store for me next. I tried to recall my last encounter with the Crew. It's always so surreal, the floating in no-space and no-time, yet feeling as if everything is solid, even more solid than here. But it's so frustrating getting so little detail from them. It's always just a hint here or an order there, without any real clear understanding. What was the last thing they said to me, my mind would try to recall in detail, but the details were always spotty to begin with.

So many times I had found myself with the Crew and every time Z was there with me. He was always with me in the higher realms. I knew him in my soul, deep in my soul. Like we had known each other since the beginning of time. He knew me, who I am. Yet every time I'd been with him, I'd been in an altered state. I would know him anywhere by his eyes. Those amber eyes. But he still was not the man I saw in my dreams, the one I know I love. He has the piercing blue eyes. His energy is different than Z's, much different. Z feels like a protector, a big brother, a close confident and someone I would trust with my life. But I want my love. Where is he? Where is my love? The alarm started blaring at 6:15. I jumped straight out of my bed and into the shower.

"I see a sign." Jazmin said as we walked through the Miami airport. "There's the group." We headed over towards the short brunette woman who had taped a sign reading "Sacred Spiritual Tours" to her carry-on luggage and placed it on the seat next to her.

"Hi I'm Jazmin Crafton and this is Arayla Weaver. We are here for the tour to Bolivia." she said as the woman searched for our names on the list of participants.

"Yeah, yes, here you two are. Do you both have your passports and entry letters with you?" she asked.

"Yes, we do." Jazmin looked at me making sure I was nodding my head. I smiled giving her yet another reassurance that I had remembered everything. She was sure I would do something to screw this up, my resistance to coming had been so strong. She wasn't going to believe I was really going until our feet hit the ground in Bolivia. Like I would do anything stupid at this late hour. I had paid the money, I was going!

There were a lot of hoops to jump through to be able to visit Bolivia. Besides the travel visa, all the shots, you also need a letter of entry from the government. This was not just jumping on a plane and flying to a tropical island. You had to navigate the politics to travel to Bolivia. I hoped the trip would be worth it. Once we were all checked in, with both the tour director and the airlines, we decided to try and find some food. There wasn't much choice. This wing of the Miami airport reminded me of the international terminal in LAX. It sucked for food choices. We looked until we found a Mexican food joint. Nothing was striking our fancy, but we knew the airplane food would be even worse and we were both starving. We had packed plenty of munchies for the trip, but we needed real food, again!

"Do you want to split an enchilada?" I asked.

"Yes, but I want to order something else too. That isn't going to be enough. Let's order steak nachos and guacamole too," she said. I just looked at her and she laughed. She was going to be a great travel partner. She was already a great friend.

Chapter 35

Sometimes the need to surrender
Is blocked from deep within
As the need to feel in control
Is culturally patterned within

To feel the insecurity
Of not knowing what will come
Can strike a nerve of panic
Residing beneath your consciousness

But once the soul surrenders
To the higher self enough
The bridge to inner knowing
Becomes stronger with every breath

There were about fifty people on this journey. Most were meeting at the Miami terminal, but a few were coming from "down under" in Australia and would join the tour in La Paz. I scanned the group. It was about eighty-five percent women and just a few men. Typical for spiritual adventures I knew. Some of the men were traveling with their partners or wives. I wasn't very hopeful with what I was seeing at the moment, that I would find "him" on this journey. I shot Jazmin a discouraging look and she just rolled her eyes.

"Can we at least get there before you decide he's not here?" she asked sternly.

Yes, I was jumping the gun, I'm sure. Maybe he was from down under and would meet us in La Paz. Maybe he was here and still out getting food. There were a lot of possibilities. I can't give up hope yet, I thought to myself. Unfortunately, I could hear myself already doubting and being disappointed. I was going to South America. It was time to get excited, put the expectations behind, live in the moment and relish the fact that once again I was embarking on an adventure!

"Let's go, it's time to board," Jazmin said with a huge grin on her face. This was going to be fun! But deep down inside I knew there was something else happening. Something else had pulled me back to South America. I'm sure that was the real reason that I had said yes so quickly, when I first heard about the trip. As we settled into our seats, I took a couple of melatonin to help me sleep. I was out before the plane took off…

Why the hell did I sign up for this? I asked myself as I heard the group leader calling us to gather. The last forty-eight hours had been hell. First, there was the eight-hour bus ride. The roads had been so bad that we literally shook the entire time. Apparently the regular roads had been closed due to rainfall, and what we were traveling on was truly awful. I had never been bounced and battered for such a long period of time. Then on top of that, the restroom on the bus had stopped working about an hour into the journey. There was nowhere to stop along the way, so about every three to four hours the bus driver pulled over and you squatted behind whatever or whomever you could find as you "relieved" yourself. It was humiliating and very uncomfortable to say the least. Thank God Jazmin had packed toilet paper in her backpack. She had taken it from the hotel in La Paz. At least squatting behind fellow travelers was better than the hellholes they actually had stopped at that said there were "facilities." Oh my God, the idea of peeing in one of those places had my skin crawling. Jazmin was a camper, so she just kind of took it all in stride.

"Geez Ray, just pee for hell's sake..." she insisted.

"I'm trying, I'm trying," I almost cried as I squatted, hidden behind five other women on the side of the road. Then we would climb back on the bus and travel for hours again. I was so far beyond mad at the whole situation, but I was trying to keep my cool.

We finally managed to get to our destination. It was a very remote village, and by remote, I mean really remote, like no hotels! The town at the bottom of Machu Picchu seemed like a sprawling metropolis compared to this. The tour had arranged for everyone to sleep in village homes. Like a hostel situation, and hostile was right! The people were nice enough, but boy the accommodations were rough. Besides, sharing a single bathroom, or more accurately a hole in the floor, with twelve other people is NOT my idea of a good time. And I had paid to come on this trip. What the heck was I thinking? This was insane. Jazmin and I were lucky. We only had to share a room with four people. I couldn't remember the last time I had shared sleeping space with someone other than a good friend, family member or lover. Talk about uncomfortable. Jazmin was trying to lay low. She knew I didn't want to come back to South America and now she was beginning to understand why.

"Today we are headed out to a very remote part of Bolivia. Sometimes referred to as the Valley of the Rocks. This is very sacred land. We will stop at two different places for ceremony and then return for another night here," the tour guide explained.

My heart sank. We have to sleep here again. I looked at Jazmin and she just cringed. She knew I was not happy, but she was trying to keep things light. In her fairy style, she was dressed in a whimsical outfit that looked like she should be dancing around in a fern forest rather than in the middle of freaking nowhere headed to some place called the Valley of the Rocks. I thought to myself, I think the rocks are in my head. Why did I ever come here? I took a deep breath and reminded myself of the strong pull to be here. And the fact that there were several really wonderful people we had met. Besides, there was the beautiful Italian hunk that I originally thought was here with his wife, but it turned out to be his sister.

Antonio and I had hit it off immediately. When we first arrived in La Paz, the tour had arranged for a buffet breakfast, as we arrived at 6 a.m. Jazmin and I had gone up before checking into our rooms. I had scanned the room and tables and headed directly for Antonio who I soon found out was with Tallia. I had liked her from the moment I saw her and well, her husband, or so I thought, was gorgeous so of course I wanted to meet them.

Once we made introductions, Jazmin knew she was in trouble. The chemistry between me and Antonio was electric, and in truth we were giving each other a hard time, in playful banter, like we were old friends, within minutes of sitting down.

"So what made you two decide to come to Bolivia?" I asked as I took another sip of papaya juice.

"We just knew we had to come. My brother and I are very connected and even though we live on opposite sides of the US, we always seem to know what the other is thinking when it comes to spiritual stuff," Tallia answered with a very thick accent.

"Where are you from originally?" I asked as I caught Antonio's eyes again and then noticed Jazmin rolling hers in delight watching the two of us. She knew me well enough.

"We both grew up in Italy," Antonio answered. Tall, dark hair, dark eyes, built, gorgeous, single and Italian. Whew, things were looking up!

"Where do you live now?" I asked both of them.

"I live in New York and my sister lives in Washington State," Antonio replied.

"So what do you do?" I continued trying to find out as much as I could.

"Well, I'm married with one son." Tallia said. "He's seven years old and very awake." She continued, "My husband is in construction and isn't very spiritual, so I keep myself immersed in the spiritual communities."

"I am a fashion photographer. I travel around the world for my work. Mostly Roma, London, Paris, LA and New York," Antonio explained.

"Wow! That sounds exciting," Jazmin said as she smiled and flirted with Antonio.

"Yes, it is," he admitted.

"Do you have a family?" Jazmin asked as she knew I was dying to know, but hadn't wanted to ask too soon.

"Yes, well, I'm divorced but I have two amazing children. One boy and one girl, seven and thirteen."

"Oh, are you close to them?" she asked.

"Yes, I love my children and I still stay on the property in Miami with their mother when I'm visiting. Since I travel so much, it just makes sense. Half my time in NY and half in Miami. We have, what do you call it, an in-law quarters behind the main house. My father used to visit and stay there, but now I do."

"You must still get along with your ex-wife then," she stated more than asked.

"Yes, we still care for each other deeply." He smiled. Hmm, well maybe this wasn't such a good potential after all. Sounds to me like he still has feelings for his ex-wife.

"How long have you been divorced?" Jazmin continued to question him trying to get as much detail as she could.

"It's been five years now. We are lucky. We still get along. It makes it better for the children."

Well, five years I thought. Maybe there is hope. But a fashion photographer? He's a player, probably with a woman in every city. Who was I kidding, several women in every city.

"How about you, what was your name again?" Tallia asked me.

"Arayla, but you can call me Ray. No I'm not married and have never had children. But Spirit is full of surprises, so I never give up hope of finding a true partner for this journey called life." I smiled.

Tallia smiled back as she was also feeling the chemistry between her brother and me. It was pretty undeniable. But it was day one of a twelve-day journey. I wasn't about to lose my heart to the best looking man on this tour. There were forty other women, at least half of whom I suspected were looking themselves. But the attraction was definitely there, so who knows? After another ten minutes or so of small talk, it was time to get back to the room and freshen up. There was a gathering of everyone in a few hours and I wanted a shower and a nap. The altitude was definitely getting to me already. La Paz is at an altitude of 15,000 feet.

"So I guess we will see you later," I paused as I got up from the table. Antonio reached for my hand and gently lifted it to his lips.

"I hope so!" he added... "I see something precious here." He lifted his index finger and touched me between my breasts.

Oh God, he is such a flirt and a player, damn I thought as his eyes locked with mine. I winked back at him and he was kind of taken back. I'm a flirt too, so watch out dude, I thought as Jazmin placed her hand on his shoulders.

"See you later," she said and we walked out of the room.

"Geez Ray, you could have cut it with a knife in there!" she complained as soon as we cleared the door.

"I know, too funny huh!" I said with a giggle.

"Girl, he's trouble with a capital T," she argued.

"I know, but this could be a lot of fun. Besides he lives on the other side of the country. What's the harm in a little flirtation? Every woman on this tour will be on him like bees to honey. And from what I gather, he will flirt his ass off with all of them." I admitted with sarcasm. "But he is hot. I mean really hot. And that accent. Damn, Jazmin," I smiled.

She just laughed. "Oh God, what have I gotten myself into! I'm not going to sleep somewhere else you know."

"No?" I replied. "Even if I could get laid by that hunk of an Italian man, you wouldn't go sleep with someone else?"

"Only if that someone else is as much of a hunk as he is!" she giggled.

"Jazmin, what would your husband say?" I laughed.

"Oh yeah, right! Like I would ever do anything like that."

"Well honey, if I can get laid on this trip, I'll go to his room," I agreed with a twinkle in my eye. We both laughed out loud. This trip was definitely looking up. Now, that breakfast seemed like a million years ago after being on the bus for days!

"Everyone gather around." The tour director said again trying to get our attention. We were standing in the middle of the town square. Everyone looking ragged from the basic accommodations of the night before. I had not even had a cup of coffee. We had gotten to the mess hall too late.

"Please, can I have your attention," she continued.

My body hurt and my head was pounding. I needed coffee and this chick was starting to get on my nerves. Just then Antonio wrapped his arms around me and swirled me in the air.

"Oh my God! Arayla, I just spent the most amazing night with you." He smiled like a Greek god, or was it Italian? He put me back down and wrapped his arms around me in an electrifying hug. As he released me, he took my face in his hands. "You are so amazing. Such an amazing Light!" he said all serious and intense.

Tallia was standing right next to him and Jazmin was watching it all in shock.

"What?" I asked confused and trying to get my head around what he was doing and saying.

"Together, last night!. You and I, we were together!"

"What do you mean Antonio?" I asked as other people were starting to pay attention as he was saying it rather loudly.

"You and me. We were together. It was so real. You have the most amazing Light. I've never experienced anything like it! We were together, connected at the heart, together as one heart beat," he replied again in his amazing Italian accent. "I've never known such love, Arayla!"

I blushed at the comment. I caught Jazmin's eyes as she looked at me like she didn't have a clue. "Antonio, slow down, what are you talking about?"

"Didn't you see me?" he asked kind of confused. "The Light that was pouring out of your heart into mine? It was beyond anything I've ever experienced." He grabbed me again and held me tight. "We were together in the higher dimension, fully connected at the heart. The love, oh my, the love I felt was powerful," he said with a grin so wide it was embarrassing.

"You're brother is very passionate and expressive," Jazmin said to Tallia.

"Yes, but I've never seen him act like this before!" Tallia responded with a smile.

"People, please, we need to get into the jeeps! Please listen for your name and jeep number. We will be traveling in groups of five in ten different jeeps to our next location. People, please!" The tour guide yelled over the crowd.

I stopped to listen for my name as Antonio continued to hold me from behind. He was 6'4" to my 5'3", so his presence was towering and he felt really, really good. I could stand there all day with his arms wrapped around me. This was crazy. Did this man just tell me he had never felt love like this? What love, I don't have a clue what he is talking about, but apparently it was a powerful experience. We were not in the same jeep and for a minute I was relieved. He tried to get the tour director to switch him and Tallia into our jeep, but she refused.

"What was that?" Jazmin asked once we were in the jeep and on the way. We sat in the very back so that the others hopefully could not hear. But everyone had witnessed it, so the minute Jazmin asked, everyone else in the jeep turned around to hear the answer. I gave them a harsh look, like mind your own business and they turned back around.

"I don't know!" I insisted. "He came out of nowhere, picked me up, swirled me around and started to say... well you heard him."

"Damn girl, I know you two have chemistry, but really." Jazmin smiled. "That was just wild."

"I know!" I grinned.

"Did you see him in your dreams or visions last night?" she asked.

"No, I barely slept at all, you know that," I grumbled.

"Yes you did, I heard you snoring!" she piped back up. We both laughed.

"I don't know Jazmin, that was intense and powerful. When he stood there holding me from behind, the energy moving through us was intense. I mean I N T E N S E. If he had not been holding me, I might have fallen over," I confessed. "But I don't have any memory of what he is talking about."

"Girl you better hold on. I see that smile on your face. What aren't you telling me?"

I just rolled my eyes and squirmed. The sexual energy was running through me like wild fire. Who was this guy? I didn't know him. I didn't remember being with him in the higher realms. But boy oh boy, whew! I mean things were really heating up. I could feel my kundalini energy starting to rise. What was I going to do now? He didn't feel like the man in my dreams. Who was he? I didn't know, but I was more than willing to find out.

The jeep started to move faster across the barren landscape. We sat in silence for a while as I tried to figure out what was going on. I know we had some kind of connection. It was there from the start, but to have him declare all of that in front of everyone on the tour. He didn't seem to be worried about it though. It was crazy. His sister had stood there watching. Her eyes never leaving the two of us. She did not seem compelled to stop her brother. On the contrary, she was really looking kind of mesmerized by the two of us. When I had looked at her with a confused expression, she had smiled like it was okay. I didn't get the feeling this was something he did often. Or if he did, not to a woman he had not spent the night with. Tallia had said she'd never seen him like that before. The whole thing was surreal and yet, something was stirring deep inside me. It was a familiar feeling. My body was reacting to him in a powerful way. The stirring was deep. Deep inside and primal beyond what I had experienced before.

"Arayla, Trust him. He is here to assist you," I heard Z say.

"Your circuitry must be able to hold all the energy. Embrace it. Feel the expansion up your spine," he continued. "We have sent you support. Allow him to help you."

"Ray, what is going on?" Jazmin asked with concern.

"What do you mean?"

"Well, your whole body is shaking."

"It is?" I asked with shock.

"Yes, girl what is happening to you?"

"Antonio… Z just told me the energy I felt when he hugged me, it's to help me expand to hold the energy. That he is here to assist me. To trust him."

"Well, he sure seems to feel connected to you," Jazmin replied.

"I feel like my spine is on fire. Like I just got hooked up to an electrical socket."

She was right. The Crew said I would always have the support I needed. I guess the support will come in many forms. At least it was in the form of an Italian hunk, I thought to myself. But his energy didn't feel familiar, at least not like what I had experienced with Z. What do they say, it takes a village… He did have beautiful eyes, yet he didn't feel like the man in my dreams either. But obviously I was supposed to trust him and that is something I don't do easily.

All the jeeps stopped at a clearing, by what I guess you could call a stream. There were llamas grazing and the landscape was beautiful. Jazmin pulled out her camera again. She was a great photographer, and I had decided I would just get all the pictures of the trip from her. I suck at remembering to take pictures and the ones I do take never really seemed to come out good. I like experiencing the moment, but I am always sorry when I come home from trips that I didn't take more pictures. Funny though, the pictures really only matter to the one who takes them for the most part.

"Stand there and smile." Jazmin took yet another picture of me.

"Girl, there aren't going to be any of you on this trip. Just me and well whatever I'm standing next to," I said with a laugh.

"I know, but I love taking pictures. You can take one of me you know."

"Give me that!" I demanded as I took a couple of shots of Jazmin with the llamas in the back ground.

"That will be beautiful." I said just as Tallia came up.

"Tallia, join Jazmin and I'll get a picture," I insisted. Tallia wrapped her arm around Jazmin and smiled. She was so beautiful. Angelic even. She was such a nice person and her energy was great. I really want to get to know her even better, I thought as Jazmin snatched the camera from my hands once again.

"Now you two," she said snapping shot, after shot, after shot. Tallia started to swirl around dancing and playing. It was fun to see her so care-free. A few of the others joined in and before you knew it we had all joined hands and were dancing around in a circle.

This was the first ceremony we had done since the trip started. All we had been doing was traveling on buses and jeeps and sleeping in subpar accommodations for days! Come to think of it, it was the first time I had seen the tour's "spiritual" leader. The one Jazmin had talked about. The draw for the tour. Where had she been? I tried to remember seeing her on the bus or at the dinner gatherings. I couldn't remember seeing her at all. That was strange, I thought.

She was beautiful. About five-foot-eight, long dark hair, thin and dressed in a flowing cream and blue… gown for lack of a better term. She was dressed like you would expect from a Celtic Goddess, not a South American native. The fabric was flowing around her as she walked into the center of the clearing. Where had she been for the last few days, was all I could think. How come I had not seen her? Who was she? Jazmin had told me she was a spiritual teacher, soul retrieval specialist, reiki master and sacred site tour leader. I had started to read her bio a couple of times before we left, but I always seemed to get distracted before I finished. I was trying to recall. She had written a couple of books on soul retrieval and had worked with a few big names in the industry. I think she was from

Sedona or something like that. I know they say she channels a group of star beings, but I can't remember who. Why couldn't I remember anything else about her? Something didn't feel right. I couldn't put my finger on it, but my radar was going up.

"Ray, what's wrong?" Jazmin asked as she grabbed my arm and started to walk towards the rest of the group.

Tallia was right there with us, but I couldn't see Antonio anywhere. "Oh nothing, must be the altitude." I said trying to sidestep her questions.

"I know you too well Arayla, don't give me that shit. What is wrong?"

"I don't know, just watch yourself. Something isn't right. Have you seen her before today?" I asked motioning toward the tour leader.

"Rowena, of course! What are you talking about, Ray? She has been with us the whole time. On the bus, at meals."

"Are you sure?" My body started to move in the other direction.

"Of course! Ray, stop being weird. She's the leader of the group for heaven's sake. Now come on, let's get into the circle. We don't want to miss out."

Jazmin seemed so irritated with me. I tried to act cool and like nothing was wrong, but Tallia was not so easily convinced.

"What is it Ray?" she whispered. I could tell from the look in her eye, she was very interested in what I was feeling.

"Haven't you seen her with us?" she asked very confused.

I shook my head no and proceeded with caution. Everyone was bringing out their drums and rattles, flutes and other music makers to start the ceremony. A beautiful woman in her fifties started to play the flute in the center of the circle. The sound started to permeate the air and the excitement started to build. The rhythm of the drums started to bring the group together in harmony and everyone sat cross legged on the ground. I sat with Jazmin on one side of me and Tallia on the other. I was glad to be sitting between them both, as my head was starting to spin, or was it the ground? I took Tallia's hand and just sat there trying to get a grip. What was happening? I couldn't seem to hear what Rowena was saying. Was it

Rowena? I think that is what they called her. Why can't I seem to focus in on her? Why don't I remember seeing her? This was crazy. Of course she had been with us. How else would she have gotten all the way out here in the middle of nowhere? I racked my brain looking for her over the last few days. She was not there. How could that be? I tried to keep my focus, but I couldn't. The ground was spinning beneath me and my head was pounding. I lay back on the ground and closed my eyes. Tallia squeezed my hand.

"Are you okay?" she asked in a low voice.

I just nodded and continued to feel the spin. Jazmin put her hand on my leg letting me know she was still there. She didn't want to miss out. I didn't' blame her. This is why we had come, to do ceremony and have this experience. Boy, this was an experience. I heard Rowena begin. "Sisters and Brothers of Light. Welcome to the land of Ancient Mu." That was the last thing I remember.

Chapter 36

So much sorrow, so much pain
Resides within the leyline streams
As sacred points upon this earth
Begin their journey back to source

To hear the cries, as history shows
The cruelty of unenlightened souls
The battles lost and rivers stained
With blood and spoilage so disdain

Each location chosen, each situation clear
As parallel timelines disappear
For each reality must be cleared
To bridge the future Gaia here

Arayla, Ray wake up!" Jazmin was shaking me.
"Is she alright?" I could hear Tallia asking.

"I'm sure she is fine, Arayla wake up!" Jazmin continued. Just then I felt the presence of someone kneeling over me.

"Arayla, open your eyes for me." Antonio said with his beautiful voice as he stroked my head. "Come back to me Arayla. I'm here for you."

I opened my eyes as his hands went behind my back and lifted me to a sitting position. He felt so nurturing, so loving, so strong. I loved the way he pronounced my name. And when he touched my back, my spine lit up with energy surging through it.

"Are you okay?" Tallia asked.

"Yes, yes, I'm fine. What happened?"

"I'd like to ask you the same question. Here drink some water." Tallia handed me a bottle.

"I bet it's just the altitude," Jazmin said trying to calm the situation. "She will be fine," she said again as she looked into my glazed but focused eyes.

I shook my head in agreement. "Yes, it probably is the altitude." I slowly tried to get to my feet.

"Here let me help you." Antonio reached for me, I was grateful for his assistance as the world seemed to still be spinning a bit. Damn he felt good. I wished he would just wrap his arms around me again.

"What is going on?" I asked.

"We're leaving, come on. We don't want to be left behind!" Jazmin said as she took my arm and led me back to our jeep. I climbed into the back seat and closed my eyes again. What had happened? I'd missed the whole ceremony. This was weird and I didn't like it. I didn't like it at all.

"Is everyone here?" the driver asked after he had already pulled into the lineup of other jeeps. Geez, what if someone wasn't here, I thought. Everyone in the front of the jeep was excited and started sharing their experiences about the ceremony.

"Isn't she awesome!" one of the woman in the front of the jeep proclaimed.

"Yeah, that was powerful. Could you feel the energy she was channeling?" another woman asked.

"Yes, and the languages she spoke. I've never heard anything like it," the third woman explained. I just listened to them all as I tried to figure out why I had gone out so hard. And why hadn't I seen Rowena before.

"Okay, spill your guts. Tell me everything," Jazmin said in a low but commanding voice. Her eyes were upset, yet searching and caring at the same time. Even though she was my closest friend, I had shared most of what had happened to me in the past, but not all of it.

"Something just isn't right. I'm sorry, but something isn't right. Until she walked into the center of that circle, I had never seen Rowena. Not once on this whole journey. Not once!" I exclaimed with a small amount of fear seeping through.

"That is just crazy. What do you mean you have never seen her? She has even sat next to us a couple of times at dinner, or at least at the same table."

"Well, I don't know what to tell you. I have never seen her before and the feeling I get is not good. Not good at all." I closed my eyes trying to get a grip. Jazmin must think I am crazy, but I know what I know. We had another hour and a half before we reached the next destination and final ceremony stop for today. I closed my eyes and leaned my head back. She grabbed my hand and held it tight.

"Ray, I believe you. I believe you. But why, why have you not been able to see her?" she asked. That was the same question I was asking myself. Why had I not been able to see her? Why had she hidden herself from me? Had she hidden herself from me? Why didn't she want me to see her? The questions kept swirling in my mind. I tried to remember Rowena speaking.

"We stand here together, united in Light." Rowena stated loudly as she stood inside the circle of people. "This holy, ancient land is the home of our ancestors. The ones who began the current cycle of time and space, these are the ancients who set into motion this cycle of learning and separation. They were the wise ones who secured this timeline into existence to allow for this great learning and experience to unfold." Her hands raised high up into the sky.

"We ask the ancients to be with us as we are present with them," Rowena continued in the center of the group leading ceremony or something to that effect. "Behold my lineage of Light as I ask for the gifts and the knowledge to be revealed to me," she requested.

Who is this woman? My mind raced. What is she asking for? Everything in my body started to freak. Something didn't feel right. I closed my eyes...

"Arayla, she is a powerful force," the Crew leader said. "She is not one to be taken lightly. She knows who you are. That is why she has shielded you from seeing her. Your Light is strong. She has come to take the codes from the grandmothers. You must retrieve the codes before she does. You must be stronger than her. You must protect the knowledge from being accessed by the wrong sources. Remember, we are with you. You must be stronger, stronger than the dark forces."

I opened my eyes when the jeep came to a sudden stop. "What's going on?" I asked anyone who would answer.

"We're stuck in the mud," the woman in the front seat complained.

"We're stuck in the mud." Another woman laughed. "Well that will make for a good story," she giggled. I looked over to see Jazmin climbing out of the jeep.

"Come on, everyone, out you go," she ordered as the women in the front of the jeep got out one by one. I stepped out into a pile of mud that went up to my ankles. I walked towards the others shaking my leg trying to get the mud off.

"Where is Jazmin?" I asked.

"'I'm over here," she said as she waved her arm.

"Is anyone else stuck?"

"Nope, most of them are ahead of us, since someone took so long getting back to the jeep."

Okay, so she was still a little upset with me. That was obvious. But

I could see there were a couple of jeeps behind us as well. Several of the drivers had run back and were starting to put boards under the wheels to try and get some leverage. At least no one was leaving us, if all the drivers were helping get us out of the mud.

"Are you feeling any better?" Jazmin asked.

"Yes. Where is Rowena's jeep?"

"Why?"

"Just wondering... "

"Not so fast missy. Are you going to fill me in on what is going on?" she demanded.

"Well the Crew just came in and told me I had to get to the codes first. That Rowena knows who I am. That she is powerful and that she did NOT want me to see her," I explained as Jazmin stood there with her mouth open.

"What? Are you telling me Rowena has been blocking you from seeing her on purpose?"

"It seems that way. That is why today was the first I have actually seen her. I know you think I'm crazy, but I tell you, I have never seen her before that ceremony," I pleaded, desperate for her to believe me.

"Why would I make something like this up?" I said. "I told you something didn't feel right as we started towards the ceremony."

"Arayla, she is a world renowned spiritual teacher. Why in the hell would she block YOU from seeing her?" She shook her head, "Ray, that just seems crazy." She started to walk away.

Just then Tallia came walking up to me. "What is going on? Is she alright?" she asked motioning towards Jazmin.

"Yes, she is just upset with me," I said as I began to lose it. I started to cry right in front of Tallia.

"What's wrong?" she asked. "Ray, something is going on and I am here to help you. I've known it since we met at breakfast. We are soul sisters and something isn't right, something strange is going on and I know you know what I am talking about." She took my arms for emphasis.

"It's Rowena. Something isn't right about her," I explained as I watched for a reaction in her face.

Tallia nodded in agreement. "I know, I feel it too," she admitted. Relief ran through my body. At least she believed me, even knew it too.

"Really Ray, I know I am here to help you. Antonio, too. He feels so connected to you. It's really got him spinning. There is something happening and we are all here for a reason."

"Ray, I want you to know that you came to me in a dream the week before this journey. You told me we would need to be strong. That we were soul sisters and once again you would ask for my help and protection," she talked with a pleading look in her eye. "You were as you are now, but different too. You are a beautiful being of Light and even my brother sees it. I never told him about the dream or that I recognized you."

"I'm here for you," she insisted. "Whatever you need. Whatever it takes. Know that." Just then the driver started yelling for everyone to get back to the jeeps. With all the drivers helping, they had managed to get our jeep out of the mud and we were ready to roll again. Jazmin was waiting for me in the back seat. She didn't say anything. She just gave me a puzzling look and turned to take a few more pictures out the window. It was going to be a long ride.

"I'm sorry," Jazmin said as she leaned over to grab her camera case.

"Sorry for what?" I asked not sure if it was because of her leaning over me to take the picture or sorry for what had happened before. She didn't respond.

"Sorry for not knowing what to think." She almost apologized. "I know you have had a lot of strange and amazing experiences, but when you are not the one having those experiences, sometimes it can be hard to believe or get your head around," she confessed. "I know you Ray, I only know Rowena by reputation. But she has a huge following and she seems to be doing great work for the planet. I just don't know what to believe." She paused for awhile trying to formulate her words.

"You say you haven't seen her. Yet, I've been right next to you on several occasions when she was there too. You say something is wrong. But we've paid a lot of money to come and work with her and experience what she has to offer. It's just caught me off guard and I honestly don't know what to think at this point." Jazmin rubbed her head.

I just sat there not knowing what to say. I couldn't convince her to believe me, she had to know it in her own heart. "You have to follow your own heart and gut," I said reluctantly. "I just know what I know and I have to act on that."

"Act on that, what does that mean, act on that?" she questioned.

"I have to follow my guidance. So if I leave the group or go off on my own, please don't freak out or be mad at me. And please don't let them leave without me," I pleaded.

"I would never leave you Ray," she said and I knew it was true. Jazmin was a true friend and I knew she was just having a hard time with it all. She would believe what she would believe, but in the meantime, I've got to listen to what I'm being guided to do. What am I being guided to do? I asked myself. And how come I haven't seen Z? He's not come to me at all this trip. Where is he? I thought to myself as we continued along behind the trail of jeeps.

"Ray, did you realize you didn't have to go out this time?" Jazmin said.

"Go out, what are you talking about?"

"You didn't go out or into a dream state this time when the Crew came in, did you?"

"No I didn't, you're right!"

She was right. The information and communication with the Crew was becoming easier, much easier. I felt a renewed sense of strength and confidence and it felt good.

Chapter 37

Within the ancient wisdom
Does the truth of life reside
As dragon, jaguar and butterfly
Hold the secrets deep inside

The myths of lost civilizations
Hold true throughout the world
Of supernatural powers
From the Cosmos, Goddess, Source

But ancient wisdom speaks to
The world in which they knew
While current science bridges
Ancient wisdom in their tubes

For all the world is illusion
Nothing more than Light and Sound
Firing in the brainwaves
Creating structured reflections of

For the truth we all are seeking
Can only be found within
When one understands the basic truth
That Light is All There Is

The landscape was breathtaking. No wonder they called it the Valley of the Rocks. It was haunting, yet somehow familiar, all at the same time. The rocks looked like everything from Egyptian statues, to birds, jaguars and even hearts. It was so surreal. How did they get that way? It was obvious they were natural formations. Everyone in the jeep was talking about it, how other worldly this place felt. It was weird driving through here, watching them roll by, feeling like I just wanted to get out and touch them, be with them. That was a strange notion, wanting to be with rocks, but I really felt like I had been here before. It was unnerving to say the least.

"What are you supposed to do?" Jazmin gently questioned me.

"I don't know yet, I just don't know," I answered with a fair amount of concern in my voice. "I just know that I am supposed to keep the codes safe and out of her hands but I'm not sure how I'm supposed to do that," I confessed.

She took my hand and gave me a reassuring smile. "Well whatever it is, I'm sure you'll know when you need to."

Come on Crew, Z, where are you and what am I supposed to do here? I thought as strongly as I could without screaming it out loud. I closed my eyes again.

The urgency was in the air. You could cut it with a knife it was so thick. I had that old familiar sensation of being in no-time, no-space. I was back with the Crew of Light, yet there seemed to be so many more present than normal. Hell, what was normal about this experience on any level?

"What is happening?" I asked the head Crew member that always converses with me, just now realizing I've never had a name for him.

"Arayla, you must remember," he said with his authoritative voice.

"Remember what?" I responded.

"How to retrieve the codes. You were there when the codes were embedded. You placed them there yourself eons ago. Remember, Arayla. Remember who you are." The intensity of the moment grew.

"Retrieve the codes? I don't know how to do that. Where are they?

What do you mean I put them there? I don't know what you want from me!" I screamed, realizing my recent sense of confidence and strength had disappeared quickly.

"Bring them safely into your matrix and secure them from outside interference. The codes are part of you, reintegrate them," he insisted.

"What is a code?" I asked realizing if I knew what a code was it would help me retrieve them and keep them safe.

"Codes are instructions. They work with the human energy matrix and physical DNA/RNA to establish the connection to source energy. It is information Arayla, very valuable information. When you have the correct codes, you are able to remember who you are. In essence, codes are the instructional roadmap for humans to remember their truth," the Crew member reminded me.

I tried to wrap my mind around what I had been told. I was there to retrieve the codes, the original codes from the Ancient Grandmothers of Mu to keep safe and out of the wrong hands. This was information to help humanity remember their truth. It was starting to make sense and the enormity and responsibility of what I was there to do began to sink in.

The jeep came to a stop in front of two amazing rock formations. One looked exactly like a puma, better known as the jaguar, the other a condor, and together they formed the most amazing heart shape within the void. It was absolutely magical!

"Ray, you're shaking." Jazmin reached over to help me out of the jeep. "What can I do to help you?" I just shook my head as I got my balance and bearings once again. The amount of energy running through my body was overwhelming to say the least and my balance was a little off. The altitude wasn't helping. The driver had informed us we were now at 17,000 ft. I scanned the jeeps looking for Tallia and Antonio. Just then I saw Rowena stepping out. Our eyes locked and a chill ran through my body. I felt weak and disoriented. Jazmin noticed the exchange between the two of us and just stood there trying to figure out what to do.

"Ray, what is happening? I just saw the look Rowena gave you. What is she doing?"

"I don't know, but I feel weak. I need some food or water or something. We need to get down by the rocks. Where is everyone going, do you know? We are doing ceremony here, right?" I asked. Just then Tallia and Antonio found us.

"Arayla, I'm here for you." Antonio reached out his arm for me to take as support. I felt safe with him, but every time he touched me the energy raced through my body. Strong, primal, sexual energy. It was a little more than I wanted to deal with at the moment, but I knew it was important to have him near.

Tallia took the other arm for support. She pointed to the group. "Looks like they are gathering in that clearing over there. Do you want to go there?"

Jazmin went back to the jeep to get water and snacks.

"What can I do Ray, what do you need from me?" Tallia asked.

"Keep me protected. Energetically, keep me protected." I whispered.

"Do you know what from?" Tallia looked worried.

"Rowena, dark forces, interference, anything that doesn't feel right. Safe from her and whatever forces she is working with," I said hoping she understood. Tallia nodded in agreement.

"I will protect you Arayla. You have my word," Antonio insisted with certainty and an air of courage. It was true, I knew he would protect me. The Crew had told me I would always have the help I needed. Antonio wasn't Z, but we certainly had a connection, a very strong connection. I was relieved that he was there with me.

We walked arm in arm down to the clearing. Everyone was bringing their musical instruments and crystals with them once again. The rock formations were so amazing and the energy coming from this place was powerful. I could feel it surging through my body.

"Can you feel the energy of this place?" Tallia said with awe.

"Yes, it is so powerful here," Antonio agreed in his thick accent.

Jazmin returned with a bottle of water and some dried fruits and nuts. "Here, eat some."

Rowena was already at the clearing with her team setting up a small altar in the center of what would be the ceremonial circle. "Gather around everyone," she requested. "Welcome to this sacred place."

"How am I going to get away from the ceremony? She will notice I'm not there." I almost shook with concern.

"Ray, place a double of yourself with us in the circle. I can help you hold that vision," Tallia offered. I looked at her with confusion.

"A double?" I wasn't sure.

"Yes, a double of yourself. Project your energy into a double so it looks like you are with us standing in the circle," she explained.

"I don't know how to do that!" I pleaded.

"Yes you do, I've watched you do it all week. I've seen you in multiple places at once. I know you can do it. I've seen it," she insisted in a calm voice. "Just intend it, believe it and it will be."

It sounded like a good idea, but I was at a loss of how to do it.

"I will help with the illusion," Tallia offered again. "I can help create the illusion so Rowena does not know."

I looked at Jazmin and she just had a shocked and confused look on her face like she could not believe what she was hearing. It did sound crazy, but Tallia said she had seen me do it all week. How could that be? I wasn't consciously doing it at all. Could I really do it? Was I capable? Just as I thought it Tallia urged me on...

"Of course you can do it. Ray, stop questioning and let's get this done."

She seemed to have total faith in me, so why was I questioning? I couldn't seem to get my head around it, but I decided to not think too much about it and just trust my intuition and my intuition said that she was right. I knew how to do it and I knew how to do it well.

"I need to be over by the Puma rock formation." I said with confidence. "I will begin the projection of my double NOW." They continued to walk towards the circle and I stopped. I placed a shield of Light around me in a full circle intending for it to keep me hidden and invisible. I guessed it was working as someone almost walked right into me. I had to jump quickly to get out of her way. She didn't see me. Perhaps this is what Rowena had done all week long so I couldn't see her. But Jazmin had, so...

My mind started to wander, but I needed to stay focused. I needed to retrieve the codes. How the hell do I retrieve the codes? I questioned again. Trust Arayla, trust. You know you can do it, I thought trying to reassure myself. Why would you be here if you couldn't do it? Why would you be told to do this if you didn't have the skills or knowledge? As I turned to walk the other way, I felt a sharp pain in my heart. Piercing and painful, I bent over grabbing my chest. I had felt this pain before, but I couldn't put my finger on when or where and then I remembered Peru.

I turned quickly to see Rowena looking straight at me. Shit, she could see me! I called out for Tallia, but she couldn't hear me. I sent her the strongest telepathic message I could and she turned, nodded and ran over to me.

"What's wrong?" Tallia asked.

"Rowena can still see me. She just sent a sharp pain through my heart. I'm sure of it," I said, freaked at the thought.

"Come back to the circle with me. We will have to figure something else out." I turned to walk back with her as Jazmin ran up to meet us.

"What is it?" Jazmin asked. I just shook my head.

"Rowena can still see her." Tallia said as we all walked back to the ceremony.

Antonio joined us and Tallia filled him in.

"I'll go to the other side of the gathering and see if I can draw some of her attention that way." He smiled to himself.

"Good idea," Tallia agreed. "That should shift the attention away from us. He's good at getting people, especially woman, to look at him." She smiled at me.

"Yes he is." I giggled trying to lighten up.

Antonio walked quickly to the other side of the circle and started to dance around and flirt with several women. That was a great distraction as everyone was watching him. His animation and sexy movements would have any woman drooling. He started to dance around with one of the women, swirling her around and being charming. It was a good plan. But I thought he was there to protect me, to help me. Maybe this was the type of protection and help I needed, maybe this was his way of giving support. Distracting everyone, shifting their focus. Hopefully it would work with Rowena too.

I released my grip on Tallia and began to consciously put a cloak of invisibility around me. I stood there for a couple of minutes just imagining that I couldn't be seen at all. I told Tallia I was leaving and to try and help keep me cloaked. I walked swiftly but easily towards the rock that resembled the Jaguar or Puma as it was called in Bolivia. I had been drawn to it from the moment I saw it. With each step I asked, how do I retrieve the codes? How do I retrieve the codes? I turned to look back at the ceremony. Rowena was in the center trying to get everyone's attention. I returned my focus toward the rock.

Rowena's grace and presence were powerful. She stood in the center of the ceremony and began to call in the forces of nature. I could hear her from where I was and knew I needed to keep my awareness in both places. Did she think I was still in the circle? I wasn't sure, but I knew that I had but a few minutes to complete the task at hand. My body was shaking from the inside out. My mind was spinning.

"Your circuitry is ready. Your connection with Antonio was successful. You are strong enough, Arayla. Focus!" I heard Z say.

My heart was still raw from the energy—dare I think "attack"—I was sure Rowena had caused. I reached the rock formation and placed my hand upon it. I could feel the energy moving through it. It was alive. It was powerful and it felt familiar on so many levels. How could that be? The Crew said I had been there before. I had been here when the codes had been embedded. What do they mean by embedded? I sat down with my back against the rock. I could still see the ceremony in the distance, but I could no longer hear Rowena's words. I could see her with her arms raised high in the air. What was she saying, what was she doing?

"Arayla, do not allow her to distract you. You must retrieve the codes, NOW!" Z said.

I closed my eyes and asked to be guided from the highest forms of Light. My heart started to race and the pain I had felt before disappeared. I tried to control my breathing, back into a slow rhythmic pace, focusing on each breath and bringing my body into a state of centeredness. I could feel the energy coming up my spine from the ground beneath me. It was like pulses shooting every couple of seconds straight up out of the top of my head. The energy continued to amplify and I could feel my body shake even more. I opened my eyes to see what was going on at the ceremony.

"Do not concern yourself with her, retrieve the codes Arayla," the Crew member instructed.

I focused once again on my heart. I said out loud, as if someone were listening and could hear me, "In the name of Divine Light. I open my matrix to receive the codes that have been kept safe in this sacred land of Mu." As I spoke the words out loud, I could see a multi-colored grid of Light expand around me coming directly from my heart. It was beautiful. The grid expanded and extended to about six feet around me in every direction. The surges of energy going up my spine continued and with each surge a flash of light moved throughout the grid. I could see my energy matrix pulsing and alive around me with my inner vision. I was glowing!

I opened my eyes and looked over to the ceremony. Rowena was pointing in my direction. I knew she was pointing to this magnificent rock formation that was in the powerful formation of the puma, the jaguar.

"Arayla, hurry, there is no time to waste." I heard the voice from the Crew again.

I closed my eyes and continued to ask for the codes. My doubt overcame me. How was I supposed to get the codes? I didn't know what I was doing. My mind raced and so did my heart. I took a couple of deep breaths to try and calm myself again. I can do this, I said to myself. I could see the grid around me. I could feel the energy pulsing through me. I WAS doing it, I thought to myself. I WAS doing it.

The sound of the drums echoed through the valley and I could feel the intensity building. God, this was a race and I knew I had to win. I had to retrieve ALL of the codes before Rowena. I could see focused beams of energy coming from Rowena towards me and this rock. God help me! I took another deep breath and surrendered. Just then my body moved into the center of the rock. How could this have been? My mind raced, but I stopped trying to analyze what was happening with my logical mind and just allowed myself to BE. I could no longer feel the rock on my back. I knew I was inside the rock energetically and maybe even physically.

I heard a voice: "We are the Ancient Grandmothers of Mu. You have returned as promised to retrieve the ancient codes. You have fulfilled your ancient promise to return in physical form to be the midwife of this wisdom. We encode these into Your Sacred Matrix of Light to hold safe and true until the alignment of the galactic center is once again full, thus ushering in the Age of Divine Light and Truth."

I started to see all kinds of things within my inner vision. The emotions that were running through me were overwhelming. I started to weep uncontrollably. I could feel the pain of the Ancient Grandmothers when the veil of forgetfulness was placed around the planet. So much pain, so much grief, as the decision was made to begin this course of evolution. I was shown—or no—I was remembering, when the decision was made to remove the grids and have humanity forget that they are connected to source energy. Remembering when the Crew decided to have all of humanity go through a process of separation to see IF they could reconnect and remember from where they came. To allow this experience and begin an experiment to see what would be required to return to the knowing that everyone is a spark of the Divine. The memories continued to flood my awareness. Remembering there was a grand design, a purpose for all of which humanity had experienced, but that it was now time to repair the fray and return the codes to ALL of humanity.

My fields began to burst with light and symbols and sounds. It was like a fireworks show inside my body and matrix. I just sat there in awe as I watched everything come into place. My body was no longer shaking, as I was unaware of having a physical body at all. This went on for what seemed like forever. The colors, the sounds, the light, the energy. It was powerful and magical and felt so right. Once it stopped I found myself propped up against the rock, safe and sound. I just sat there with tears streaming down my face.

"Arayla, you have done well. The codes are now safely embedded inside your matrix. You must keep them safe at all costs," the Crew member said with a very pleased and relieved tone.

I continued to sit there trying to comprehend all that I had just experienced. All the pain, emotion, wounds, wars, destruction, manipulation, interference that this world had been through. This is the precise location where the decision had been made and the Jaguar seal had been removed from the planetary grids of Gaia. Of course this is where the codes must be returned. But what did that mean? I was sure I had retrieved the codes. I watched them embed into my energy matrix. I listened to my own thoughts and how crazy it sounded. But I knew they were there, I just didn't have a clue what I was supposed to do now. Keep them hidden and safe, Arayla, I thought to myself. Keep them hidden and safe!

Chapter 38

To hear the call of destiny
The body must be clear
Of all the holographic junk
That influences your fears

Your soul will remember
The promises you made
Before you came to body
Within this Earth-bound maze

Listen to your inner child
Listen to your soul
For destiny is calling you
To find your way back home

I was tired, weary, worn out at a level beyond what I could even explain. It seemed like my body was breaking down on every level, and the depth of exhaustion I was feeling was overwhelming. Going back to work in the real world and trying to deal with all the mundane details of regular life felt so draining. My life in the higher realms, the spiritual realms had become so much more real than my 3D life.

I knew what I was doing was important. I could feel it in my bones, but I just couldn't seem to rebuild my energy. I need rest, time to rejuvenate and rebuild myself, I thought to myself, not even really knowing what I meant by rebuilding myself. I needed a vacation. A real vacation from everything! One that didn't include moving in and out of different dimensions. But with recent events I didn't feel I could really let go and just relax. Especially after the encounter with Rowena in Bolivia. I had felt the dark energies. I knew they were real. Now it seemed like something or someone was always watching me, just at the edge of my awareness, waiting to pounce.

I remembered the experience over the Nazca Lines, learning to self-monitor my systems. I really did feel like someone or something was constantly trying to infiltrate my system, my matrix, my "computer." The Crew just kept reminding me to keep the information safe and pure. To keep my guard and shields up. To protect myself and the codes from all outside influences. I knew what to do, but it was like I couldn't get enough power or energy to make it happen. I asked Z for help, but it didn't seem to be enough.

I was lying at home in bed wishing I had someone to just protect me for a while so I could rest, when the phone rang. It was Antonio. The timing could not have been better. Our connection was strong and he had proven worthy during our encounter in Bolivia. He seemed to understand the spiritual world and on some level instinctively knew I was working with the Light doing something important for humanity. I had only given him bits and pieces of the story while we were in Bolivia. I kept the details pretty much to myself. But he had sworn to protect me then, so maybe he could do it now. We had kept in touch over the last few months. He was always traveling for his work. But he would call me often just to touch base and reconnect. Although the heat and passion that was so evident in

Bolivia had never developed into anything physical, much to my dismay, the love and compassion we felt for each had stayed strong.

"Antonio, I'm so glad to hear your voice," I exclaimed.

"My Arayla, how are you my Goddess of Light?" he said with such sweetness. He always referred to me as his "Goddess."

I giggled. "I love when you call me that!" I responded with as much sex appeal as I could muster.

"You sound tired."

"I am! More than I can ever remember. Everything seems to be just too much for me right now. I need a vacation!"

"Well, I am here for you, Arayla. What can I do for you?" he asked.

"I just feel like I can't let my guard down and it's really taking its toll."

"Why, what are you feeling?" He was trying to understand.

"I don't know. I feel like I am being watched all the time. Not by someone in the physical, but more like someone or something in another dimension. I keep having vivid dreams of battles and like I'm being chased," I said, trying to convey why I felt the need for protection.

"I wake up feeling like I haven't slept at all and I always seem to be looking over my shoulder half expecting someone ready to attack me." As I explained, I felt a wave of exhaustion come over me again.

"I knew something was up with you. You have been in my dreams and meditations recently. More than normal." He laughed, alluding to the possibility that maybe he did have passionate dreams about me.

"Oh really?" I wanted to know more.

"Seriously, Arayla, I can protect you. I will place a circle of protection around you. You are safe with me," he explained. "You know we are deeply connected. You feel it too! I know I've protected you in many lifetimes." I could hear the smile on his face.

I stopped to think about what he was saying. Could he really protect me from afar? Our connection had been strong, but it was strong when we were physically together. Was he strong enough to protect me when he was thousands of miles away? And had he really protected me or was it just that he could provide distraction? It seemed crazy to ask someone for protection from your dreams and visions. But it was real. It was happening in another place, another dimension and I did need protection, someone to watch my back.

"I don't know Antonio. I just don't feel safe and I am just so tired. I was supposed to go away for the holiday weekend, but I don't even have the energy to do that." I was sure he could hear the exhaustion in my voice.

"Arayla, I am here for you. I've told you before. I will protect you. You can relax. You can really rest and know that I've got your back," he insisted with such sincerity and desire to help.

"Antonio, are you sure? Do you even know how to give me protection?" I asked hoping that it might be true.

"Yes, I will protect you. I promise I have the skills to keep you safe. Take the long weekend and relax, rest, rejuvenate and replenish your soul. I will watch over you, keep you safe and secure. You have my word," Antonio promised.

"You're sure you know what you are doing?" I questioned him again.

"Yes, I promise. I will keep you safe and protected. You know how deep our connection is. You know how much love I feel for you. Our heart connection is beyond anything I've ever known. Rest well, my friend."

"Okay, I will touch base with you next week. Thank you for this. I really need someone I can trust to help me. I really need to unplug from everything for a while," I spoke with gratitude.

"Perhaps once you feel rejuvenated again, we can go on a vacation together!" he said.

"Yes, that would be wonderful Antonio! Thank you!"

As we ended the phone conversation I laid back on the bed remembering Bolivia and Antonio's response to me. He had declared his love to me in front of everyone. Claiming our hearts had been connected with such immense love. I wondered what that would feel like with someone in the physical. The closest experience I'd had was in another dimension of reality with a jaguar of all things. Someday, I thought. Someday I will find him, the man in my dreams with those beautiful deep piercing blue eyes.

I rolled over and fell into a deep sleep. Deeper than I had in weeks. It was such a relief to have someone like Antonio watch over me. It was so comforting and welcomed and I vowed to really let myself rest. I mean really rest for the first time in I couldn't remember how long. I wasn't even sure if I really knew how, but I was going to give it my best shot.

My dreams were full of struggles and swords, evil and Light, good guys and bad guys all mixed up into a whirlwind of sounds and flashes. I sat up straight in my bed at 3:33 a.m. drenched in sweat and disoriented. It took me a couple of minutes to realize I was safe in my own room. I tried to shake off the visions in my dreams. I lay there wondering if Antonio was having the same kind of experience clear across the country. I tried to send him a telepathic message, wondering if he would get it on some level. I crawled back under the covers and about an hour later finally fell back to sleep.

I had four days off. It was strange. I didn't know what to do with myself. I hadn't really taken any time off except for my travel vacations, which always ended up being anything but relaxing. Toni was having a barbecue over the weekend, so I was planning on going there, but the rest of the time was free. Truly free. I spent most of the time sleeping. My body was really worn down, more so than I had really realized. But even as I rested, I didn't feel like I was really sleeping. I would wake up knowing I had been out working on the grids, repairing, fixing, protecting and fighting with someone or something.

By the second day, I started to feel strange. I couldn't really place my finger on it. I just felt different. It seemed like I wasn't hearing Z or my guidance. Then I thought, it's just part of taking "time off." That this is what it felt like when I really stepped away from it all for some much needed rest, so I decided not to worry about it. Besides, of course I was always connected to Z. That would never change, right?

By Sunday, I was feeling really out of sorts. I was glad I was going to Toni's for a barbecue. I really felt like I wanted to go to connect with people. The house had seemed intensely quiet the last two days. I felt disconnected from the world and a gathering with good friends and food seemed like a good idea.

"Ray, is that you?" I heard Toni yell from the back patio.

"Yep, it's me," I responded.

"Did you bring your potato salad? I've been craving it all day!" Toni asked.

"Of course I did. Gotta have potato salad with ribs. How are they coming?" I asked as I watched her lift the barbecue lid to baste the ribs with another coating of sauce.

"They are going to be melt -in-your-mouth good!" she exclaimed. "We have about ten more minutes before we are ready to eat."

"Guess I timed it well, then!"

"Yeah, why didn't you come over earlier? What have you been up to?"

"I've just been sleeping mostly," I responded. "I've been feeling a little weird lately."

"Weird? More weird than usual?" Toni asked half laughing as it came out of her mouth.

"Yeah, I guess that is a valid question. Yes, more weird than normal. I just feel kind of strange. Disconnected. You remember Antonio? The guy I met in Bolivia?"

"You mean the Italian hunk?"

"Yes. Well he said he would give me energetic protection so that I could really relax this weekend."

"What? What do you mean protection?"

"Well, I've just been feeling really overwhelmed and exhausted and I needed some help. He called the other night just as I had said out loud that I needed some 'time off' from everything. He offered to put energetic protection around me and so I agreed."

"Do you think that was a good idea, Ray?" Toni questioned.

"I thought so at the time, but now I'm not so sure. I feel weird and disconnected somehow. I thought it was just because I was really letting myself relax, but now I'm not sure what I'm feeling." Now I was worried. A wave of panic rushed through my body.

What had I done? Could I really trust Antonio? We had such a strong connection, but did I really know him well enough to give him so much access to me? Why was I feeling so disconnected? Shouldn't I be feeling stronger instead of more disconnected? Why wasn't I hearing Z? I was starting to get really upset and Toni could see it in my eyes. I promised to retrieve the codes. I did and if I lose them now what will happen, what would the ramifications be? Geez, it all sounded so crazy.

"I'm sure it will be fine, Ray. Relax, he promised to have your back, right?" she said.

"Yes, he said not to worry, that he had my back." But I was worried and the realization of what I had done made me sick to my stomach. I decided I was overreacting. Why would he promise to have my back and then not make sure I was protected? It didn't make sense. I needed to learn to trust people more. I decided to let it go and try and enjoy the evening.

The next morning I sat down to go into mediation and nothing! Nothing! I couldn't get connected to anything. Not my higher self, not Z, not the grids. It was like I was in the dark void. I panicked. I picked up the phone and called Antonio. When he answered, my heart sunk. I knew, I just knew.

In his broken accent and with as much apology as he could muster, be began to tell me how he had decided to pull his protection from me over the weekend. He said he had been guided to remove it for my own good. That it was not his role to protect me. That I had to learn to protect myself. When I questioned him as to why he didn't call me and tell me he had pulled the protection, why he had not bothered to just let me know out of plain courtesy, he just came up with reason after reason of why his actions were noble.

As I placed the phone down, the panic started to overcome me. What had I done? I felt as if I had been betrayed at the deepest level possible. I had let my guard down completely thinking that someone I trusted was protecting me. I had placed myself into Antonio's hands and he had left me exposed to whatever was trying to mess with me. How could I be so stupid? I was in shock from the betrayal of a close friend, in shock from feeling more disconnected from my higher self and guidance that I could remember and in shock that I had allowed myself to be so vulnerable, especially when I knew there was something trying to access my energy fields and information.

My connection was gone. I didn't even know how to process that. I had placed my trust in him. How stupid was I to have left myself so vulnerable. I just sat there and cried. I had never felt so lost, so betrayed, so disconnected in my life.

I cried out to Z, but nothing. I couldn't hear a thing. I tried to convince myself it was all just a bad nightmare and I would wake up tomorrow and everything would be fine. But I knew better. I knew I had gotten myself into a mess and I had no idea in hell how I was going to fix it. How could I fix it if I wasn't connected? I had forgotten what it felt like to not be connected to Z, to my higher self, to the Crew. I called Toni in a state of pure panic and desperation.

"Ray, breathe," she said. "We will figure this out. You have to settle down. Being this emotional isn't helping." I knew she was right, but I couldn't help it. Everything was wrong. Everything was falling apart. I was ready to quit. I was ready to pull the plug. Never had I felt so ready to check out of this place.

"What am I going to do Toni?" I screamed. "I don't know what to do!"

"Have you asked for help?" she asked.

"Of course I have, but I can't hear them. I can't hear my higher self, Z, or the Crew at all!" I screamed back at her with tears streaming down my face.

"We will figure this out. Z would not leave you. He's still with you, we just have to figure out how to fix this."

"I feel like all my wires have been cut. Like I've been severed from my guidance. Like someone came in with a sword and cut every connection, every wire, every thread of Light I had to source." I sobbed.

"So really what we need to do is reconnect you." Toni was calm and matter of fact.

"Yes, but do you know how to do that Toni?" I screamed.

"Well, not with you in this emotional state I don't!" She screamed back.

I knew she was right. I had to get a grip, but my emotions were all over the place and I felt like my world was crumbling. How ironic was that? I felt my world was crumbling because my spiritual connection was missing. The spiritual realms had become more real than my real life. I couldn't imagine living in this world without my connection. I knew Z would help me find a way, even if I couldn't hear him right now. I knew in my soul he was still there. I just had to figure out a way to reconnect.

"Ray, I keep getting that you need to go to Kona. You will be able to reconnect there." Toni said.

"How can I do that?" I exclaimed, thinking of all the reasons why I couldn't go running off to Kona right now. "I don't have the money for that or the vacation time, but there is something calling me there."

"So when have you ever let the logical side of things influence you, Ray? It's not a good time to start now! You know what I am saying is right, all logic aside. You have to figure out how to get to Kona. You need to be in the water and let the island heal you." She said it so confidently. Toni, the logical one, telling me to cast all logic aside and go to Kona, now.

I knew what she was saying was right. The water always heals me. As I was sitting there trying to figure out how I would be able to pull it off financially and with work, the phone rang. I picked it up and on the other end was an advertised recording announcing my chance to win a trip to Hawaii. I hung up the phone and laughed. I was going to Hawaii. Too bad I didn't actually win the all-expenses-paid trip, but the sign was pretty clear, all the same. Maybe I couldn't hear Z right now, but at least I could hear the advertisement on the other end of the phone...

The air is different in Hawaii, thick, exotic, you can feel it as it penetrates your soul. As I walked down the stairs off the plane, I felt like I was home. It seemed weird arriving in Hawaii alone. It's a place for romance with lovers and once-in-a-lifetime adventures with family. I was here to reconnect, heal and repair the damage that had been done to my circuitry when I opened up and allowed someone else to "protect" me. What a fool I had been to think I could let my guard down. Never again, I vowed never again would I be so foolish.

I had chosen to stay at the Hilton in Waikoloa Village. It was a sprawling resort which required a boat ride to get you to the different sections of the hotel. But it was beautiful and captured the essence of a forgotten Hawaii through the artwork that graced the walkways. Although it took a good twenty minutes to walk to my room, it was worth it, and the fresh air and smells of the exotic flowers made the experience even more perfect. I unpacked, undress and curled up on the plush king-sized bed.

I woke up in a pool of sweat. The bed looked like it had been thrashed and I felt worn out before my day even began. After showering and purchasing a very expensive cup of second-rate coffee, I was on my way to the ocean. The bellman who had delivered my luggage the day before told me about a secluded private beach which allowed public access. There were only twenty-four spots for parking and once they were full, they were full. I was feeling lucky, hoping I would be able to spend the day there and was relieved when the cute guy at the guard gate handed me the pass. I made my way down to the sandy beach, covered myself with sun block, put my hat on and walked out into the clear pure water.

The Queen's Bath, as it is called, is one of the only places on the island where it is soft sand all the way into the water. It feels safe and secluded and it's easy to let myself just float without worrying about the waves or current taking me away. The rock juts out in the distance, making a sanctuary of calm water protected from the forces of the ocean. The last time I was here, I had gone farther south to a different beach and gotten my butt kicked by the current. I tumbled at least twenty times before someone helped me get to my feet and out of the water. It shook me to my core and was not an experience I wanted to repeat. I needed nurturing and healing this time and this peaceful place was just the ticket.

The Queen's Bath always drew families, as it was easy and safe for children to play in. So the giggling of small children and teenagers alike filled the air. But with a limited number of cars allowed in, the crowd was small relative to other beaches on the island.

The moment my body touched the water, I let out an audible sigh. The water, my one true healer. Nothing soothed me more than being submerged in water. I let my body float effortlessly as my mind started to clear. I could feel my body relaxing. Here is where I would rebuild my connection. Here is where I would heal. Here is where I would find Z again. I slipped into a deep state of relaxation and started to pray.

I stayed in the water for hours. Nothing. Nothing was coming through. By the end of the day I was in a panic, wondering if I had really messed up this time. What if I couldn't reconnect? What if I couldn't rebuild my circuitry? What if I was going to have to live without my connection to Z, the Crew? I tried to calm myself down, but I could feel the emotion building. I couldn't fall apart. I was in paradise. You can't fall apart in paradise I told myself, knowing full well, it didn't matter where I was on the planet. If I felt disconnected, I was going to fall apart!

I was sunburned, hungry, ready to cry and frustrated that I wasn't feeling any more connected than when I got on the plane to begin with. All of my prayers seemed to be going unanswered and my depression was really starting to rear its ugly head. I had gathered up my towel and bag and was ready to head back to the car when I noticed her. She was standing across the beach right by a palm tree. Her gaze was strong and her eyes, although too far away to see clearly, shot right through me. I knew her. Her strong Hawaiian stature and long dark hair were so familiar to me. She looked right at me, right through me actually, nodded her head and then gave me a great big smile. I knew her, but from where? Had I seen her at the hotel earlier, had I met her before? She was hauntingly familiar and then I knew. I looked back towards her, but she was gone. My heart warmed and in that moment I knew. I knew everything would be all right. She was the sign that my prayers would be answered.

I came back to that same spot, the Queen's Bath, for the next five days. Slowly my connection to Z got stronger and stronger. Each day as I was ready to leave, the mysterious Hawaiian woman would appear in the distance to reassure me. I wasn't even sure if she was real, if she existed on the physical level or just in my inner vision. My last day on the Big Island, as I was submerged in the water, I sent out a declaration to the universe. I said out loud, with all my strength, power and conviction... "I ask that everything which is not FULLY aligned with MY Highest Good, MY

Truth and Destiny be released from my life with absolute ease and grace!"

In what seemed like a flash, my connection to Z and the Crew was restored. I knew my body was still floating in the warm water of the Queen's Bath, but I was once again in no-time, no-space, standing in front of the Crew with Z by my side.

"Arayla, the reconnect and recalibration is almost complete," the Crew member said.

"What happened?" I said with what I'm sure sounded like panic. "I couldn't connect. I couldn't hear or see you! I was completely severed from everything!" I continued sounding frightened, but actually relieved to be with the Crew again.

"Arayla, calm down," Z said as he took my hand.

"What do you mean calm down? That was the most scared I have ever been! I couldn't see you, hear you, feel you. It was awful." I said with tears in my eyes. "How could I have been so stupid?" I asked.

"You always get so emotional, Arayla!" Z seemed so nonchalant about the whole situation. "You were never in any real danger. I was always there with you. This was necessary."

"What was necessary? To scare me half to death and frighten me to my core?" Now I was angry at his lack of concern.

"It was necessary to fully sever your connection. We needed to completely unplug you from the system, download the codes into the new grid and then reconnect you so you could be connected at a completely different frequency with a new improved security program. Don't you see? It needed to happen just as it did. Humans are always thinking the worst, when it was always part of the plan," he said again in that rational and reassuring voice of his.

I could feel the tears running down my face as I floated in the warm water of the Queen's Bath. Tears of joy. Tears of relief. Tears because I realized I was never really alone. Tears because, although I still didn't get it, I realized Antonio did not betray me. He followed the guidance perfectly.

I could hear Z's voice in the distance, "Arayla, there is much that needs to be done. Breathe me in. I am forever with you."

Chapter 39

Within the Matrix of the Light
The patterns will unfold
The grids, the colors, the balls of Light
Forever will be told

For in this special time frame
The universe concludes
That from those whose hearts can bear the Light
True happiness exudes

For faith in not the answer
But a necessary tool
As physics plays a role within
Your journey through and though

Be still within the moment
Be strong within your Light
The pathway will be given
In perfect time each night

Each memory you uncover
Each truth you shed to Light
Brings you one step closer
To ever lasting life

I took a deep breath and everything became vivid. I knew exactly what had to be done.

"Arayla, are you ready"? Z asked as I saw the twinkle in his eye.

"Yes!" I answered with a level of confidence I had rarely felt. I braced myself for what I knew was going to be a fast paced and wild ride. Anchoring my feet firmly on the ocean's floor under the Queen's Bath, I drew in another deep breath. It was if the ocean floor had opened and swallowed me whole. I felt a rush of energy like I was falling, free falling, but I knew exactly where I was and where I was going. In an instant, I found myself at the portal opening of the North Pole. I could see the Light move with me through the core of the earth connecting Kona with the North Pole. I sent a pulse of Light through my body, and then the seal, anchoring it firmly. Then I took in another deep breath.

As the ground opened, the darkness pulled me deep, deep through the core of Gaia. The energy sucking me through the tunnel was electrifying as I watched the Light move with me. I again was in warm water, only this time I was in the waters of Bimini. My heart was racing and the energy moving through me caused my entire body to convulse, but I felt in complete control. I anchored the Light through my body and then the seal, sent a pulse through Gaia and took in another deep breath.

The ground dropped out beneath me once again, as I traveled with lightening speed through the core of the earth, this time to the South Pole. Anchoring the energy firmly, I shot through the tunnel again finding myself back in the Queen's Bath on Kona. I knew the first layer was complete. I could see the diamond pattern anchoring North to South, Kona to Bimini, Lemuria to Atlantis, the past, the present, the future...

Bracing myself for the next layer, I dug my feet into the sand beneath me and inhaled again.

First to Bimini, then to Sacramento, down to Machu Picchu, back to Oklahoma. The speed of movement through the earth's core was dizzying, but with each place the Light amplified. At each location, I anchored the Light with my body and then through the seal. I was moving so fast, it was all I could do to recognize and remember each place. I had traveled to each location in the physical. I had placed my feet firmly on the ground, intuitively knowing that I would anchor "something" someday at each of these spots. I just never dreamed it would be this. Oklahoma, to Joshua Tree, down to Bolivia and the Valley of the Rocks. Even in a flash, I could feel the power of the Jaguar rock where the Ancient Grandmothers had been. Bolivia back to the South Pole, straight through the core of the planet up to the North Pole and back to Kona. My head was spinning, but my body was strong. Strong and anchored with a stability that seemed perfectly natural to me. I felt energized and alive and I liked it. Allowing my body to relax for a minute, I heard his voice loud and clear.

"Arayla, you're not done. You've only completed the subterranean grid. Now you must complete the galactic grid," Z instructed.

Realizing what he was saying, I braced myself, anticipating the intensity of what I knew was coming. I was ready. I was prepared, I thought to myself and it was true. I was prepared and it felt good to feel so confident. For so long I was just flying by the seat of my pants. Now, I felt like I knew what I was doing.

"Are you ready to REALLY fly?" I heard him chuckle.

In a flash of light my body shot up, high into the ethers. I flashed back to the experience of being high above the Nazca lines and felt a jolt of exhilaration flood my body. My heart raced as I zoomed through the grids of Light, high above the earth, in a pattern mirroring what I had just traveled within her core. Bursts of light, in so many colors I couldn't begin to name them, exploded from my heart as it anchored through the symbol on my chest. I was flying, flying high above the earth, traveling from place to place upon the grids of Light.

As I felt the warmth of the Queen's Bath gently on my skin I opened my eyes. Was it complete? I asked myself, half expecting to zoom somewhere else at any moment. Taking another deep breath, I sank deeper into the water and into my body.

"The anchoring is now complete," the Crew member proclaimed.

"Now that you have completed the first part of your mission, the codes can begin to reintegrate into the planetary grids for all of humanity. It will take the humans many years to fully integrate these new codes, but a Golden Age of Divine Love and Truth has now been set into motion," the Crew member declared.

"There will continue to be opposition, forces which do not want humanity to remember who they are, what they are capable of. You must continue to be strong. To keep the grids and codes pure and clear from outside infiltration. The subterranean and galactic grids must bridge before the next stage can begin," the Crew member explained.

"Bridge, how will they bridge?" I asked out loud, hoping I would get an answer.

"Through you, Arayla," Z said with such tenderness. "Through you."

"What do you mean, through me?"

"Why do you think we have sent you to all these places?" Z asked as if my question was ridiculous. "You ARE the bridge Arayla. You are the human vessel which bridges the dimensions."

"That is why I have gone to all these places? Traveling between the dimensions to bridge and anchor the Light?" I exclaimed as the pieces started to fall into place.

"I have always said it," Z laughed.

"You've always said what?" I asked.

"She Travels Light."

Chapter 40

Before this Divine illusion
Before you sparked your Light
We sang in perfect union
In sacred soul delight

This journey was created
To bring the mystery
Of what individual thought forms
Could possibly conceive

We made our plan together
In total harmony
For in the end
Our hearts would blend
For all eternity

Arayla, wake up. Please wake up." I heard, but it was faint, like it was coming from miles away. "Ray, please come back to us," the voice pleaded. I felt someone's hand in mine, but it wasn't Z's.

"She has to wake up. It's been five weeks, but I have such hope. I just know it in my heart. She will come back." My mother was speaking to Toni who was with her in the hospital room. The realization came that it was MY hospital room.

"Bonnie, I can't believe the doctors can't figure this out. They still have no idea why she went into this coma. I wish there was a medical reason because it might make some sense..." Toni continued.

Bonnie responded with a nod of her head. "She just slipped into the coma. One moment she was talking to me and the next she was gone," Bonnie said with tears rolling down her face.

"You know Ray is strong. She will come out of this. You have to keep the faith. She is way too stubborn not to," Toni exclaimed with a slight laugh. "I've known Ray for a long time. She's a fighter."

"I know, it's just been so long. Five weeks is a really long time, Toni. The doctors are so confused. And all that strange stuff she has done. Sitting up and screaming at us in that gibberish. Making all those really loud high-pitched sounds. It's like she is possessed or something. It's scary. I don't know what is happening to her. She moans and cries like she is in such pain and then she's silent again. It's all just too much. To watch your child go through something like this. When there is nothing I can do. Nothing!" Bonnie started to cry.

"I know, but you have to believe, have faith that she will pull through this. Faith that if she were going to die, she would have done so already. You don't come back from being pronounced dead three times without a strong will to live, Bonnie. Remember that. Ray is a fighter. She's strong and healthy," Toni argued and with that comment Bonnie laughed.

"Yes but if she is strong and healthy, why the hell is she lying here in a coma?" she demanded. It was a valid question that multiple medical specialists had not been able to answer. After running every test in the book, they were no closer to figuring out what was wrong. Bonnie had even gone to a psychic to try and get answers. The truth was, she was losing faith and scared that nothing would bring her daughter back to her.

"Arayla, try, try and come back to us," she begged while patting the back of her daughter's hand.

"Bonnie, why don't you go home? I'll stay with her tonight," Toni offered as she looked at Bonnie, seeing the stress of these last few weeks written all over her face. No one had really rested since this had all started, but Bonnie had taken the brunt of it all.

"Go home and rest, get some good food, take a bath and then you will be fresh again for tomorrow," Toni said with a reassuring voice.

"Okay, you're right," she resigned. "Toni, you've been a real friend through all of this. With her father gone and her siblings spread across the country, there really hasn't been a lot of support except for you. You know how much this means to me and Ray, right?" Bonnie said as she picked up her purse and headed towards the door. She stopped and turned back to Toni, "Do you think she will ever come back to us? Do you think she will really ever wake up?" Bonnie asked without really expecting an answer. She passed Dr. Sounding as he entered the room.

"Mrs. Weaver, how is our sleeping beauty doing tonight?" he asked.

"No change yet," she responded.

Dr. Sounding picked up the chart, made a few notes and placed it back in the holder. He walked over and put his hand in mine. I could hear everything. Standing over me he gently touched my face. "Arayla, it's time to wake up. Can you hear me, Miss Weaver?" I heard him say.

"Yes, I can hear you. I'd know that voice anywhere!" I said, but no one could hear me. The words weren't actually coming out of my mouth. Just then I opened my eyes to see his beautiful blue eyes looking down at me.

"Well hello there, beautiful," I heard him say. Toni jumped up and ran after Bonnie.

Bonnie asked, "What, what is it?"

"Her eyes are open, she opened her eyes!"

"Arayla, can you hear me? Arayla, open your eyes for me again," Dr. Sounding asked.

"Sweetheart, it's mom. Can you hear me?" Bonnie said, making her way to the bed.

I just blinked, wondering why no one could hear me. Where was I? What was going on? My body felt really weird. I could see my mom. She was crying. Why was she crying? Wait, where did he go? I wanted my man! I wanted to see those beautiful blue eyes again. I closed my eyes and a flash of white light filled my vision. I heard a voice loudly echo through my head.

"You must return and remember the truth of who you are!" he demanded.

Return where, remember what truth? I wondered as something was poking my eye and geez get that bright light out of my face would you! I yelled, but my lips weren't moving.

"Her pulse is good. Blood pressure's normal. Temperature's normal. EKG is normal. Arayla, can you hear me? Arayla, can you respond please?" I heard the nurse standing over me say.

"Squeeze my hand, Arayla, you can do it. Squeeze my hand. I can see those beautiful eyes of yours. Squeeze my hand please."

I saw Dr. Sounding shake his head, no longer looking at the nurse on the other side of me. "Arayla, do you know who I am?" He asked again.

"Of course, you're Max," I responded, but then he asked me again.

"Arayla, can you respond? Do you know who I am?"

"Yes!" I yelled, "I know who you are!" I said, but he still couldn't hear me.

"Let's get her in for more testing. Her pupils are responsive. Her vitals are good. We need her to respond." Dr. Sounding continued to squeeze my hand hoping for a response.

"Arayla, speak to me honey. I'm right here. Speak to me if you can," Bonnie pleaded.

Toni took Bonnie's hand. "She'll be fine, Bonnie. She'll be fine. She's a fighter, see."

I was trying figure out where I was, but all I could think was,

"Where is Z?"

About the Author

From managing the corporate world to exploring new dimensional levels, Raquel Spencer has traveled an extraordinary path to a new understanding of the many planes of existence. A graduate of California State University-Sacramento with a B.S. in Business, Spencer worked with Fortune 100 companies for more than twenty years. Her life profoundly shifted after waking from a five-week unexplained medical coma in 1985. The coma marked the beginning of her own personal awakening.

In 2009 Spencer left the corporate world to become a full time metaphysical and spiritual teacher with clients throughout the world. She has been recognized by world renowned spiritual forerunners, North and South American shamans, Hindu priests and Tibetan Lamas alike as a "key player" in the advancement of human consciousness. Today, she teaches and supports a growing audience of metaphysicians, truth seekers and initiates worldwide through workshops, conferences, special events, private one-on-one sessions and small group journeys to sacred sites.

Raquel writes: *"I have spent my life navigating between worlds. My personal experiences have assisted with developing a level of compassion, wisdom and the multidimensional understanding to be an effective Spiritual Teacher, Healer and Energetic Channel for our times."*

Insightful, compassionate, intuitive and with a great sense of humor, Spencer's personality is down-to-earth even as she brings us into highly advanced levels of human potential. *She Travels Light* is her first novel—this fast-paced story was written to inspire readers by expanding our knowledge of metaphysics, multiple and parallel dimensions and to move beyond our current perceptions of reality.

Visit her websites at:
www.RaquelSpencer.com and www.SheTravelsLight.com